Fog

Ken McAlpine

iUniverse, Inc.
Bloomington

Fog

iUniverse books may be ordered through booksellers or by contacting:

iUniverse
1663 Liberty Drive
Bloomington, IN 47403
www.iuniverse.com
1-800-Authors (1-800-288-4677)

ISBN: 978-1-4697-9166-1 (sc)
ISBN: 978-1-4697-9168-5 (hc)
ISBN: 978-1-4697-9167-8 (e)

Printed in the United States of America

iUniverse rev. date: 4/27/2012

Fog

To Kathy, who has always believed.

1

They ran across the sloping deck like marionettes, arms and legs akimbo, and when the waves caught the sailors, their arms jerked out, snatching at the night, before they disappeared without a sound.

The rude cold filched her breath. When the waves rushed toward her, foaming and leaping and rumbling across the deck faster than any man could run—she knew this now— she drew what breath she could and felt her body clench. The waves carried their own wicked cold, so cold it burned, but the fizzing blackness they brought was worse, shutting her away in the darkest loneliness on earth. She believed in God. She prayed for the time between the waves, when the wind screamed and the snow made angry locust clicks but the stars hung peacefully and were still. She imagined the stars were angels, waiting.

She supposed she might not die. Father had tied her to the mainmast, carefully folding her arms across her chest. The rope had cut into her, although she no longer felt its bite. She had watched his hands proudly, the beautiful fingers expertly cinching the knots, but there was something different in his face. Mother had believed in God, but Father trusted no one, not even God, and when he finished his tying, he fell against her and pushed his lips to her ear and told her to keep her secret close and fight for her life. He prayed a lie, promising God he would do anything if he gave her safe passage, and then asked her to forgive him for what he had done to her. She accepted everything, kissing his eyelids, and when the waves swallowed them she felt his arms about her. Finally, a wave smothered them and, as if he didn't care anymore, he was gone, and she almost gave up.

Far above her, the last sailor regarded the red pinprick of lanterns on the shore and loosed his fingers from the icy rigging. He fell like a pinwheel in a faint breeze, and when he struck the *Asia's* deck, he gave an odd little hop. He was a quick-handed boy, marvelous at jacks, but now he lay twisted in an impossible shape, sliding down the deck to join the black waves lumbering to shore.

The great wave rose in the same way her friend had fallen, with queer slowness. It kept rising, gray front streaked with white, until she wondered if she was sinking. She said good-bye to the stars, closing her eyes and squeezing Miss Lolly to her chest.

The deck shuddered. She was swallowed again in iron cold. She felt herself tipping, the mainmast splintering away, and she was swept easily into the sea, riding for a moment as if on the softest mattress. And then she was spinning, turning over and over, her lungs screaming for air in roaring darkness that never gave way to show the stars.

She wanted to die, but she fought to live because Father wished it, and it was possible that God listened to everyone's prayers, even Father's.

On the beach, Captain Edwin Merton's agonies were many. His mistake had seen his ship, his crew, and his only child into the sea. The wave that had deposited him ashore had snapped four ribs and a femur. Crawling toward the great cliffs, he had felt the separations only as mild burning; cold and shock had served as anesthesia.

At the foot of the cliffs, he had lain for a time, confused. With all the sensations clamoring for his attention, it was difficult to concentrate on any one matter until the angel arrived, holding the reins of the great white horse. The angel had dissolved behind the passing curtains of white, so that at first Edwin Merton thought it a hallucination. But when the angel crouched beside him, the breath behind the brilliant smile was rancid. The knife sliding down his midsection brought a stench equally as real, and blood filled his mouth as he turned his cheek to the snowy sand.

The blade's deft workings brought him great focus. Yet even as he suffered agonies he had not thought possible, he recognized the justness of his punishment. He shouted agreement, raining oaths upon himself and powers that would see a child to such an end. The angel brushed his cheek tenderly with downy knuckles and spoke encouragement in his ear, lauding him for atoning for his sins, but it was only his daughter's voice he heard; after a pause, the angel returned to cutting. The angel was an artist, skirting the organs that sustain life, touching the places that chimed. There were partings, tuggings, burstings, sour nausea, regret. Snow caressed his organs. Lifting his head, he saw his body's warmth, a steamy wavering in the dark, not quite a soul.

The punishment was just, but the pain was too great. Captain Merton set his will against the knife. His will was strong; his raging only aided his demise.

His end caused the angel a melodious sigh. Applying the knife carefully, the angel removed the organ that mattered. When he finished, he buried Captain Edwin Merton with the same precision that had ushered his end.

Hewing to nature's course, child outlived parent. Two miles south of Edwin Merton's grave, at the foot of the Cape Cod cliffs, Isabella Merton, spread upon the wooden table in the day house, looked up into a boy's eyes. The boy had sad eyes, but not so sad that Isabella forgot her own troubles.

After all her efforts, she was certain. "I'm going to die," she said.

Above her, the boy kept staring, his mouth making strange motions. She thought of her father and the broken sailor, and her mother with her helpless eyes and phlegmy cough. Nothing could be done. This understanding brought a sleepy comfort.

"Don't be frightened," she said. "It can't be helped."

She pressed her chin to Miss Lolly's head, feeling the coarse wood where the hair, once flower-petal soft, had torn away. Everything grand, now ruined and spoiled.

"Miss Lolly and I were going to be the talk of New York," she whispered. "We were going to ride in a steam elevator. I hate the sea."

A kettle whistled merrily. She tried to keep thinking about the elevator, but her legs, which had only tingled at first, were warming. It was not a comfortable warming like the morning sun against your skin, but a fast-rising heat, as if she had stepped too close to a fire. When the big man drew back the canvas, she saw her legs and she knew something terrible was rushing up on her.

The big man had lied to her, although his lies, like his face, had been kind. She and the big man had played a game, pretending they hadn't seen the truth. The silent boy hadn't played. She liked the boy for not lying, nearly loved him for the way he looked at her as if they were best friends, but when he reached for Miss Lolly, she had to scold him.

When the big man placed the handkerchief, rolled like a sausage, in her mouth, she closed her eyes and bit down hard, and her heart scampered.

There was a creaking, like a wagon wheel starting to turn. The pain was shocking. Almost as quickly, a deadening flowed over her. The black ocean, the fire in her legs, her faithful doll, they drifted away. The wooden table became her hilltop swing. As she rose and fell, the wind tickling her ears, she gazed again beyond the farthest edge of England's green fields, toward the grandest country in the world, a place where stalwart men and upright ladies dressed in the latest fashions and danced to music played on electric phonographs and rode in steam elevators, up, up, up, beyond the birds. It was sore disappointment to have sailed across the ocean to find instead an America so loud and foul-mannered. America didn't deserve her secret. She wasn't going to change the world. She was just going to die.

When dawn came, only the ocean raged, as the jagged remains of the *Asia* lay dark against the gray November sky.

2

The storm that saw to the *Asia's* end passed to the west. Ferocious cold pooled in its wake, gripping the Cape for a week. In Wellfleet, Chatham, and Provincetown harbors, the winter of 1882 cemented its already considerable reputation by crushing a dozen dories in ice. In the marshes, jagged blocks of ice as big as men lay strewn about, and the creeks and channels shone milky white. Even Ezekiel Donne, who in all seasons walked about the dunes in his underthings, remained inside. At the Cape's far tip only the wild dogs padded through the Provincelands, moving like lethargic shadows.

On the eighth day, a wan sun appeared and the Peaked Hill Bars surfmen buried the *Asia's* dead. A steady wind blew from the northeast, jostling the smaller limbs of Provincetown Cemetery's lone oak, the sound like bones scraping.

The men had built a fire first, hoping to thaw the frozen ground, but it proved nearly fruitless.

"Better luck burrowing under a nun's knickers," said Willie Bangs, bouncing his shovel off the stubborn moraine.

Still, they proceeded with muted curses. Eight sailors, glazed with the same crust as the frozen earth, waited for their single grave. The girl lay in the supply wagon twenty yards away. The wagon was no more than a wood slab resting on spoked wheels; without sides, it allowed a clear view of the small pine coffin.

Daniel Cole frowned on delay and swearing. Captain Daniel Cole, keeper of Peaked Hill Bars Lifesaving Station, always insisted on a prompt burial, but weather and circumstance had forced a rare exception. The Atlantic had been slow in relinquishing the dead; burying made no sense until all the bodies were collected.

The *Asia's* crew washed ashore over the course of a week, the surfmen transporting the bodies to Peaked Hill Bars Lifesaving Station in the supply wagon. Thoreau, the brown bay gelding, strained as the wheels slipped in the sand. The lifesavers stacked the bodies outside, cinching a canvas tarp tightly over the pile. The wild dogs normally kept to the desolate Provincelands, but winter's deprivations drove them farther afield.

On Captain Cole's order, the girl remained in the day house just away from the main station, her body packed in snow and wrapped in canvas. The corpse proved inconvenient. Resting near the edge of the high sand cliffs, the day house served as a lookout for ships in distress. The single room, with its potbellied stove and table, was already cramped, and although the girl was small, the table was smaller. Performing day watch, the surfmen had to move gingerly to avoid bumping the protruding canvas.

Each man handled the inconvenience in his fashion. Frank Mayo and the Swede, Martin Nelson, kept their backs to the corpse at all times; Mayo because he cared little about any death, save his own; Nelson in a doomed attempt to forget. Antone Lucas, the diminutive Azores islander, was consumed with avoiding his reflection in the windows: seeing one's reflection in the presence of a corpse was invitation to die next. Hedging his bets, he kept one hand jammed in his trousers pocket, squeezing a lucky acorn. Ben Maddocks prayed for the girl's soul. During his watch, Willie Bangs engaged the girl in amiable conversation; it was rare to pass time with someone who never interrupted. Cole relieved young Hiram Paine of day watch, a rare exception to duties executed to the letter.

Though the men were unhappy about digging, they were glad to be rid of the bodies.

Willie watched Captain Cole walk to the supply wagon. As Cole bent to the coffin, Ornish Helms sidled toward the keeper.

Provincetown's undertaker, Ornish Helms had supplied the pine box. There was no time to craft coffins for the sailors, and more pertinent, no one to pay for them. There had been no money for the girl's coffin either. Cole had had to summon his ample powers of persuasion to get Ornish to donate the girl's box.

The thin undertaker approached the wagon slowly. It amused Willie that most people approached the keeper in the same wary fashion, as if engaging a mad dog or an irate spouse— not, in Willie's experience, that there was much difference.

But when Cole turned away from the coffin, Ornish Helms fairly leapt forward. The keeper stood still while the undertaker's hands danced in the air.

Willie rested his shovel against a weathered headstone and rubbed his wrists. "No doubt lamenting another heinous financial slight resulting from his generous nature," he said. "Why we had to bury these men on a day when the ground is balkier than a deaf mule is beyond me. It's not like they were going to sit up and walk off in a huff if they weren't accommodated."

"They might walk off at the rate you're digging," said Frank Mayo.

Normally, Mayo enjoyed listening to Willie. The man's tongue was lively and its waggings produced amusement and distraction in a job that saw little of either. But Mayo's every joint ached, and Willie's desultory digging wasn't improving his mood.

"The dead could outshovel you and get us out of here sooner," Mayo added.

"They're welcome to up and lend a hand," said Willie, "though I doubt they share your concern with time."

The other men had stopped digging. They stood silent, displaying hangdog faces. Their dour mood made Willie's spirits rise.

"The rest of God's creatures appreciate the moment," he said. "I'd wager they even appreciate a day as miserable as this. But not man. Even in our happiest moments, we're rushing off somewhere else. What's our hurry?" His eyes swept the cemetery. "Here's what we're rushing to."

"Bad luck to speak of death," muttered Ben Maddocks, crossing himself and commencing to dig again.

"I don't know if you're paying attention, but I doubt our luck could turn much worse," said Willie. "But as these gentlemen would no doubt heartily attest, even the worst moments are worth living. Still, you have to step back and notice them. Keeping your eyes on the ground is fine work for cows and moles."

"Maybe you'd like to explain your philosophy of leisure to Captain Cole," said Mayo.

"God knows I've tried," said Willie, glancing toward the wagon. Ornish Helms was still waving his hands at the keeper. "The man isn't much for philosophy, as we all well know. He isn't much for any of the world's pleasures that I can tell."

"That would include an afternoon in your company," said Mayo, resuming his digging.

The rest of the men took up their digging too.

"You'd be surprised who enjoys a lengthy afternoon in my company," said Willie, snubbing his shovel. "You could start by asking some of the women you've courted."

Frank Mayo possessed tousled, wheat-colored hair and a like-hued mustache, lovingly tended. "The women I court might be interested in you as a museum piece," he said.

"Women enjoy an older man," Willie said. "He's more apt to pay attention to their needs, rather than his own reflection."

"You need to pay attention to digging, or we'll be burying these men in the dark."

Despite himself, Willie jumped. In ten years of service under Daniel Cole, Willie had never gotten used to the man's approach. He walked like a deer and, more annoying still, rarely announced himself. Had it been any other man, Willie would have sworn he was the butt of a subtly crafted joke.

Willie forgot his good mood. "I wish you'd quit walking like a wisp of fog. Man my age can't take too many starts."

"You won't die of overexertion," said Cole, taking up a shovel.

"I prefer to parcel my energy wisely."

"It would be wise to be gone from here before nightfall," said Cole.

"I'm at home in the dark," said Willie. "Just ask Mayo's ladies."

Several of the men laughed softly. Cole glanced at Hiram. The boy shoveled silently, a burlap sack at his feet. Cole felt Willie's eyes on him, but he ignored the surfman's stare.

Cole had left Antone Lucas to man the station. Before they left for the cemetery, Willie had come upstairs to Cole's quarters to ask that Hiram stay behind too. Willie had argued that even a blind man could see the girl's death had shaken the boy deeply; to have him dig her grave would be callous and uncaring, a sign that man was no better than the beasts. Cole had ignored the inference and the request. Death was part of their job. The sooner the boy grew accustomed to it, the better off he'd be. Hiram had walked the two miles to Provincetown cemetery with the rest of them.

Willie resumed digging, his mind on the boy. At seventeen, Hiram had already seen his share of life's fickle cruelty, but the boy still brimmed with energy and wonder. He was sad at times, and this was to be expected, but when he was absorbed in the present, he fairly boiled with curiosity and life. He reminded Willie of the electric ball that had careened through one of the station's windows during a lightning storm. The apparition had hummed about the station for an instant before buzzsawing back out the window, leaving everyone's hair on end. When Hiram joined the station as winter man two months earlier, hired to bolster manpower in a season that saw an average of two shipwrecks a week along the Cape's shore, he had infused the station with life. The men had taken to him instantly.

Since the wreck of the *Asia*, everyone had tried to shake Hiram from his gloom. Martin had baked a cherry pie, but the pie lay untouched for three days until Martin finally allowed the men to eat it. They tried cards with equivalent luck. Hiram was the luckiest card player any of them had seen, with consistent good fortune that would have been irritating and suspect in any other man. But Hiram didn't care whether he won or lost, and so his luck was endearing, though not to Antone, whose own luck with cards was equivalently bad. During calm weather, the two played poker deep into the night, matchsticks piling beside Hiram, hissed curses piling on Antone's lips.

Life, however, possessed an unfathomable deck; the boy had been dealt an unexpected card.

Maintaining a semblance of digging, Willie eyed the bodies curiously. Frost had turned every man pale, but they were still clearly sailors, their faces burnished by sun and wind, their hands scarred. The sole exception lay a short spit off Willie's right boot. The man was shaven-headed, with astonishingly large ears. Even in a frosted state, it was clear the elements had only recently gnawed his face raw. With the exception of a purpled coin-size mark in the center of his right palm, his hands were smooth, the nails tended. Fastidious to the end, the man had washed ashore wearing hand-sewn leather shoes and a silk vest, firmly buttoned. He was a good ten years older than any of his companions. Willie guessed the man was either an unlucky passenger or, more likely, a shipping company minion; perhaps an accountant, maybe even one of the ship's owners. Whoever he was, Willie doubted he had envisioned an end like this.

Willie felt sorry for the men, but he was more intrigued by the puzzle their bodies presented. By their youth and dress, all but the elephant-eared man were clearly sailors. But if the bald man had not been the captain, then one face was missing.

Under most circumstances it was not at all unusual for bodies to be lost to the sea. Given time, pushed by wind and current, bloated bodies often sailed off for the horizon. But the storm that had claimed the *Asia* had possessed an extraordinarily fierce northeast wind. The onshore wind, abetted by the tremendous surf, had driven virtually everything but the *Asia* herself ashore; the beach had been littered with lumber, tangles of rigging and sail, even a bilge pump that weighed the rough equivalent of an ox. Eventually, they would receive the crew list from the shipping company, but at the moment, it appeared one body had possibly bucked the elements, swaying now somewhere on the sea bottom.

Wherever he swayed, the missing man had at least escaped with his dignity. The *Asia's* crew was now outfitted for the circus. Once again, the Woman's National Relief Association had provided burial vestments, and again no apparent accounting had been given to size. The largest sailors strained to burst their buttoned jackets, while the hands and feet of the smallest disappeared inside pants cuffs and jacket sleeves, as if they were already receding in death. It was true the Woman's National Relief Association had limited means and could not provide for every variation of the human form. But it was also true the organization was comprised primarily of widows, many of whom had suffered unhappy marriages.

Done with the men, Willie's eyes walked the cemetery. Even by graveyard standards, Provincetown's final resting place was a sad and meager place; a half-acre of sandy dirt and wiry grass, treeless but for the solitary white oak at the cemetery's eastern edge. Headstones and wood crosses, canted at innumerable angles and stained like rotted teeth, drifted on the loamy rise and fall of land. There were no mausoleums or grand monuments. Times were never easy on the Cape. What money there was went to the living.

In Willie's mind, the cemetery possessed one saving grace: from its heights, it offered a resplendent view of Provincetown's steepled churches and jumbled buildings, and the wharves, lined with all manner of vessel, poked like thumbs into Cape Cod Bay. Willie did not miss the humor in the cemetery's location. It perched, patient as any predator, gazing down on the bustle of ignorant victims.

Though few gave thought to their own inevitable residence, many enjoyed the prospect of seeing others lain to rest. For the past hour, a steady stream of townspeople had arrived in wagons and on foot. Nearly sixty people now stood murmuring in groups. Many came to pray because it was the duty of churchgoing folk, but it was also true that a dead child was rare.

Willie noted one conspicuous absence. Reverend Marmaduke Matthews was head of the Presbyterian Church. The largest church in Provincetown, its towering steeple pointed bright white into the sky, an illuminating finger reminding all that God watched their every move. Marmaduke Matthews was also Provincetown's largest minister. Within the walls of his church, the reverend, aided by his great bulk, issued booming scoldings, well-attended by the God-fearing. If one believed Marmaduke Matthews, hell was a crowded place, but the Devil had space enough remaining.

Reverend Matthews rarely bypassed a funeral or a crowd, both providing opportunity for driving yet another fiery lance of retribution into the rotting hearts of sinners. Still, Willie was fairly certain the good reverend would miss this chance. For reasons Willie had never fathomed, Captain Cole despised the minister, and the keeper's distaste, when openly manifested, provided a snort of brimstone itself. A funeral of today's magnitude would be a sore temptation, but Willie doubted the reverend had the nerve for it.

Daniel Cole noted Reverend Matthews' absence with relief. He detested religion as man had molded it. The ministers he had known lavished their attentions on the rich and the dead, distracting themselves, now and again, to berate the rest of the hard-working populace. They also prattled on, a particular inconvenience on a day as cold as this.

Cole saw he was not to escape aggravation entirely, however. As they finished squaring the mass grave, a tall figure cloaked in a black robe moved briskly in their direction. On the Cape, two things were certain: men died in shipwrecks, and Widow Addison Doane, doyenne of the Relief Association, oversaw their interment.

Widow Doane stepped up to Cole. She clasped a worn Bible in her hands. Although her frame was as spare as bamboo, her neck retained a repository of loose skin that, at this moment, swung from side to side as she took in the men.

"Keeper Cole, you'll bury the girl first."

Cole stood stiffly. "I will see to it."

Widow Doane nodded curtly. "You are a man who sees things through."

Cole held Widow Doane's gaze, but Willie saw his friend's knuckles whiten on the shovel. It wasn't just Widow Doane. Women made Daniel Cole uncomfortable. His friend had loved once, but now it was as if he had forgotten what to do in even the simplest circumstances.

Willie knew women found the keeper attractive. Though a head shorter than most men, he was square-shouldered and powerfully built, yet he retained the lithe movements and clear-sighted gaze of a boy scooping frogs from a creek. He considered the world through dark eyes made darker still by a shock of coal-black hair. The collective effect was one of sobriety and sadness. Women found sadness irresistible, and though they might swoon briefly at the feet of a romancer, in the end, seriousness was what their practical nature desired. Several of the whores Willie knew at the Cork and Barrel had expressed curiosity regarding the captain, and certain of the Cape's distinguished widows allowed word to circulate that they considered the keeper a worthy match. But Cole showed no interest in anyone. That mute indifference had been instilled in a man whom women desired was, in Willie's mind, proof again that God liked things lively.

Widow Doane was not among Daniel Cole's admirers.

"Reverend Matthews will not be attending," she said. "I am assuming you will be conducting the service, Captain Cole?"

"Yes."

"I have prepared a sermon."

"It won't be necessary."

The widow dipped her chin slightly as if she might charge. Instead she said, "The girl is dressed in the dress we provided?"

"I saw to it myself."

"She looks natural?"

"As best as can be expected."

"Has she been marked in any fashion?"

"Only her legs."

The ache of not knowing shone in the widow's eyes. She waited, but Cole did not oblige.

"Her legs?" she said finally.

"They were broken."

"Poor child. Did she suffer greatly?"

"Only she could have told us."

"Are her injuries adequately concealed?"

"She is amply covered by the dress you supplied."

Willie peeked into the coffin. The dress was big enough for a grown woman. It bunched in great folds at the girl's feet, like a rose pedestal.

"The coffin is sufficient?" asked Widow Doane.

"Yes."

Widow Doane shot a tart glance in the direction of the undertaker, standing long-faced beside the supply wagon.

"I hope that miserly man's needs are as simple when it comes time for his own funeral," she said, and with a cluck, Widow Doane departed.

Cole turned to the men.

"Place the shovels out of the way. We'll start the service in five minutes."

Hiram had absorbed the unfoldings with numb disinterest, but now the moment had come. Bending, he picked up the sack at his feet. Walking to the supply wagon, he felt the brush of mourners, but for all he knew he was parting wheat. He ignored the skinny undertaker too. His hands and legs shook.

Hiram took the doll from the sack, the satin dress smooth against his fingers. He had washed the dress in a kitchen pot late one night, taking down the rusted iron and pressing it smooth. He placed the doll on the wagon. The dishwater afternoon turned the bright red dress cheerier still. He stared at the doll for moment, the bald spot where the hair had been torn away, the lopsided smile, as if the left side of the mouth had assumed death's sadness.

Leaning over the coffin, Hiram willed his eyes wide. For a week now, the girl had tormented his dreams, her eyes probing his. Now her face was peaceful, and, with her eyes shut, accepting. Hiram knew this was another lie.

When he reached for the doll, it was gone.

"She's pretty," said a small voice. "Even bald."

Hiram could not breathe. His heart galloped in his chest.

He turned. He was not hearing the dead. The girl was no more than five. She stared up at him, nearly swallowed up in a pile of jackets and a woolen cap.

The doll swung in a mittened hand.

"Mother is afraid of the cold," she said. "My brother died of pneumonia. He was three. I'm wearing two pairs of wool knickers. They chafe."

Hiram tried to smile. "You're Mrs. Parson's daughter," he said.

"Emilia."

"Hello, Emilia."

The girl turned to the coffin. "Are you her father?"

"No."

The round face lost and regained hope in almost the same instant.

"Is her father ... *dead?*"

"Yes."

"What about her mother?"

"Her mother isn't here."

"Mother says women don't have to prove themselves by taking foolish chances at sea." The girl held the doll with both hands, studying it. She looked up at Hiram. "It's her doll?"

"Yes."

"But you have it now." The girl touched a chipped cheek gently. "You could give her to me."

He had vowed to do this one thing. To falter again would be almost laughable.

"The doll is all she has left. She needs it to help her rest."

"To help her *soul* rest. That ... " the girl jerked a mittened thumb at the coffin, " ... is food for worms." Her chapped lips pursed thoughtfully. "Her soul would know." The mittened hand rose. "I understand."

"Thank you," Hiram said, taking the doll.

"You're welcome." The girl tugged a corner of her wool cap. "She can't speak anymore," she said, and disappeared into the crowd.

Hiram nearly called after her. He was a coward and a fool. The dead had no use for dolls. If the girl could speak, she would laugh at him. Leaning over the casket, he placed the doll gently in the crook of an arm. The doll smiled up at him, but the girl did not.

They buried the girl first. Pale sunlight bathed the cemetery in apathetic light, but in the shadows thrown by the oak's thickest branches, evening already held sway. The living shivered. The floor of the grave was already glazed with frost.

Cole had fashioned a cross, whittling two pieces of birch to clean white bone and fixing them together with fishing line. Bending, he drove the cross into the jumbled earth.

Willie and Martin placed the coffin beside the grave. The mourners pressed forward, jockeying for a glimpse.

Cole had wanted the coffin shut, but Widow Doane had insisted the coffin remain open until it was lowered into the grave; the gathered, she said, should know the heartless capriciousness of the devil sea. Cole thought the sentiment ridiculous, like showcasing a plough for farmers, but he kept silent. Having once denied Widow Doane the chance to speak, he had realized the danger of forcing her to relent again.

Willie and the Swede slid the lid into place. Willie nailed the lid shut. The hammering in the frozen stillness was sharp and loud. Several mourners, veterans of the war, hunched at the first report. The surfmen lowered the casket with ropes, bumping it to rest.

After the sailors had been rolled as delicately as possible into their mass grave, Cole spoke.

"These sailors knew the risks of their profession. Their deaths were a risk willingly shouldered. The sadness here is in the loved ones left behind." Cole bowed his head.

The mourners, caught off guard by the brevity of the sermon, shuffled and whispered before following suit. A child giggled.

Widow Doane began reciting the Lord's Prayer.

Cole spoke over her. "Children are a different matter. They do not choose their fate."

Cole watched for a moment as the oak's thinner branches, nudged by the freshening wind, assumed a mocking bob. "Someone had their reasons for taking this child to sea in winter. May they live with those reasons in whatever eternity awaits them."

Cole turned to the surfmen. "Fill in the graves."

3

The walk back through the Provincelands took the exhausted men over an hour. They trekked silently among the great dunes, sobered by cold, death, and the effort of spading frozen earth. Sand squeaked beneath their boots. Overhead, the day departed.

They rounded the final dune as the lifesaving station basked in the last light of the setting sun. The two-story building's sharply angled cedar-shingle roof, topped by the lookout tower, was coated with frost. The last light turned the frost soft pink. The men had no interest in nature's brush strokes. All eyes were fixed on the light through the ground floor windows and the dark wisp of smoke rising through the metal funnel on the roof.

Antone had stoked the potbellied stove for their arrival. Now, the men crowded about the stove, thrusting stinging hands as close as possible to the hot iron.

The sight of the islander standing in his suspenders and an undershirt irked Willie.

"You missed a fine outing," Willie said to him, turning the backs of his hands to the stove. "I hope you didn't find it too tedious and discomfiting amidst this tropical torpor."

Antone shifted uncomfortably. "The stove is too hot?" he asked.

"It is for one of us," Willie said.

Antone had arrived at Peaked Hill Bars six years earlier on a fine fall morning, sitting straight-backed atop the carriage from Wellfleet, battered trunk in one hand, seven-foot hickory-shaft harpoon in the other. With great and silent ceremony, the dark-skinned man, harpoon rising two feet over his head, had handed Captain Cole a scrap of paper on which was scrawled the word *work*.

A cursory glance was enough to see the arrival was too small for lifesaving work. Not wanting to bruise the man's dignity, Cole allowed him to stay the night. The following morning, Antone had marched silently beside the surfboat as the men drove the boat to the water's edge for the morning's drill. As they pushed the boat into knee-deep water, to everyone's surprise, the silent man swung nimbly over the gunnel, taking up Mayo's oar. More surprising, Captain Cole allowed him to remain at the oar. They made several dozen runs in and out through the surf, which, on that day was appreciable, comprising jumbled breakers five to eight feet high. Mayo's oar was closest to the stern; only Cole, standing at the steering oar was farther astern. Through the splash and spray, each surfman had watched the dark-skinned sprite maneuver the oar as if it were part of him. On the final run, Cole let him take the steering oar. Here too, he performed impeccably.

Cole had hired Antone on their return to the station. That afternoon, the islander had pantomimed his request to Martin. Cole was presented with a second scrap of paper on which Martin had scrawled *I am your loyal servant*.

After six years, Antone's command of English had improved, but it still possessed holes into which Willie liberally poured salt.

"You missed funeral services summarily orchestrated by our pithy keeper," Willie said.

Antone looked to Martin.

"The funeral was short," Martin said.

"Piss off," said Willie.

Martin smiled.

"Surfman Bangs is upset," he said to Antone.

"Yes," said Antone, catching the spirit. "He is heating up."

"It's like watching a dog discover its balls," said Willie.

Ben Maddocks roused himself. "There is no call for coarse language," he said. "Coarse language is a step down the Devil's path."

"At least it's warm there," said Willie.

Ben regarded Willie benevolently.

"You are tired, but God's creatures must act appropriately in every circumstance." Ben raised his eyes to the oak beams squared off beneath the roof. "When the storms of life are raging, when the world is tossing me like a ship upon the sea, thou who rulest wind and water, stand by us."

"He's the only one with a donkey's patience," said Willie.

No one agreed or disagreed. The men only stood by the stove, nodding to sleep on their feet.

Daniel Cole did not follow the men inside. He rarely felt the cold anymore, and what cold he felt, he shouldered as his due. He walked to the edge of the cliffs and looked out at the ocean. The Atlantic, dark and disorderly beneath the first stars, ran to a disappearing horizon.

He stood, considering the *Asia.* They had done what they could. The seas had been too heavy for a boat rescue. Even with a dangerous addition of gunpowder, repeated attempts to fire a line to the *Asia* with the Lyle gun had been beaten down by the heavy snow and fierce onshore wind. They had been forced to wait for the wind to slacken or the waves to push the ship off the outermost shoal and into range of the line. But the *Asia's* keel had remained fixed and the storm's fury had spiraled to even greater heights, a foul child feeding on its own hellish tantrum. The crew had perished. The girl, washed ashore still bound to the mainmast, had lived long enough to die in their hands. They had accomplished nothing but a burial.

Cole knew their hands had been tied, but failure gnawed at him. Staring out at the water, he felt a profound weariness. In the ten years since the first lifesaving stations had been constructed on Cape Cod—nine stations stretching along the shoreline from Monomoy in the south, to Race Point near Provincetown—hundreds had been rescued. Magazines and newspapers trumpeted these rescues in reports that Cole found overblown and often inaccurate, but there was no denying lives had been saved. But nature cared nothing for their accomplishments. Ships and storms kept coming, and sailors and passengers fell from deck and rigging, the ocean swallowing their screams. Cole often felt as if he were standing in a fast-moving river, struggling to stay on his feet while crying souls swept past, their arms outstretched.

Far below, the beach was ghost gray. It was time for the first patrol. Peaked Hill Bars sat between North Truro's High Head Station, four miles to the south, and Race Point Station, three miles to the northwest. Each night, in three shifts—sunset to eight, eight to midnight, and midnight to four—two surfmen left the station to patrol, one walking northwest along the great curve of beach, the other going south. Halfway between the stations, they met surfmen from High Head and Race Point. Exchanging a metal token to mark their meeting, the surfmen turned back for their respective stations.

Looking toward the station, Cole saw Willie approaching, hunched against the cold.

Willie stepped up beside him and began rolling a cigarette.

"The first patrol has left?" Cole asked.

"I took care of it."

Cole accepted the offered smoke. They smoked for a time in silence, enjoying the cool rush of tobacco. Cole usually preferred to be alone, but on this troubled night, Willie was a welcome presence.

Willie blew a smoke ring heavenward. "I'll bet a pair of Frenchmen are ruminating on this same water," he said, watching the ring rise and fade in the cold air. "Frenchmen are a pensive lot. They sit at cafes all day, sipping wine and discussing why Swiss cheese has holes. We don't ruminate enough in this country. We're too damn busy building a future."

Cole watched his own smoke ring.

"You'd make a fine Frenchman," he said.

"I'm a bored Frenchman," Willie said. "When you talk to yourself, there are few surprises." He brushed an errant ash from his knee. "Plenty of times, I'd kick my grandmother's shins for just one enlightening discussion. It's a grand world, filled with politics and poetry and music and women, and we crawl about this spit of sand, mindless as flies, repeating the days. I suspect you'd make a fine conversationalist if you said something that wasn't an order."

"Maybe then you'd listen."

Willie blew another smoke ring. "I'll bet the Frenchmen are sharing a bottle of wine," he said wistfully. "German," he added.

"What?"

"The bald man's shoes," said Willie. "They were German. Very expensive. The man had fine taste."

"How would you know that?"

"I read the fashion magazines."

"Why a man who wears tobacco-stained long johns and ten-year-old wool trousers reads fashion magazines is a puzzle to me," Cole said.

"You can educate yourself about things without taking them up," said Willie. "Maybe you could read about curiosity."

Cole's mind was already clamped on the shoes. They had caught his attention when they found the bald man on the beach. It wasn't that the man wore dress shoes, although that was unusual. What was odd was a drowned man fully dressed. The *Asia* had not gone down quickly. Those on board had had ample time to consider their end. Most men, faced with plunging into the sea, stripped off everything that threatened to drag them under. At the very least, they removed their boots. The bald man had washed ashore with his shoes firmly tied, each button on his silk vest securely fastened. It were as if the man had calmly dressed for his own funeral.

But this was only a trifling oddity, turned askew and pressed vainly into an increasingly strange puzzle. There were stranger, more inexplicable facts. The girl, for one. Children traveled on passenger vessels, not on merchanteers, and they rarely traversed the entire Atlantic on winter's treacherous seas. Martin had reported the girl's accent was English; she had died far from home. Someone had taken her to sea at considerable risk. Considerable risk was rarely undertaken without opportunity for like gain, but what could possibly be gained from the ferrying of mundane cargo? From the pieces of lumber washed ashore, the *Asia's* assignment appeared no different from that of countless vessels wrecked along the Cape. That the girl was aboard spoke of something else. The ship, too, was built for speed, her lines fine, her composite light. There was no reason to race across the Atlantic with a cargo of lumber. Cole suspected the *Asia* hadn't carried much lumber at all.

The missing captain vexed Cole too. He had waited out the week, certain one of the stations to the south would find a body, but no report had come. It was possible they had recovered all the bodies. Perhaps the well-dressed man had been the captain. Cole knew of instances in which company owners bestowed a captaincy to a family member or relative, staffing the vessel with an able first mate to keep the ship on course. But instinct told him this was not the case. He was almost certain the captain was not among the dead they had buried.

There was a last matter, in Cole's mind, that was no puzzle at all. When Antone had first sighted the *Asia,* she was heading north under full sail, her rigging set to beat upwind. The foolish risk had seen to her end. The overpowering headwinds had poured into the full sails like fists, driving her back onto the shoals stern-first. From the beach, they had heard the thunderclap-slatting of the sails as the canvas finally tore away, madcap ghosts twisting wildly through the air. A captain would beat upwind under full sail in such conditions for one reason: safe harbor close at hand. But the closest harbor was Provincetown, several miles to the north. Cole had no doubt the captain, whoever and wherever he was, had believed salvation was at hand, until the sea ended the chances and lives of everyone on board, including a child.

The thought sickened Cole. Again, he contemplated the black belief that evil had its way with the world. He picked up Willie's words slowly, like a gull's distant cries.

"It's senseless worry, Daniel. It was a hellish storm, and no one, not even Daniel Cole, could have thought their way around it. Only God himself could have saved that girl. Sadly, God is the only person who doesn't take orders from you."

Cole said nothing. His mind followed the *Asia*, beating upwind.

"There are plenty of men who believe you control fate," said Willie, "but I hope you're not one of them. It was poor luck, pure and simple. That ship found herself in a bad place. The outcome should surprise no one, least of all you."

Cole knew there was no sense postponing the inevitable. "And the boy?" he asked.

"What about him?"

"You didn't come out here just to cheer me up," said Cole. "You think it was wrong bringing Hiram to the cemetery."

Willie blew a smoke ring. Cole recognized it as punctuation.

"It's your enviable job to make decisions, Daniel. Since we're alone, I'll allow that more times than not, they're right."

"I worry that may be changing."

"Doubt is part of the human condition, and so are you."

The human condition, thought Cole, was precisely what stymied him. He needed help, and as much as it pained him, the man beside him might provide it.

"Why do you think Hiram is taking the girl's death so hard?" Cole asked.

Willie shrugged. "Only he can tell you. If you want my guess, death is a particular shock to the young. You and I aren't young anymore." Willie waited.

Cole smoked, the ash glowing bright.

Willie said, "He lost his sister at about the same age. I never heard the particulars."

"I don't know what happened," said Cole.

"When you ask for help, you can return the favor."

"Nellie and Samuel Paine were private," said Cole. "Their daughter's death was their business."

"Nellie never said anything to you? If I believed you were capable of having a friend, she would be the one." Willie felt bad as soon as he said it. "You were good to her when her husband passed."

"I did what anyone would do."

Willie did not miss the omission of particulars. "Fine then, keep your opinions to yourself," he said. "Whatever the circumstances, I'd wager his sister's death is part of Hiram's trouble now. I'd also wager that making him attend that mopey ceremony didn't perk him up much."

Cole awaited further haranguing.

Instead, Willie gave a slow chuckle. "By God, the expression on Ornish Helm's face when he saw the girl was priceless. You'd have thought he'd just been told that people had decided to up and stop dying. Fussy as he is, he couldn't have done a better job. Right down to the bow, you didn't miss a trick. Maybe you should take up undertaking. It's a natural sideline."

Cole had removed the ribbon from the small box he kept in the bottom drawer of his desk. He had tied the ribbon countless times, Julia sitting, hand mirror in her lap, gazing out the window at the sparkle of Shetland's Pond with the comfortable look children have, certain their world is safe. It was their game; he tying the ribbon in myriad forms, Julia lifting the mirror to give each creation focused study before requesting a change. He still felt the cool strands of her hair slipping between his fingers.

It had taken him four tries to tie the bow in the girl's hair. When he finished, it was all he could do to not sink to his knees.

"Should I have let Widow Doane speak?" he said.

"If you had, we'd still be standing there," said Willie. "You and I don't agree on many things, but I agree there's no sense lingering over the dead. They don't care for long ceremonies any more than the living do."

"Some people take brevity to be disrespectful."

"However they take it, they expect it from you. You're as predictable as the tides."

"It's a mistake to think you know anyone," said Cole.

"I know the gathered didn't pine for a sermon from Widow Doane. The only person with a greater love for the sound of scripture is Reverend Matthews. If words were money, the king of Persia would be polishing that man's shoes." Willie pretended to consider something on the end of his boot. "Marmaduke's a queer name, isn't it?"

Willie was hoping to draw his friend's mind away from his troubles, but he was fishing too. It was true Cole had no love for man's religion. Equally true, Marmaduke Matthews' mouth was always open, and no one disliked chatter more than Daniel Cole. But these were not reasons to hate a man. Even now, Cole's face hardened.

"I suspect Marmaduke sounds perfectly natural to him," Cole said.

Having raised the topic, Willie was genuinely curious. "It sounds like old English," he said. "Maybe it means 'tireless tongue' or 'stupendous bag of wind.' "

"Those strike me as apt descriptions of other men."

"I hope you have a direct line to God, because there's one minister who won't be praying for your soul," Willie said.

"Reverend Matthews' prayers don't count for much," Cole said.

"You know who God listens to?"

"I've seen no proof God listens at all."

"One can always rely on Daniel Cole for a cheerful thought," said Willie.

Two lights appeared on the beach.

Cole was mildly alarmed that he had forgotten. "They're late," he said.

"Take it out of my hide," said Willie. "I told them they could rest an extra fifteen minutes if they walked faster. In case you hadn't noticed, they spent the better part of the day banging their joints against frozen ground."

From this distance, the lanterns twinkled prettily. They made their way to the water's edge, stayed close a moment longer, and then separated north and south.

"A last peck on the cheek," said Willie. "Do you ever wonder if anyone is looking down on us?"

"Who would be looking down on us?"

"The deceased," said Willie.

"The dead are gone." Cole hoped that would be enough, but of course it wasn't.

"Practically speaking, I suppose they are," said Willie. "They're not at your table eating, or warming your bed, or getting on your nerves. But I've often wondered if a piece of them stays behind. Not a ghost, but some spark that isn't extinguished. Maybe now and again it peeks in to see how its loved ones are doing. Or maybe it just peeks to be nosey."

"If there is a heaven," said Cole, "I'd think every scrap of the deceased would run from this world screaming."

To Cole, heaven was a dreamer's wish. There had been a group in Barnstable called the Come-Outers who'd walked along the tops of fences to avoid the sidewalks thick with sinners. As far as Cole could see everyone sinned, no matter where they walked.

Willie was now doing what he usually did, namely, annoy him.

"That something as magnificent as the human spirit can be wholly snuffed in a blink is hard to swallow," Willie said.

"I'd have thought you'd seen enough death by now to know that's exactly the case."

Willie ran a thumb along his stubbled jaw. "I'm not so sure I like the idea of my loved ones watching anything they want. That would take some of the pep from my sails. Plus, I'd have to arrive in heaven prepared for a tongue lashing."

Cole's irritation turned to amusement. "You'll go to heaven?"

Willie scowled. "Why not? I've performed a few indiscretions, but it's never been to the detriment of anyone else. It's not like heaven is only inhabited by whitewashed saints and the virgins I never tended to."

"Heaven's admission standards are as loose as your morals."

"Joke all you want," said Willie, "but I think a part of you believes in the hereafter. Or wants to. Why else would a man spend every Saturday in a cemetery? By now, you've memorized the view."

The weight in Cole's heart never left him, so it couldn't return.

"You can't punish yourself forever, Daniel. Sara would be the first to tell you that communing with headstones is untoward punishment and plain unnatural too."

Cole was too tired to muster anger. "What would you propose I do?" he asked. "Go with you to whore and drink in Provincetown? I can't say that's much of a life. It's none of your business how I spend my time. But I'll tell you it's peaceful at the cemetery, and I can escape from conversations like this one."

Willie dropped his cigarette, squashing it under a boot. "Suit yourself," he said. "You're a stubborn goat. The rest of the men admire that, but I see it as fear of change."

"You're free to see what you like."

"I'm just trying to get you to see beyond the next coat of paint," said Willie. "Afterlife or no, there's more to life than this life."

After Willie left, Cole stood considering the dark water. One mistake—a boat turned broadside, a misstep among coiled lines, a back turned to a panicked sailor—and water's caress would provide ablution. Those very mistakes, and hundreds of feckless permutations, killed men regularly. Sometimes in the middle of a rescue, while the steering oar wrenched like a terrified animal in his hands, he would absorb the unfolding carnage with detached curiosity. The black heavens, the leaping waves like wildly snatching hands, the surfboat angling dangerously, the men pulling frantically at the oars, all of it became a siren call. How easy to lean, to slip overboard, a moment's discomfort as the body reflexively fought to save itself, and then nothing.

But then he would return to nature's yowl and see the strained faces of the men, their eyes fixed on him while they put their fear into the oar. He was their shepherd in a cathedral turned inside out and screaming. He could not walk away.

He turned for the station.

That night, Hiram stumbled outside, bladder brimming. Rounding the corner of the station, working sleepily at his pants buttons, he nearly stepped on the dog. Hiram heard frantic scrabbling, followed by a guttural growl.

The dog was so ragged-ribbed it looked as if it would blow away. Instead, the ratty animal bunched, haunches quivering, unwilling to give up the ground beneath its feet. Its head was lowered, its bared teeth glistened against sagging gums, and the hairs on its back spiked stiffly. Wild dogs never attacked anything bigger than a cottontail rabbit, but something here was different. Dog and boy stood, panting steam.

Hiram felt his hands drooping idle at his pants buttons. He raised them slowly. The growling rose with his hands.

The movement was a blur. The dog made a short hop back, its body performing a snapping, near miraculous reversal in midair. It was running before it struck the ground, disappearing into the night so quickly, Hiram might have questioned its presence if not for the hammering of his heart and the smell of something rotten in the frozen air.

He peed facing the dunes, his hands shaking.

He was still shaking as he lay in his cot. He looked up into the dark rafters and listened to the men snoring, the sound a growling itself.

Only when he began to scold himself for his pointless fear did he realize where the standoff had taken place. The dead sailors were gone, but a starving dog did not see it that way.

4

The next morning before breakfast, Cole was surprised by a knock on his door. Surfman Lucas and Surfman Nelson stepped into his quarters. The two men stood before his desk, rigid as trees, the islander a sapling, the Swede an oak.

"We have a request, sir," said the oak.

The paralyzed men reminded Cole of grouse before a flush, but Cole refused himself a smile. Both men were fine lifesavers. They deserved his respect.

"Please proceed," Cole said.

Martin stepped forward, bumping against the desk. "We wish to take Surfman Paine into town," he blurted.

Cole stifled his surprise. Outside of extenuating circumstances such as the burial of the *Asia's* crew, only one surfman at a time left the station, and only on his day off. The islander and the Swede were obsessive about regulations, but they were also closest to the boy.

"Three of you," said Cole, just to be sure.

"Yes, sir," said Martin.

"May I ask why?"

"For Hiram's spirits, sir."

Cole's mind moved quickly over the facts. Seas were calm, the barometer steady. There were no drills today. Wednesdays were devoted to upkeep and repairs. Painting could wait; rope needed splicing, but that was easily handled by the remaining men. He would have liked an explanation, but Martin and Antone had earned his trust.

It also countered his judgment, but he was growing tired of being judge. Perhaps, he could embrace change.

"Be back by mid-afternoon," he said.

Antone had explained his plan to Martin, who, to his credit, had agreed with only minor protest. The three lifesavers left for Provincetown after a breakfast of sorely burnt beans; they alternated cooking, and Ben was perhaps the worst cook in the entire United States Lifesaving Service. As the station dropped from sight, Hiram took a last look over his shoulder, half expecting to be called back, but saw only a few gulls watching from a roof corner.

Hiram desperately wanted to ask where they were going, but he had vowed to remain silent, and as they walked he clenched his jaw tight. Martin was silent too, but Antone filled in for both of them, jabbering about long-ago whaling hunts, the fine points of scrimshaw, and a cousin in the Azores who was pregnant by a married man. Antone interrupted this discourse periodically to question Martin's courage. Martin ignored the insults, walking vacant-eyed along the rutted path that led toward Provincetown. Despite his vow to remain angry, Hiram began to feel sorry for Martin. He had never seen the Swede so mournful. Hiram wondered if Ben's beans were troubling his stomach.

Reaching Provincetown, they proceeded to the home of Widow Caroline Mayhew. The mansion was one of the grandest in town, the long drive lined with cypress pines that whispered as they passed.

It was not yet eight, the air still heavy with night's frost, but the door swung wide with Antone's first rap.

"We are here for the contest," stated Antone formally.

Hiram was baffled, but Widow Mayhew was perfectly comfortable with this remark. She was also comfortable standing before three men in bright red wool knickers. The old lady was close to eighty. Her lipstick-covered mouth, which matched her knickers, made a loose circle. Hiram guessed it was a failed smile, supported as it was by three teeth.

She took a long look at Martin. To Hiram, she looked like a woman deciding on a dress.

"You're a big fellow," she said, nodding appreciatively. "I favor big fellows. Mr. Mayhew was a big fellow. That was satisfying."

To Hiram's shock, Widow Mayhew gave Martin a sly wink.

"In days gone by," she continued, "I would have made you weak-kneed, but alas, as you can see, time has reduced me to nothing but elbows and knees." She turned her attention momentarily to an elbow, brushing free a clump of hair. "Damn dog. Blind and foul smelling. Age is unkind to every species."

Stepping out to the porch, she closed the door behind her, placing the clump of hair in a potted plant by the door.

"We have business to discuss," she said to Antone.

Antone and the widow went down the steps and out onto the frozen grass. The widow was barefoot. Hiram watched them confer. Once, Widow Mayhew turned back to the porch to take a long look at him.

Martin continued to face the door as if hoping someone else might answer. Widow Mayhew trotted nimbly up the steps, passing by on her bone-white feet.

Hiram couldn't help himself. "Are your feet cold, ma'am?"

The widow regarded her feet happily. "Once brown as bark and twice as tough. I went walkabout in nothing but these feet. The Aborigines, you should know, are quite advanced in their views of this world. Our haughty Mr. Kipling calls them the lesser breeds, but he is woefully misguided, and a pansy and snoot as well."

With that, she shut the door in their faces.

Hiram was completely rudderless. He had long heard that Widow Mayhew was crazy as a loon. Those rumors were now firmly cemented. But, Martin's chalky complexion aside, his companions seemed comfortable with the strange unfoldings.

Antone bounced a punch off Martin's arm. "We see a world wonder!" he said. "Find your courage. You are not being hung."

"Maybe you could take my place," Martin said.

"Impossible! You're the big fellow!"

They walked along the side yard. There was a large corral behind the mansion, fencing in a half-acre square, but the animal at the center of the corral was not a horse. It stood upright on enormous haunches, taller than any man. As they approached the fence, a tiny head, like a disproportionate afterthought, jerked about to regard them. Steamy wisps chuffed from the black nostrils on the creature's snout.

Widow Mayhew was waiting at the fence, an ankle-length wool coat over her knickers. Her feet were still bare. Climbing up on the lowest rail, she gave a single war-like shriek.

The creature disappeared. At least Hiram thought it disappeared. It no longer stood where it had been. There had been a slight rustle of straw beneath the plank feet, then nothing but a curling wisp of dust.

Hiram saw the kangaroo, thirty yards from where it once stood, moving along the far edge of the corral with impossible leaps, each takeoff and landing marked by a dusty explosion. Then, just as abruptly, the great animal was standing before them, filling the air with steam and a horse-like smell.

Hiram felt his jaw unhinge. He had seen photographs of kangaroos in schoolbooks, but the photographs were fuzzy and taken from a distance, so that the animals appeared to be cute, cuddly creatures. The animal before him was not cuddly in the least. It was at least eight feet tall, with a chest like a barrel. Sharp claws were affixed to its spindly arms. Its snout, making its way down to them, contained horse-size teeth.

"God almighty," whispered Antone.

Martin mumbled something.

Widow Mayhew announced, "Wundurra. Aboriginal for warrior."

Reaching into the bag in her hand, Widow Mayhew produced a carrot. "Of course, *you* know that," she cooed at the animal.

The kangaroo bowed forward, taking the carrot delicately in its tiny clawed hands. Rising, it held the carrot to its snout as if it were commencing to play the flute. In an instant, the carrot was gone.

The kangaroo accepted a second carrot, again executing a stately bow and gingerly taking the vegetable from the widow's hand.

"Might we all have such table manners," Widow Mayhew said. "In most instances, kangaroos are the gentlest of creatures. On our very first meeting, Wundurra nuzzled my ear. Mr. Mayhew gave him to me as an anniversary present. Wundurra hated my husband from the outset, kicked the stuffing out of him on more than one occasion. We kept him nonetheless. One must keep a woman happy."

Hiram knew that wealthy families on Nantucket and the Cape collected curiosities from around the world, but he had not imagined they'd be breathing.

Martin stared transfixed as the kangaroo dispatched a third carrot.

"You'll have more of a chance if you start breathing," Widow Mayhew told him. "Give him a scratch. He's harmless now that he's finished eating. The only thing that truly upsets Wundurra is someone tampering with his food."

Martin slowly extended a hand. The kangaroo bowed. Verifying the absence of carrot, it pushed Martin's hand away with its snout.

"It appears you've been rebuffed," said Widow Mayhew. "Wundurra has never had much love for men. I suspect he sees you, too, as a rival for my substantial charms." Widow Mayhew clapped her hands together. "What a grand morning! It's been far too long since men fought over me."

She turned to Antone. "Three dollars to you, should your man last three minutes. Three dollars to me if he is knocked silly, though with most men, it's hard to tell."

She reached into a second bag at her feet. "Your man must wear these," she said. She handed the boxing gloves to Martin. "I'd advise you retract your punches quickly. It's not the original pair. I believe Wundurra thinks they're melons."

Widow Mayhew gave a bow not unlike the kangaroo's. "Now man and animal will battle for lady and honor. And perhaps an extra carrot."

Martin gave Hiram a sickly grin.

Hiram smiled back at his friend, his own dry mouth forming a grimace. "You don't have to do this," Hiram whispered. "I've seen the kangaroo. That's enough."

"Oh, but every creature has its shades," said Widow Mayhew, "and so bears examination in every light. Wundurra has never injured anyone beyond recovery. At worst, a clawing and a nasty welt or two. The unavoidable hurt is to the purse."

Widow Mayhew swung open the gate. "No time like the present, handsome knight."

Martin entered the corral, boxing gloves already up. The kangaroo had repaired to the distant fence to consult a noise in the woods. Its head swung about with the gate's closing creak. In four loping bounds the animal was on Martin. The Swede shouted. There followed a brief flurry of upper limbs.

Martin stood with his head against the kangaroo's chest, locked in place with a spindly arm. With its other arm, the kangaroo applied several cuffs to the top of Martin's head before losing interest.

Martin deemed it best to remain still. Man and beast stood in the gauzy sunlight, their labored breaths mingling in the frosty air.

Widow Mayhew frowned. "Frozen with indecision. I am reminded of my wedding night."

A crow's cry rang from the woods.

Widow Mayhew regarded the pair sadly. "I think Wundurra is smitten with him." Consulting her pocket watch, she snapped it shut. "An agreement is an agreement," she said.

Again, she issued the strident cry. The kangaroo broke away so quickly that Martin nearly fell. The animal circumnavigated the corral in eye-doubting bounds. For a horrible moment, Hiram was afraid it was coming around for a second attack, but the kangaroo halted before the widow, its great chest heaving. Dust rose.

Wagging a finger, Widow Mayhew handed over a carrot. "I should deprive you of three dollars' worth of carrots. Warrior. What a crock!"

She produced a purse. Fishing out three coins, she handed them to Antone.

Martin had climbed the fence and was now walking unsteadily toward the drive.

"Too unnerved to stay for tea," said Widow Mayhew, watching his broad back sadly. "Perhaps, another time."

Hiram moved to follow his friend.

"Young man," she called after him.

"Ma'am?" Hiram said.

"Come here."

Widow Mayhew still held the coin purse. The lipstick mouth formed a straight line. Hiram wondered if she was going to ask him to try his luck. He didn't want to box the kangaroo. This time, the animal might not be so disinterested.

"For you," the widow said.

She placed something smooth in his hand. Six inches long, the snake was adorned with alternating bands of white and yellow. The artist was precise in his carving, but crude with the paint. Reddish brown daubs splattered the sinuous form, spotting many of the bands.

"Carved from red gum root," said Widow Mayhew. "Australia was settled by English convicts. Fine people, the Australians. Their criminal heritage provides them ample backbone and a sense of fun. But it's the Aboriginals who are truly fascinating. A race like no other, they've been in the country since before time began." Her hand still rested on his. "No surprise, the Aborigines have no regard for time." The hand withdrew. "But few people believe crazy old ladies, now do they?"

The way she looked at him made Hiram profoundly embarrassed.

"As you turn older, the old become wiser," she said.

Hiram looked down at the carving. "Thank you."

When he looked up, Widow Mayhew was watching him.

"It's not a trinket," she said. "It is a reminder that there are things beyond us, and that life may extend beyond this unhappy place. The Aborigines celebrate death as a passage to something better. I prefer their outlook, though I confess a dour Anglican upbringing dies hard. Lacking though he was on certain fronts, I miss Mr. Mayhew terribly."

Something crept into her eyes that made her older still. "However it unfolds, death is part of life. And life, as death reminds us, is precious and not a day to be wasted."

Turning on a bare heel, Widow Mayhew strode to the house.

Antone and Hiram caught Martin at the end of the drive.

Antone wrinkled his nose. "Tonight, you sleep with Thoreau."

That night, sitting on his cot, Hiram stared at the carving in his palm. They had learned about Aborigines in school. They were scrawny fellows, blacker than midnight, who carried sticks sharpened to spears and ran about naked, much to the amusement of everyone in class. He had never thought of them as anything more than caricatures on the pages of a book.

The carving in his hand was feather light, as if it were already lifting away from this world.

5

A week after Martin's bout with the kangaroo, the men were presented with a natural wonder of a darker sort. News of the grounded whales reached Peaked Hill Bars an hour before dawn, with Ben Maddocks bursting into the station to announce life was fleeing the sea.

"Only because it's your watch," grumbled Mayo, propping himself sleepily on an elbow.

The stranded animals were pilot whales, better known on the Cape as blackfish. Beachings of larger whales were not uncommon along the Cape, the great creatures willfully driving themselves ashore. But the large whales came ashore one at a time, each to meet a solitary end. Not so the blackfish. By the time the men arrived on the beach, a dull sun was balancing on the horizon. In the creeping light, shadows still filled the dry sand hollows, but a sheen had already spread out on the wet sand left by the receding tide. On this glistening surface, dozens of blackfish lay dying. The largest stretched nearly twelve feet, while the infants, who breathed their last in quicker heaves, were as long as men. Their bodies collapsed like dark butter. Now and again, an animal issued a hoarse cough, a vapor tendril exiting a blowhole. A faint northerly wind carried their dying sounds.

When Ben had burst into the station, Hiram was excited. Outside of old photos his father had shown him, he had never seen a pilot whale. But here on the beach, all excitement was gone. He was no stranger to the demise of wild things. Plenty of times, he had played a hand in their end. Every boy hunted in the marshes. But the geese, yellowlegs, and Eskimo curlews he brought down were solitary birds; as they fell, their companions winged on. Here, the entire flock had fallen to earth on its own accord. He imagined the whales, powerful forms vectoring up from dark, comforting waters, sensing the shallows and the first tug of the waves, pushing aside their shrieking instinct as they crossed the innermost shoals, pressing against each other in terrible encouragement until their undersides grated against the sand and until no impulse, for or against, could alter lonely death.

The surfmen walked among the whales, each alone with his thoughts. Hiram stood by the supply wagon with Captain Cole and Willie. The keeper had decided to bring the wagon for the smaller fish—cod and perch—which followed the blackfish ashore. They, too, lay on the wet sand, some still flopping. Fresh fish would be a welcome relief from salt pork, dried beef, and overcooked beans, but no one was moving to pick them up.

Gazing at the field of dead and dying whales, Cole only wished to be gone. Thoreau snorted in his traces, unsettled by the scent of death. A biting wind rose. Hiram turned up the collar of his oilskin.

Cole spied the scuttling figure as Willie spoke.

"He was probably here to welcome them ashore," Willie said.

Hiram followed the men's gaze north. He saw nothing but dead whales, lining the wet sand like fat cobblestones. Then he caught a glimpse of a man's head. It bobbed above a distant whale, disappeared, and then reappeared.

"Cutting his mark," said Willie. "He'll see a tidy profit this morning."

Captain Cole was silent.

Hiram followed the bobbing head. The man was uncommonly short. The sloped backs of the largest blackfish rose to the average man's thighs, but when this man passed behind the whales, he disappeared almost to his waist. He didn't walk. Instead, he moved from whale to whale in bursts, rolling queerly from side to side, like a ship on the sea. It was a hypnotic motion, carrying him across the sand like water.

As he moved closer, Hiram saw he was mildly humpbacked.

"Maybe we should notch a few whales before he owns the lot," said Willie. "He'd enjoy the competition."

"I'll see no profit in death," said Cole.

"Rumor has it the old buzzard has fortunes cached in the dunes, but scraps for coins as if his next meal depends on it," Willie said.

The keeper leaned forward, his dark eyes fixed on the approaching figure. "He enjoys the scent of death far more than the heft of a coin."

They stood at the southern edge of the dying whales. A lone blackfish lay ten yards behind them. The man passed by without a glance. Crouching, he applied the fishing knife to the whale, etching a circle above the right eye.

Once finished cutting, he walked directly up to them. "If wild things could speak ... " the man said. "A singular thing to see to one's end."

The voice was deep and mildly mournful, like an organ note, richly struck. The man stood with the sun at his back, the face beneath his ratty bowler in shadow. Stringy gray hair fell to the man's shoulders, curling greasily on the humped back. The hump forced his head forward slightly, so that he appeared to be waiting on a secret.

Willie spoke casually. "You're up early, Pomp."

"The inability to sleep is one of the few blessings of age," Pomp said. He wiped the fishing knife on his trousers. The blade was more needle than knife. The blood was black in the gray light.

The bowler dipped. "Keeper Cole."

The captain said nothing.

The man's kneecaps nearly faced straight out to the side. Hiram had never seen legs so bowed.

Pomp studied his legs as if he had just discovered them dangling from his waist. "Nearly enough clearance for a Union Pacific locomotive," he said. "It would be a fine thing to piss on progress."

Pomp turned and the shadows left his face.

Hiram jerked.

The man looked like an ape. Brow and lower jaw thrust forward. The wrinkled skin appeared half rotted; in places, the pigment was black. It was as if someone had pulled a canvas sail from a fire and molded it to the man's skull.

His lively gray eyes walked over Hiram. "I fear today's youth are ill-prepared for life's possibilities. Our species grows soft, and I worry things will only get worse. But we must believe in the next generation, mustn't we, Keeper Cole? You and I can't play ringmasters to the circus forever."

The old man did not look at Cole. He smiled broadly at Willie, displaying fine white teeth. "Our mutual friends at the Cork and Barrel have missed your charms."

"I've been occupied," said Willie. "This happy job leaves little time for lollygagging."

Willie spoke easily, but Hiram did not miss the slow beat of the words.

"Drilling and burying," the man said. "Shouldn't one negate the other?"

"Life can be a circus," Willie said.

The old man cackled. The other men had gathered nearby. Their faces were blank, but their hands fidgeted.

"When life's pleasures take a backseat to burying, something has gone awry," Pomp said. "One of many reasons I prefer to take orders from myself. Frankly, I've always been surprised to see you subordinate to another man. A free spirit knows no reins."

"I require another man's orders to keep me from wandering too far afield," said Willie.

Pomp regarded the captain bemusedly. "Always the observer, Keeper Cole. Silence is a sorely undervalued trait. Most men live to hear the sound of their own voice, and when they die they have heard nothing at all."

The old man looked out at the blackfish. "A vast and lovely shoreline, yet it often seems too small for the both of us, does it not Captain Cole?"

"We do not cross paths often enough," Cole said.

The responding laugh was a wild dog's bark. "Your sense of humor remains undiminished." The old man spread his arms to the beach. "A gift from providence. The Lord is good."

"The Lord most often sees to those who see to themselves," said Cole.

This bark was sharper still. "You and I know the same God, Captain Cole."

"Even a man as industrious as yourself will be hard put to remove all this blubber and boil it down," said Willie.

"On occasion, industry must succumb to reality. I'll sell the whales as they lay, and let the sleepers do the cutting."

"It takes some effort to be first on the scene so often," said Cole.

The gray eyes returned to Cole slowly. "Life is a race, and Daniel Cole is never more than a step behind. Only time outruns us both."

Pomp held up the fishing knife. He turned it slowly, the thin steel reflecting light. "These blackfish come ashore, and not one of us knows why. An enthralling matter, the seemingly happenstance vagaries of life."

"I didn't think you lent much import to life, unless it serves you profit," said Cole.

"I've found that most life merits little concern at all." He sheathed the knife. "There are exceptions."

The old man stepped past Cole.

Thoreau stood so quietly, Hiram had forgotten about him. Willie had named the gelding after the famous Massachusetts writer. It was Willie's contention that, if not for the physical hurdles presented in filling out paperwork, Thoreau would be running the station. Like his namesake, the gelding had little patience for man. Only Ben had gained his affection. Outside of feedings, everyone else who approached him risked a vicious kick.

To Hiram's astonishment the old man walked up to the horse and began stroking his flank.

"A magnificent creature you are," Pomp crooned. "I could take you away from this menial existence and give you the life you deserve. Though it is insulting to affix a price to wisdom and spirit, perhaps these men might be convinced to indulge my whim."

Pomp ran a palm along Thoreau's neck. "If I recall correctly, twenty years back, old man Rich cut his mark in seventy blackfish and sold them for two thousand dollars. I plan on embarrassing his profits. Everything I earn from the sale of these whales, for this horse."

Hiram's mouth fell open.

"The horse isn't for sale," said Cole.

Pomp did not turn from the gelding. "You bought this horse out from under me. Samuel Mullet, wasn't it? Stupid man, even duller than his namesake. So anxious for your approval. " The old man gave Thoreau a last tender stroke. "Perhaps, you and I will elope under their noses, lovers into the mist."

Two wagons approached from the north.

Pomp turned, touching a finger to the rim of the bowler. "My first customers. I hope they're prepared to pay for their sloth."

They watched Pomp walk away. Making his way to the blackfish closest to the sea, the old man raised an arm, circling the knife like a lasso.

"Never one to linger," Willie said, but there was no humor in the words.

That evening, Hiram followed Willie outside. It was nearly dark. A scrim of deep blue, the last tincture of day, traced the ridgelines of the dunes. Hiram stood at a polite distance, while Willie peed with his eyes shut, a look of pleasure on his face.

Willie hitched up his pants and turned. "Short on entertainment?"

"Who was he?"

"Not a face one loses in the crowd, is it?"

Even now, Willie was undecided. He'd debated all afternoon, and he still didn't know what to tell the boy. It was wise to know your enemy, but judging from the way Hiram tossed and muttered at night, the boy had enough nightmares already.

Willie made up his mind. "He frightens me too, Hiram." Before Hiram could protest, Willie said, "You've never seen him, have you?"

On the beach, the old man's presence had stripped away everything but the moment. But as soon as he left, the exact question had struck Hiram like a thunderclap.

"How can that be?" Hiram said.

"I don't have an answer," said Willie. "We live in a small place, and he's not a man easily overlooked. Pomp lives alone in a cabin in the Provincelands, but he's no hermit. He enjoys life's pleasures more than the next man. But you see him only when he chooses."

In the shadow of the station, Hiram couldn't see Willie's face clearly, but he knew the older surfman was watching him.

"He's not like us, Hiram. It's not much of an answer, but it's the only one I have." It was a lie, but for now a lie would suffice.

"He mocked Keeper Cole," said Hiram.

"I rest my case."

"Would he have paid that sum for Thoreau?"

"It wasn't about money."

Overhead, the stars winked. For once, Willie did not feel like winking back. The boy had a bucketful of questions, but there was only one thing he needed to know.

"Better you don't see him, Hiram," Willie said. "There are things darker than this morning."

Hiram followed Willie up the porch steps. He nearly spoke when Willie stopped to open the door, but doubt made him hesitate. And then Willie stepped into the station, and the opportunity was gone.

Hiram stood in the doorway.

"Take all the time you like," shouted Mayo. "We can use the fresh air."

Hiram heard himself mutter an apology and felt the door close, but he wasn't inside the station, he was back on the beach, in the wind carrying sighs and the stink of death.

He was sure the old man had been studying him.

Late that night, Cole sat at his desk attempting to sort out what he knew.

He had mailed his report to the United States Lifesaving Service in Washington, meticulously notching most of what he knew of the *Asia's* demise. He had little faith in Washington's bureaucrats, but it was possible his report might reach someone who would see something he had missed.

Cole turned the mahogany owl in his hand. The paperweight had been presented to him for ten years of service, but wisdom, it seemed, came to him less often these days. He worried, too, that his emotions were fogging his ability to see the *Asia's* circumstances clearly. The girl's death had shaken him more than he liked. At first, he had been able to maintain control over his emotions, even in the face of inconceivable loss. Standing before the blackened foundation of his family's cottage, the other fishermen silent behind him, he had willed his tremblings to a standstill, forcing himself to see the smoky tendrils not as two pure spirits rising but as the wood smoke they were. He had laid out the facts like cards and assigned fault where it clearly lay. Only later that night, when he had returned to the cottage alone, had he allowed himself weakness. Now weakness threatened to thwart him.

Looking up from his desk, Cole eyed the frosted window and the night beyond. He was tired of death. It tainted everything, always lurking like a great beast just beyond the firelight. It seemed to Cole that most of his life had been occupied with death, and the only escape in sight was his own.

His gaze ran along the rows of leather-bound journals packed tidily along the wall, ten years of meticulous record keeping—surf conditions, weather, barometric pressures—notched each day at sunrise, noon, sunset, and midnight. At times, he felt the logbooks mocked him, filled as they were with factors outside his control. Wrecks were also noted. Death inhabited the pages too.

The logbooks marked time, and in the winter of 1882, times were changing. Out west, the vast prairies of buffalo had been wiped out, and the Indians largely tamed. On the seas, the whales had been hunted nearly to extinction, pursued now to the farthest reaches of the South Pacific and the Arctic. The cod fleets and mackerel schooners that had once jammed the harbors of Wellfleet and Provincetown had dwindled, disappearing with the same inexorable decline as the fish they had once hauled from the sea in unfathomable numbers, shimmering silver columns, salted and drying in the sun.

This was progress as man defined it, and, often, it made him restless and more than uneasy.

He went to the window. Patches of snow gleamed pale in the moonlight. His eyes went to where the cliffs fell away, to the utter darkness beyond. The morning after the *Asia's* demise, he had walked the ridgeline, although he knew he would find nothing. Hell's storm had erased any hope of tracks.

He made no note of this in his report. Reports were about facts. But he would not neglect his suspicions when it came to determining the truth behind the *Asia's* end. Innocent men and a child had died. He knew, too, it would not end here.

Turning the owl slowly, he watched its lacquer surface catch the moonlight. But it was not the owl he saw. It was a fishing knife, held up to the bleak dawn, gathering light from nowhere, its shimmering like laughter.

6

The Cork and Barrel sat two blocks back from Provincetown Harbor, separated from the waterfront by a ramshackle row of fishing shanties and the loamy slash of Bradford Street. For reasons no one could discern, a stuffed buffalo head was mounted above the entrance, an ugly, weather-thrashed creature with a pugnacious gaze. The handiwork of an alcoholic taxidermist, the animal was cross-eyed, condemned for eternity to witness twofold the shabby bleakness of Bradford Street.

Pomp enjoyed the buffalo's nonsensical air, just as he favored the Cork and Barrel's proximity to the water. The smell of the sea never left the dim interior, though more pungent smells often stifled it.

Pomp watched Rummy arrange bottles behind the bar. The scrawny owner moved back and forth, shaking his head and muttering as if refusing himself a loan. A long forgotten patron had dubbed him Rummy because his distaste for liquor was rivaled only by his distaste for humanity. Now few knew his real name.

Pomp always sat at the same table. Set at the pub's rear, the table faced the door, allowing him to watch the customers' comings and goings. The table was close to the bar, a once gleaming mahogany circle now chipped into runic relief by the broken teeth and bottles of fishermen and whalers. The table was also near one of the few windows. In warm weather, the window allowed the rattle of wagons and the ringing of ship's bells to spill happily in, and some of the stench of vomit and cheap tobacco to eke out.

On this winter morning the pub was quiet, the only sound discrete murmurings and the occasional chime of glasses: three local ship owners finalizing a business matter at a nearby table.

Rummy had yet to deliver a whisky, but Pomp didn't mind. He sat enjoying the quiet and the sweet taste of commerce gone right. The blackfish had turned a finer sum than he had imagined. He had come to celebrate, but he was not disappointed to find the pub empty. His own company would suffice until someone interesting arrived.

He watched the businessmen, their faces illuminated by a failing candle stub. Even in broad daylight, the pub was in a state of gloaming. A few lanterns hung from the ceiling beams, but they were far flung and rarely lit. Oil cost money.

That Rummy studiously ignored him amused Pomp.

He did not have to raise his voice. "I don't know why you don't find another line of work. I've never seen a man look so miserable."

Rummy was bald; his age, anyone's guess. A life inside his squalid pub had turned his skin pale and seen his eyes' wane. He was too cheap to buy spectacles. When someone addressed him, he squinted furiously in their direction.

Rummy halted his arranging to do so now. "I'm busy, in case you can't see," he said. "If you need to talk, buy a whore."

Few men insulted Pomp, but it was senseless to take any insult from Rummy personally. The man disliked everyone.

"It might do us all more good if I bought you a whore," said Pomp amiably. "Your sour attitude infects this place."

"We can't all live on our wits," said Rummy, disappearing behind the bar. He resurfaced holding a bottle of whisky and a tumbler. Coming around the bar, he held the bottle at arm's length as if it were about to strike him across the face.

He placed the tumbler in front of Pomp and poured until it was half full. "If your tongue is occupied, it can't wag at me."

Pomp laid a hand on the bony wrist. "Leave the bottle."

"It'll cost you."

"I'd have it no other way," said Pomp. "All part of my plan to see you to retirement."

Scowling made Rummy squint all the more. "It's all I can do to stay ahead of everyone trying to cheat me," he said.

Pomp laughed. "You can tell that to the other turnips who frequent this place, but I'd guess you've got a tidy nest egg tucked away. You could retire to Boston this afternoon, buy yourself a hundred pairs of spectacles, and find your sense of humor."

Rummy shivered visibly. Any talk of his own money made him painfully nervous. Because he rarely spoke, many assumed him slow-witted, but Pomp knew Rummy had a deft head for figures. Pomp harbored a genuine fondness for the skinny barkeeper. He knew all too well how people judged a man by his appearance.

Pomp tipped the whisky. "To wolves in sheep's clothing," he said as Rummy stalked off, muttering.

Pomp did not miss how the ship owners stole glances at him or how they had smiled uncomfortably when he came in. He watched them with disinterest. Most men were dullards and cowards. He knew they had their suspicions, just as he knew they would never voice them. It was the rare man who acted honestly.

A draft swept through the pub. Pomp looked to the door. William Barnabas and Otis Watkins stood blinking in the half-light before making for his table. As they passed, the ship owners nodded greeting.

Barnabas and Watkins were Cape Cod's most successful wreckers. The Cape's wreckers took advantage of what natural misfortune brought them. Wrecked ships meant wood and iron, ship's wheels, spars, deadeyes, shackles, chock cleats, nails, and more. Sails, rigging, and nets were hauled back to barns, repaired, and resold. Iron was reforged. The wreckers kept their wagons at the ready, filled with knives, axes, and crowbars, and they were not alone. News of a grounded ship traveled like buckshot. Informed of a ship aground just a month earlier, a Chatham minister had abruptly concluded his sermon with the admonishment "Start fair!" and dashed out the door, his parishioners at his heels.

Few were quicker to a ship aground than Barnabas and Watkins. On several occasions, they had nearly stripped an entire vessel before their fellow wreckers arrived. None knew the Cape's weather or shoals better, and few possessed a keener sense of impending disaster. The shelves of their Provincetown chandlery groaned beneath the weight of salvaged goods.

Now, each man crossed the pub in his own fashion. Exceedingly tall and thin, Barnabas took great strides, forcing Watkins, equally short and stout, to shuffle briskly to stay abreast. Though both men were the same age, Barnabas' hair was snow-white while Watkins' scalp sprouted dark, curly ringlets. The effect was that of father and corpulent son.

Arriving at the table, Watkins flashed a cherubic smile. "A calm morning presents the rare opportunity for business associates to enjoy a relaxing drink," he said, eyeing the whisky.

"I don't believe we've been invited to sit," said Barnabas.

Pomp gestured to the empty chairs. "Forgive me," he said, "but it's a luxury to see you gentleman wait on anything."

Rummy brought two more glasses, placing them on the table and leaving without a word.

"Long-winded fellow, isn't he?" said Barnabas.

Pushing at a wayward ringlet, Watkins was already casting a moony gaze toward the staircase near the front door. "Will anyone be joining us?" he asked.

The ladies lived and worked on the second floor. The three men could hear the groan of pipes, the women washing up after servicing the early-morning shift of randy fishermen.

"My associate," said Barnabas, "you may recall, is ruled by schoolboy genitals."

"Lucky fellow," said Pomp. "But I'm afraid he'll have to content himself with whisky for now. Abby is reading the morning papers. She won't be down until afternoon."

It was common knowledge that Otis Watkins yearned for Abby Hierdal's Nordic charms. He had pursued her for years, and she had refused him in kind, Watkins' wife being one of the few Provincetown ladies who treated her with courtesy.

Watkins stared at the stairs. "Do you think she engaged a man?"

"She's a working lady, like the rest," Pomp said, not unkindly.

Watkins hauled his eyes from the stairwell and set them forlornly on Pomp.

"She's your friend," Watkins said. "You could speak with her."

"Or you could pass her a note in class," said Barnabas.

Watkins looked down into his tumbler. "She smells like a garden after a spring rain."

"Fertile ground," said Barnabas, "upon which you will plant no randy seed."

Abby was not slender. In fact she was decidedly plump, with ample hips that melded promptly with a swaying bottom. Often, she hiked up her dress, poked a finger into a snowy thigh, and scolded herself for her weakness for figgy duff pudding—a collection of butter, flour, sugar, and raisins boiled in a bag, to which she added homemade honey. But her open manner was also like honey, striking men with singular force. She regarded the world with a child's frank gaze and addressed it in the same manner. But Pomp knew she was no simpleton. Abby was living testament to women's complexity.

It lifted Pomp's spirits to see a grown man behaving like a love-struck youth. "A poet's soul and an industrialist's bank account," he said. "She might reconsider your advances if you stopped feigning poverty."

"Abby doesn't care about money," said Watkins. Glumly, he added, "A pox on my wife."

"Everyone cares about money, my merry friend," said Pomp. "I shouldn't have to tell you that. Tell me what you're worth, and I'll pass the information along and throw in what a ladies' man you are to boot."

The whiff of business returned Watkins to his senses. "I suspect most of the Cape is far more interested in what you have squirreled away," he said.

Pomp tipped his glass to the men. "Junk by another man's measure."

"Give us a gander and we'll be the judge," said Watkins.

Barnabas laughed. "Better odds of Miss Hierdal rushing down to satisfy you on this table." Turning to Pomp, he said, "My partner forgets his manners when he is drunk with love. Your business is your business, until you deign to discuss it."

Pomp made no attempt to fill the silence.

Barnabas said, "There was a meeting last night at town hall about the canal. We expected to see you there."

Pomp had known about the meeting, but meetings regarding the canal had been held for twenty years. They reminded Pomp of a traveling circus, arriving at intervals to make lots of noise and leave nothing but dried shit in their wake. Miles Standish had first proposed digging a great canal along the backside of the Cape in the 1600s, connecting Cape Cod Bay and Buzzards Bay and allowing vessels to avoid the treacherous Atlantic shoals entirely. Since then, dozens of entrepreneurs had taken up the call. Yet the earth separating the bays remained firmly in place.

"I'm certain the canal is half finished by this morning," said Pomp.

"They're going ahead, and this time they won't be tripped up by money or politics," said Watkins, radiating a different anxiety. "There's too much at stake. There's certain to be plenty of arguing and conniving, but this outfit aims to see the canal built. A no-nonsense sort named Henry Whitney spoke. He called the canal a scheme of national importance. Everyone cheered."

"That's because Mr. Whitney hasn't asked them for money yet," said Pomp. "I attended the same meeting ten years ago. Everyone chattered like hyenas. Unless you count stock-jobbing, nothing's transpired since."

"They mean it this time," said Barnabas. "They have capital of four million dollars."

The figure was news to Pomp. Such a sum boded substantial resolve. For a moment his spirits dipped. He let the whisky rest on his tongue, listening as the wreckers recounted particulars of the meeting with mounting misery.

"The canal would save ships sailing between New York and Boston seventy miles of dangerous passage," concluded Watkins dejectedly. "It would finish us."

"Only captains who fell asleep would run aground," added Barnabas.

In a single doleful motion, the wreckers reached for their whisky glasses and drank them down. They looked like small boys denied dessert.

Pomp laughed. "Here's what I see in my crystal ball," he said. "A few piles of landfill, and your orator, Mr. Whitney, running for his life, while investors shout for his head on a gaffe."

Pomp poured three whiskies and raised his glass. "Bully to man," he said. "May he always undermine his own progress."

The whisky fired Pomp's throat. His heart flamed with it. Closing his eyes, he heard the shouts ringing again in his ears, the mouth spewing blood and tissue, bellowing the great man's name through howling agony and wind. It was as if the *Asia's* captain was speaking from inside him. Perhaps, he did live on. Even with his organs displayed to the skies, the man had possessed admirable vitality.

Eat a man's liver, and you assume his spirit. Pomp smiled. It would do to have the strength of many. He knew this would be a winter to remember.

7

The timing of the arrival of Captain Colin Daintree, United States Revenue Cutter Service Inspector of Life-Saving Stations, was inopportune—Daintree arriving at the Wellfleet train station as a powerful storm gathered over the Atlantic, with most of Wellfleet's fishing fleet far out to sea.

Cole had never met Captain Daintree. He vowed to greet the man with an open mind, but past experiences with the Lifesaving Service would make this an effort. Though the Lifesaving Service was administered by Sumner Kimball, an honest and forthright man, few of Kimball's subordinates were cut from his cloth. In Cole's opinion, the bureaucrats had created, and then neglected, a host of problems on the Cape.

When the first lifesaving stations had been established, Washington chose the keepers and allowed those keepers to pick their crews. Washington had selected dutiful keepers, but they had picked keepers with no sense of duty too. Over the years, unsavory keepers and surfmen had been winnowed out by the rare decree from Washington and the hard realities of the job: men of weak moral character did not relish difficult, dangerous jobs. But bad seeds remained.

In Cole's mind, the worst of the lot served as keeper of Race Point Station, two miles to the north. John Kilbride and his men had been a thorn in Cole's side for ten years. As a boy, John Kilbride had been a liar and a cheat, and his disposition had only grown bolder as he became a man. Kilbride stood well over six feet, and he was built like a blacksmith's anvil. He had been a drunk and a sorry excuse of a fisherman. He was unchanged as a keeper. He spent much of his time away from the station, patronizing the bars and whores of Provincetown. During several violent nor'easters, Kilbride's crew had not patrolled. Cole was also fairly certain a Race Point surfman had stood by while a trap fisherman's boat sank and the man drowned. Cole had darker suspicions regarding Kilbride, as well, but these he kept to himself.

After the trap fisherman's drowning, Cole had gone to Race Point and confronted Kilbride. Kilbride had denied any wrongdoing on the part of his man. Returning to Peaked Hill Bars, Cole had then written Washington, outlining Kilbride's negligence in detail. Over the next month, two similar letters followed. They, too, brought no response. Cole stopped writing.

Now the Lifesaving Service was sending an emissary. In keeping with the maddening habits of bureaucracy, Captain Daintree had not stated the purpose of his visit in his letter; he had merely demanded Cole meet him at Wellfleet Station.

Cole could only hope the captain had come, in part, to remove John Kilbride. This hope alone sent Cole to the station, though he made the trip against his instincts. He had awaken at four to a falling barometer. First light had revealed an Atlantic wild with cross-chop, a sea of whitecaps beneath a blood-orange sky.

Standing on the train platform at noon, Cole watched the wind bend the tops of the pines. By now, Willie had sent two men out on patrol. Should a ship run aground, Willie would ably handle matters.

Wellfleet's fishing fleet was a far more worrisome problem. The fleet had sailed for George's Bank two days earlier. On the Cape itself, the full ferocity of the storm had yet to be gauged, but Cole had no doubt the fishermen already knew what they were up against. Depending on their outbound progress, the boats might be too far out to sea to make a run for home.

Cole knew most of the men. He had fished with them before he became keeper. They would recognize the first signs of inclement weather, but he knew few, if any, of the captains would turn for home quickly. Their livelihood rested on taking chances. Empty holds left families hungry.

Cole had been in the same situation himself, making decisions any sane man would deem reckless. Many times, Sara had greeted him at the dock with a tongue-lashing after a harrowing return, although even as she questioned his good sense and hers, they both knew her remonstrance would make no difference. He would sail again in foul weather; she would berate him again on his return. It had been as much a part of their life as the bed that always followed, the act of love furious for the relief it contained.

With Julia's birth, Cole's risk-taking had increased. He continued fishing after he became keeper, pushing out every Saturday, which was the keeper's day off, to supplement his meager lifesaving income. With one day's opportunity, he had paid scant attention to the weather.

He was fishing when the cottage had burned to the ground. The fire had started on the roof, likely an errant spark from the fire he'd built before he left. As he walked through the morning darkness to Wellfleet Harbor, the wind had risen quickly, clawing loose fall's last leaves. He had nearly turned back, but Sara was an early riser and he needed to get his lines in the water. His wife and daughter were probably dead before he was beyond sight of land. The roof had collapsed, killing them while they slept. Sailing into the harbor that evening, the huddle of fishermen on the dock had sent something numb into his head. He had run the skiff right into the dock.

That night, he slept in the ashes of Julia's bedroom. The numbness had never left.

Now, Cole considered the dark sky. The train was already fifteen minutes late. Grit blew in sinuous trails across the tracks.

Washington's emissary did not improve Cole's mood. Colin Daintree was a fussy man, sporting a pencil-thin mustache and dress blues. Stepping delicately to the platform, he gave Cole a terse nod. "Our transport?"

Cole indicated the wagon. Captain Daintree walked toward Thoreau. Cole fetched the man's valise from the platform.

They rode side by side, absorbing the bump and sway of the rutted road. When Cole raised the subject of Kilbride and his crew, Captain Daintree waved a thin hand.

"I am familiar with your complaints. The conversation can wait."

The road passed first through the woods. The trees blocked the brunt of the wind, but above the bare treetops Cole saw the black-bottomed clouds gathering. Cole clicked the reins, Thoreau quickening his pace. The men could drag the surfboat or the Lyle gun down to the beach in the beach cart, but the horse did it faster and left the men with energy they needed.

As they moved into the open dunes, the gusting wind threw sand in their faces. Captain Daintree sat erect, mustache twitching. At regular intervals, he removed a silver brush from his coat pocket, briskly sweeping at the sand.

Cole's mind ran through the possibilities. The fishing boats farthest out at sea now knew the full fury of the storm. Sails had been taken in and double-reefed. Perhaps not yet aware of the storm's full bloom, the boats closer to land were making preparations to wait the storm out, lying under the foresail carrying the bob jib.

Nothing could be done for them, but Cole still fumed. He was away from his obligations, performing the duties of an errand boy, riding beside a man who, it appeared, wouldn't recognize a storm until it poured down his throat.

By the time they arrived at Peaked Hill Bars, the wind was tossing cannonballs of grit. As they stepped from the wagon, fat raindrops began to fall. Within seconds, the clouds opened.

Captain Daintree ran for the station. Cole unhitched Thoreau and walked him to the stable. He checked the water bucket and pitched the horse some hay. Passing the wagon, Cole picked up the soggy valise.

When Cole entered the station, Captain Daintree was standing stiffly in the middle of the room. The men had stopped their card game to regard the dripping designate curiously. Cole noted that

Frank Mayo and the Swede were gone. The men all had their boots on.

Willie smiled. "Now I can concentrate on my cards," he said.

"Be prepared to leave your winnings," said Cole.

Placing the valise at the designate's feet, he went upstairs. Entering his quarters, Cole went to the window. Through the splattered pane, the ocean leapt and frothed as if it were contained in a great pot violently shaken by an unseen hand. No ships were visible, but Cole knew full well that men were suffering the cold, bounding seas.

A scraping interrupted his thoughts. Turning, he was surprised to see Captain Daintree seated at the desk. The designate produced a box from the valise. He removed a slender cigar. Striking a match, he brought it to life with a succession of brisk puffs.

"A fine, and still dry, smoke," he said.

Cole removed his oilskin from its peg beside the window.

"Captain Daintree, I must be brief. A storm is on us, and it's worse than I thought. At any moment we could be called to action. I'm hoping you've come to replace Keeper Kilbride."

The mustachioed man regarded the glowing end of his cigar.

"I'm afraid, Captain Cole, matters are not quite so simple. We did receive your letters and their quite serious accusations. In delving into the matter, we came up with a not unsurprising result. Keeper Kilbride denies your claims. In fact, he accuses you of fabricating lies. He tells us that, for reasons known only to you, you harbor an irrational animosity toward him." Inhaling, Daintree held the smoke for a long moment before releasing a gray cloud. "Your word alone is hardly enough to mete out justice."

Cole had a sudden urge to smash the cigar into the smug face, but he stilled his anger. At this very moment, the fishing boat captains were deadening their emotions.

"Captain Daintree, I have no time for games. Wellfleet's fishing fleet is at sea. I will repeat myself once, as clearly as I know how. John Kilbride is a drunk, a liar, and a menace to shipping. Appointing him keeper was a fool's mistake that has led to several deaths and will lead to more. If you don't remove him, the responsibility will rest on your shoulders."

Captain Daintree gave the cigar an idle flick, depositing ash on the floor. "Other than your own men, who obviously possess a certain prejudice, has anyone else directly witnessed this purported negligence? Do we dismiss Keeper Kilbride solely on the grievances of another station?"

Captain Daintree removed the silver brush from his vest pocket and brushed at a trouser knee. "I do not presume to be rude, but surely you do not believe I have traveled all this way to discuss a matter as trivial as Keeper Kilbride?"

Cole's anger was gone, smothered in disgust. He had spent his life among purposeful men. This dandy had no direction and less sense. "Captain Daintree, your ignorance forces me to be blunt. It's obvious you have spent no time around the sea. How you came to your position, I won't guess. But had you ever experienced a winter storm, you would realize they rarely draw a crowd. We are the only witnesses to John Kilbride's incompetence because we are the only ones present. You may talk to my men. They will answer you honestly. They accept my orders, but I don't own their souls. Now if you will excuse me, I can't waste any more time."

Cole walked to the door.

Captain Daintree sprang to his feet. "Sir! I have made a long and arduous trip! We have a matter of national significance to discuss! I demand your attention!"

Cole turned. "Your demands hold no sway in my station."

Captain Daintree's moustache twitched madly. To his credit, he calmed himself. "You must understand," he said. "Our country's future is at stake."

"I am concerned with more immediate matters," said Cole.

"The *Asia* carried an item of global significance, one that will advance mankind's cause and chart a new direction for the world. Is that immediate and important enough to concern you, Keeper Cole?"

"Not unless it can bring the fishing fleet home safely," said Cole, stepping through the door, shutting it, and turning the key in the lock.

Downstairs, the surfmen stood stone-faced. Upstairs, Captain Daintree shouted.

"Well Daniel," said Willie, "there goes your chance at a linen life in Washington."

For a brief moment, Cole drifted outside himself. The wind rattling the windows, the drum of rain, the men alert in the dusky light, the heightened pace of his own heart. Outside of Daintree's shouting, it was a satisfying stage. He was precisely where he wanted to be.

The wind threw rain against the windows. Thunder rolled.

Crossing himself, Ben Maddocks said, "May God save them."

"He may require help," said Cole.

When the time for his midnight patrol arrived, Hiram, worming into his boots at the edge of his cot, was surprised to see Ben standing by the door in his oilskin. Willie, stuffing his stocking feet into his own boots, was readying for the northward patrol.

Willie looked over from his cot. "He's going with you. We don't have to agree with authority, Hiram, but we have to obey it." Leaning forward, Willie whispered. "Don't take it out on Ben. He volunteered."

Hiram walked to the door. Ben took down a second Patrol Lantern and handed it to him.

"One man's decision does not determine another man's character," Ben said.

Hiram's face burned.

Before he could speak, Ben put a hand on his shoulder. "We must stay together. It will be easy to get separated." Ben dipped his head, lips moving silently. Lifting his head, he smiled. "It storms like the Devil, but it remains the Lord's handiwork."

The frozen rain pelted against their slickers, hard as bird shot. Descending the steep cliff path, Hiram was certain a gust would toss him into space. Ben walked a few steps ahead, bent nearly double. Ahead of them, Willie crouched in the same fashion. Hiram leaned into the cliff face, carving a sandy furrow with a shoulder.

As they walked to the water, the wind backed slightly, but when they turned south it blew full in their faces, hurling suffocating curtains of rain and sand. Hiram tilted his wood shingle to shield his eyes, but a gust slapped it against the bridge of his nose. The pain made his eyes water, blinding him further. Beside him, Ben put his shingle back inside his oilskin. Hiram followed suit.

They walked so that their shoulders and elbows bumped. Hiram tried to look for ships, but it was pointless. The ocean had gone mad. Enormous waves ran in nonsensical directions, their frothy tops sheared loose and flung in contrails along the surface so that the Atlantic resembled a heaving, snowy plain. The world was a continuous roar.

They spotted the High Head surfman long before he should have appeared, coming toward them at a half-run. They stopped to exchange tokens. The wind nearly sealed Caleb Jessup's hood in front of his face, but Hiram still saw the pimpled cheeks form a grin. They had been schoolmates and friends. Caleb's family raised dairy cattle. Every day, he had come to school smelling of milk and manure.

Caleb handed the token to Ben. Then he leaned into Hiram. "I want a chaperone!"

"You still smell like a turd!"

Hiram glanced quickly at Ben, but the surfman was busy trying to stuff the token in the pocket of his oilskin, which flapped like a crazed crow.

The instant they turned north, Hiram could barely control his legs. Shoving at their backs, the wind forced them into Caleb Jessup's half-run. The sand against their backs made the wild crackling of a fiery blaze.

A mile from the station, a different sound reached Hiram's ears. He yanked on Ben's sleeve. Apparently, Ben's hearing was keen; he was already bug-eyed. Though it didn't seem possible, the sound rode easily over the wind, a hair-raising keening. A weight crawled into Hiram's chest and limbs. He shot a look over his shoulder, glimpsing only darkness. He turned back toward Ben, suddenly glad for his company, but Ben was gone.

Ben was twenty yards down the beach, running full tilt, his arms making wind-milling circles, as if clawing at the air would gain him more speed.

The unholy noise rose several decibels.

Hiram ran without apology, taking great, awkward strides, each one threatening to throw him forward on his face. The keening, hung now with a terrible yearning, was still gaining. When Hiram drew alongside Ben, the wind-milling surfman was shouting madly, spewing spittle and curses.

Somehow, Ben picked up his pace. They ran, matched stride for stride. Just off their heels, the howling rose to a triumphant shriek. Ben screamed and spun about. To Hiram's surprise, he stopped and turned too. They stood, denying themselves their final breath, as the black form bounded through the rain. In its eagerness, it defied gravity, leaving the beach in ground-gobbling vaults.

Issuing a final expletive, Ben threw up his hands. Without thinking, Hiram grabbed Ben's wrist and yanked him to the ground. The empty barrel arced through the air where their heads had been, its open bunghole whistling furiously as it passed.

They rose to their feet slowly, staring down the beach. The barrel had already bounded out of sight. Hiram felt a buzzing through his body and the glorious explosion of his own hot breaths.

He cupped a hand behind Ben's neck, yanking him close. "Coarse language is a footfall down the Devil's path!"

Ben's lunatic grin filled Hiram's world. "Turd sniffer!"

They stood, foreheads touching, supporting each other in the tempest.

8

The storm's ferocity was rivaled by the speed of its departure. By dawn, the skies were clear. The ocean continued to run wild in every direction, but the night's southeasterly gale fell off to a stiff breeze.

All but one of the fishing fleet was lost—twenty-seven boats and nearly one hundred men. The sole survivor, the *Water Witch*, captained by Matthias Rich, had turned for the Cape just in time, edging around Race Point and into the lee of Herring Cove with only a severe case of sea sickness on board.

The others fell short. Two days after the arrival of the *Water Witch*, a second boat returned, this time to Nauset Bars. Moving at the pace of the tide, she arrived keel to the sky, crew drifting in her cabin. More bodies began washing ashore that night, rolling at the water's edge like restless sleepers.

The Cape's populace flooded the beach. Old women sat on driftwood and stared to the east. Their husbands walked circles around jagged timbers, resurrecting memories of their sons. The wives of the sons walked too—something had to be done—trailed by frightened children. Three children, the oldest no more than five, stood beside a kneeling woman who screamed oaths at the sea. The wreckers brought their wagons but had left their tools at home. Barnabas and Watkins brought candies for the children. Ezekiel Donne kept his distance. Clad in long johns, he walked slowly, jiggling the leather coin purse that always dangled from his loop of rope belt.

The lifesavers worked alongside the wreckers. Cole divided the men into two groups of three, dispatching Captain Daintree too. The bureaucrat had lost much of his pluck. When Cole assigned him to walk the beach with Mayo and Antone, he simply nodded, though he sputtered briefly when Cole placed him under Antone's command.

"Captain Cole. Your man is colored."

"That and more qualified."

Ben, Antone, and the designate walked north; Hiram, Willie, and Captain Cole south. Cole left Mayo to man the station.

Over the years, they had collected their share of bodies, but they were strangers. This time, there was no detachment in their work. Virtually every face brought a shock of recognition, and about the gray visages, already nibbled by creatures of the sea, swam the faces of family members. Carrying the corpses to the wagon, the men stared at their feet.

The surfmen discovered the first body before they even had time to separate. The man lay on his back at the foot of the cliff path, arms at his side as if sleeping.

Willie and Antone gazed down at the mutton-chopped man. It seemed to Hiram that some understanding had just passed between the two surfmen.

"There will be others," Willie said.

The next body was less than a hundred yards away, a gray-haired man with a peaceful look and a small scar on his right temple. To Hiram's surprise, Willie knelt beside the body.

When he finished praying, Willie gently touched the scar and rose to his feet. "No harm in asking," he said, brushing sand from his knees. "Jesus died for sinners, and this fellow certainly qualified. He had a weakness for cards and ladies, but he was the gentleman we all should be."

Far down the beach, someone wailed in terrible anguish, as if they were being slowly turned inside out. Hiram wished it would stop.

Willie didn't appear to hear. He watched the peaceful man. "He earned that scar in a scuffle between two headstrong boys. He gave me the beating I deserved, but I left my mark. Even then, there was no satisfaction in it."

A raft of skunk coots rested on the ocean's surface just beyond the breakers. As each swell passed, the tiny black and white birds rose in mass, before disappearing behind the breaker's oily back.

The wailing continued. Hiram watched the birds.

"I've seen my share of death," Willie said, "but this day takes the prize."

The coots rose and fell, their coming and going like a sly wink.

That night, Hiram slipped the carving from the chest under his cot and stepped outside, walking past Thoreau's stable and into the dunes. When he was out of sight he sat in the cold sand and cried. He was embarrassed, but he was alone. The cold made the tears heavy.

Hiram knew death was part of the lifesaver's work. He had prepared incessantly for his first encounter. Alone in the equipment room, splicing rope, standing lookout in the day house, surrounded by the snoring surfmen, he had conjured every manner of gruesome end. Skulls were crushed to pulp by falling masts, limbs severed by flying lines. Sailors spun slowly in the dark, their screams giving way to silver bubbles.

When Martin had burst into the day house cradling the canvas bundle, Hiram had been wholly unprepared. He had stood stupidly by the stove, a log in his hands. When Martin placed the bundle gently on the table and pulled back the canvas, Hiram had felt the air leave him.

The girl's face was so white it might have been bone. The protruding bones were darker, and the splintered ends darker still, stained with blood that seeped reluctantly from the ragged openings below each knee.

Again dark eyes had stared at him, puzzled and disappointed. This time, though, the pursed lips voiced their disappointment. "I'm going to die."

Despite the howling storm, Hiram heard every sound. The rubber-hiss of Martin removing his slicker, the girl's stutter-step breaths, the drip of melting snow, a tap, tap, tapping, like someone walking away.

The weary voice had made Hiram ache.

"Is New York far?" she'd said. The girl had waited patiently.

He had searched frantically for words, but it was like rummaging around in an empty sack.

Martin had stepped up beside him, speaking cheerily, as if the three of them were strolling about a summer fair. "New York isn't far at all," he said. "It's only a short trip by boat or train."

"I prefer the train."

"Excellent choice," he said. "The train serves delicious desserts from a fancy sweet cart."

"Éclairs?"

"Éclairs are their specialty."

"I love éclairs."

When Martin started smoothing her hair, the girl closed her eyes. Martin moved away.

Hiram had watched a trembling finger caress the doll. She was bleeding faster, and the blood was giving her away.

The words were a whisper. "My father gave her to me. Miss Lolly and I were going to be the talk of New York. We were going to ride in a steam elevator. I hate the sea."

More than anything in the world, he had wanted to speak. He had leaned forward, hoping words might fall out, but words deserted him. Steam rose drowsily from a pan on the table.

Martin had plunged his hands into the pan with a grunt. "Hold her tight, Hiram."

He had wondered if the skinny arms would collapse in his hands, but they jerked with shocking strength when he reached to pull the doll away.

"No."

Martin placed the rolled kerchief in the girl's mouth. She had known what to do. The perfect nostrils made small flarings.

Martin looked down at her like the father he was. "You are the finest patient I have ever had," he said. He did not look away.

There was no choice. Setting the bones made a terrible grating. The girl's head jerked from side to side. She spit out the cloth in a burst of blood. The light in her eyes drained away and then winked out, like the slow shutting of a door.

Sitting in the sand, Hiram saw the slack faces of the living and the dead. Truro alone had lost sixty men. Hiram imagined the fishermen in the capsized boat, clawing at the cabin walls, jerking at latches that refused to budge, swimming as hopelessly as goldfish in a bowl.

He looked at the carving in his hand. The snake was nicked and gouged, a childish carving for a childish boy. It was foolish to believe in a better place. This world of death and despair was all there was. He snapped the carving and threw it into the dark.

9

The funeral for the deceased fishermen was the largest and saddest in the Cape's long and somber history. Even the day dawned bone-weary.

The service took place at the Presbyterian Church in Provincetown. While the crowd assembled inside the church, Reverend Marmaduke Matthews conducted his final preparations, repairing to the outhouse behind his cottage to rid himself of apprehension and a portion of his oversized breakfast. It was true he enjoyed nothing more than an audience, but it was also true that before every sermon, his mouth turned to ash and his stomach bubbled like stew on a stove. Today, with virtually the entire lower Cape wedging their way into his church, his stomach pranced like a yearling colt. The sermon was shaping up to be the biggest of his career. The outhouse was a good distance from the church. A few moments in its dim sanctity would let him collect his thoughts and dispel his turmoil.

He was staring at his feet, making revisions to the sermon's opening, when he felt cold lick his thighs.

The bright wash of light blinded him. A dark form stepped through the open doorway. The door shut quickly, and a bony joint banged against his knee, but Marmaduke couldn't move, much less stand and yank up his trousers.

Shock didn't render him speechless for long. "How dare you." He began to sputter additional threats.

"Quiet," the voice said.

The threats died in his throat.

"You'll pardon my choice of meeting place, but it seems our best opportunity for privacy."

Marmaduke did his best to gather his wits and his vestments. "Could this not wait?" he asked.

"No. I shouldn't have to remind you that this is not overly pleasant for me."

After the reverend's first blinks, the old man took shape rapidly. This did not quell Marmaduke's unease. The old man's humped frame always struck Marmaduke not as a handicap but as a threat, a coiling before release. They had worked together for nineteen years. Pomp had threatened him only once, at the very beginning, with an oblique innuendo at that, but the knife's delicate peelings and the river otter's near-human pants had ensured his loyal silence.

There were times when Marmaduke believed he was born for the cloth. He recognized evil.

"You are enjoying the conjugal visits?" the old man said.

Marmaduke said nothing.

"I believe I have a knack for finding women who satisfy," said Pomp.

The minister shifted, his thighs rubbing together like milky hamhocks. It could not be easy coupling with such a man.

Pomp made a mental note to provide Abby additional remuneration. He had decided to tell the minister as little as possible. He knew the man feared him too much to betray him, but he also knew the minister's tongue wagged without surcease.

"I know your minions await your words of solace," Pomp continued, "so I'll be brief. Word has reached my ears that could see us to untoward wealth."

Pomp saw the transformation on the minister's face. Greed still trumped fear. "I need you to direct similar eagerness toward any news regarding the recent misfortune of the *Asia*. I have reason to believe the vessel was carrying an item of considerable value. Unfortunately, its whereabouts remain a mystery. Any light your God-fearing citizenry might shed on the matter would be appreciated."

The old man had come to see him in a stinking outhouse on a frigid winter morning. Marmaduke had to force himself to calm. "The nature of this treasure?"

"The precise answer perished with the crew," said Pomp.

Marmaduke's mind raced. "This vessel … " he chose the words carefully, " … was she a casualty of fate?"

"That detail is not pertinent."

"Has anyone else shown an interest in this matter?"

Pomp had to give the man credit. When not hypnotized by the sound of his own voice, he possessed a sharp mind.

"I can't be certain, but I believe our friend Daniel Cole may be aware of this prize. As you know, it was his station that failed the vessel." Pomp leaned slightly to one side, hoping for a breath of fresh air through one of the wider cracks. "And, so, this unfortunate meeting place. A representative of the United States Lifesaving Service sits in your church. I don't believe he journeyed to the Cape for your sermon. The designate provides us providential opportunity. Find a way to speak with him. In your Lamb of God fashion, do what you can to learn what he knows. I doubt he'll tell you much—bureaucrats don't even trust themselves—but he won't be here long, so we must do what we can. I will attend the service out of respect for the deceased, but I can't approach him. As you well know, our community has no shortage of busybodies. If news of even the most innocent encounter between myself and the designate reaches Keeper Cole, it could make things more difficult for everyone."

Pomp gave the minister a meaningful look. "The good keeper and the rest of the Cape must remain unaware of our interest."

Marmaduke's shifting produced a jiggle of thigh. "It might help my questioning if you provided me with additional counsel," he said.

"Don't eat so much rich food," said Pomp.

The church swelled with humanity. Front to rear, the pews were full, mourners clinging to the edges of overflow benches. The spectrum of Cape society pressed uncomfortably together. The owner of the glassworks sat beside Ezekiel Donne, who showed his respects by wearing a silk vest and trousers, which he'd put on in an alley two blocks from the church.

Cole let all the surfmen attend; he remained at the station. Willie and Hiram somehow found seats four pews from the pulpit. Willie took his seat beside a short, wiry man with a bushy gray beard that descended to his lap. The two men exchanged whispers, and the man gave Hiram a friendly nod.

Hiram had hoped to scan the congregation for his mother, but he was wedged so tightly between Willie and a woman with breath like vinegar that he could not turn around. His mother no longer went to church, but Hiram thought she might make an exception today. Many of the fishermen and their wives were her friends.

Time passed. Two pews forward, a woman made a low moaning. Willie and the old man conferred in whispers. Hiram spied Captain Daintree sitting straight-backed in the first pew, the shoulders of his winter dress blues sporting gold epaulets that looked like pinioned squirrels. Hiram felt his feet fall asleep.

At last, the door behind the altar opened and the resonant notes of the organ sounded before quickly dying away.

Reverend Matthews strode forth, trailed by two nervous acolytes. Reverend Matthews' vestments were pure white, a series of cloaks draped precisely one upon the other so that it looked to Hiram as if the man had been the sole recipient of a Godly snowfall. The field of white was broken only by a gold sash that squared across the Reverend's broad shoulders before falling, in two elegant banners, nearly to the ground.

Reverend Matthews stepped to the pulpit. After a brief silence filled with shifting from the audience, the minister solemnly raised a hand and made the sign of the cross. His face was somber, but in his eyes, Hiram saw Godly joy.

The great baritone filled the last empty spaces. "And when they had taken up anchors, they committed themselves unto the sea, and loosened the rudder bands and hoisted up the mainsail to the wind, and made toward shore. And falling into a place where the two seas met, they ran the ship aground, and the forepart struck fast and remained unmovable, but the hinder part was broken with the violence of the waves."

The words ran about the walls. Reverend Matthews' gaze swept the congregation. To Hiram's alarm, the minister's eyes fixed briefly on him. The great head turned away, and Hiram wondered if he had imagined it.

Reverend Matthews made the sign of the cross. "Acts 27. The shipwreck of Saint Paul. Blessed be the sheep of the Lord."

He stepped around the pulpit and raised both hands. His boom dropped an octave, and his voice assumed a tone of grandfatherly kindness. "My dear, bereaved flock. Our sorrow is bottomless. These are times that try us mightily. Times that make us question ourselves, our lives, the very roots of our belief. We are, for the most part, an upstanding, God-fearing community. Yet, for his good reasons, our creator has dealt us a painful lesson in the transience of this earthly life."

The moaning woman burst into tears. The woman beside her gave a nervous little cry and fairly leapt on her.

Reverend Matthews lowered his affectionate gaze. "Let her sorrow, Mrs. Dunbar. Her soul is afflicted with grievous pain, and the poison must be spilled in the manner that comes naturally. With time, she will see the light."

The reverend turned back to the congregation. "It is difficult to find words in times like these. But in his every action, our Lord presents a lesson."

The lesson, it seemed to Hiram, was that man could just as easily drown in words. He tried his best to follow the sermon, but eventually the words became a drone. Many of his fellow parishioners, Hiram saw, had begun to slouch. The bearded man leaned against Willie, snoring softly.

Hiram maintained a façade of rapt attention, but his eyes wandered over the pews he could see. His heart actually jolted, as if someone had reached inside him and given the organ a hearty bump. Once awakened, it hammered away.

The angelic beauty sat at the far left end of the second pew, so that the sun slanting through the stained glass lit the billow of amber hair piled atop the swan neck. Her attention wandered too. Turning her head, she looked to the stained glass window. The movement loosed a ribbon of hair. It fell with a slow, ladle sweep across the bare nape of neck. Hiram knew he must stop staring, but his will snubbed him. It was not the prayer God wanted to hear, but Hiram asked that they would cross paths after the service.

Slowly, Hiram became aware of the silence. The dozing parishioners were startled awake by a burst of song from the choir, and then the entire church was singing, the sound coming to Hiram's ears like waves to the shore, and Reverend Matthews was striding down the aisle, the acolytes in measured pursuit. As they moved past, the mourners flowed in behind them. Hiram watched helplessly as the heavenly beauty joined the procession. She passed his pew looking straight ahead, a divinity in the unwashed current.

Hiram started to follow her, but Willie pinched his elbow.

"We can save ourselves," Willie said.

Exiting the opposite end of the pew, the bearded man hot on their heels, they walked to the rear of the church and out a side door that Hiram hadn't seen. Steps deposited them into a small yard beside a woodpile and a rusted stove covered with glistening patches of ice.

The bearded man shook Willie's hand. "It's the wise man who notes all points of egress," he said.

Hiram fairly ran around to the front of the church, but by the time he rounded the corner, the river of mourners had pooled into an indistinguishable sea.

Willie stepped up beside him. "By God, I believe that man's wind could breathe life back into every one of those fishermen. That door is genuine salvation."

The minister stood at the church entrance, greeting the line of those less fortunate. The crowd continued to spill into the churchyard. The sun had broken through the clouds, and the sea of bodies lent their own warmth to the gathering. Several men engaged Willie in conversation. A few of the men spoke to Hiram, but he barely heard them or his own responses, as his eyes raked the crowd.

Hiram's heart stopped. "Willie."

Pomp stood less than twenty yards away. He had traded patchwork canvas for a dark blue suit, but he still wore the ratty bowler. He was talking to Ezekiel Donne who, to Hiram's astonishment, was also dressed in a suit and listening raptly.

"A gift, to commune with the unreachable," said Willie. "I doubt anyone else could persuade Mr. Donne to put on pants and keep them on."

"Why is he here?"

"Why shouldn't he be?"

"If he's as dark as you say he is, he shouldn't be at church."

"He didn't come for the service. But few of the men we lauded today were saints, though most were fine company."

Pomp laughed and Ezekiel Donne clapped his hands and grinned madly. Several mourners shot the men disapproving glances, but neither man paid any mind.

"No doubt, the most interesting conversation for miles," said Willie.

"They're rude," said Hiram, although he had always felt bad for Ezekiel Donne. Calling him rude made Hiram feel worse.

"Did you notice anything about the bodies on the beach?" Willie asked.

"No."

"So many corpses, so neatly composed, so far from the tide line?" Willie still watched the two men. "Pomp was first again. We each pay homage in our own fashion."

The church bell began to ring. The crowd fell silent, the men doffing their caps, the women bowing their bonneted heads. The bell tolled eight times, the fishermen's earthly watch concluded.

As the last of the ringing drifted away, Ezekiel Donne gave a donkey's bray and began a high-stepping jig. Pomp placed a hand on Ezekiel's shoulder and the thin man fell forlorn and silent, like a scolded child.

Marmaduke Matthews had stationed himself at the entrance as quickly as possible, but several clots of mourners had still beaten him to the front door, making their escape.

Now the sun fell full on the front stoop of the church. Marmaduke felt a faint prickle of nervous sweat. He let the line run past quickly, greeting each mourner with a firm handshake and Godly smile, listening as they complimented his sermon, though he saw their compliments did not reach their eyes. Weathered faces filed past, testament to life and lament, until, looking down the line, he spotted the face he sought. The designate was being harangued by Isaiah Hatch. Isaiah was a notorious dullard with no interests outside of himself. Marmaduke watched the codger's shiny bald head bob in enthusiastic agreement to his own words.

By the time the designate reached for Marmaduke's outstretched hand, his clenched jaw acknowledged his ears' severe battering.

Marmaduke produced his most reverential smile. "Welcome to our Cape, captain. It's an honor to have you here. I regret your visit coincides with such sad circumstance. Understandably, it dilutes our welcome considerably."

"I would have turned for shore," Isaiah Hatch said, speaking to the back of Captain Daintree's head. "Clear signs the sea gives. Foolish to ignore them. Learned that lesson well in my time at sea. Salty as cured cod, I was."

Reverend Matthews retained the warmth in his smile. "Mr. Hatch, perhaps you would allow me a moment with this gentleman?"

"Certainly," Isaiah said. "Happy to have you join us."

"I wish to speak to our distinguished visitor alone," the reverend said.

"Oh."

Placing a hand on the designate's elbow, Marmaduke steered him down the steps and around the corner, where they were largely out of sight.

He discarded the reverential smile for one of confidentiality. "Unwise to be seen playing favorites," he said.

The designate watched him. The man had a queer habit of briskly brushing his sleeves.

"Captain Colin Daintree, am I correct?"

Marmaduke did not miss the flicker of suspicion. Regarding man's behavior, Pomp rarely erred.

Marmaduke held out his hands. "Few distinguished persons visit our provincial backwater. Such news spreads as quickly as man turns to sin."

To his credit, the bureaucrat did not buckle beneath the platitudes immediately.

"Should you be neglecting your congregation?"

Marmaduke knew the man was right. To ignore his duties for too long would draw suspicion. He gave a chuckle. "God's truth be told, they're thanking God I'm gone. However, I mustn't allow them too much neglect. Let me start by saying I have the profoundest respect for the lifesaving service. Our cape's bravest men dedicate their lives to its aims, but," he lowered his voice and winked, "I have also known many of these men my entire life. I know many of them require sage oversight."

He had made the proper read. The thin man nodded curtly. "Ours is a job that often goes unappreciated, reverend. It is no easy matter overseeing the corps. They are quite capable, and as you noted quite brave, but a strong back and heart is not always matched by an equivalent mind. They often need direction."

"I have some experience in the matter. We are both, in our respective fashions, shepherds of men."

"I suppose we are."

"You are a friend of Sumner Kimball's?" the reverend inquired.

"A fine man."

Marmaduke noted the subtle distinction. "I'm certain Superintendent Kimball employed only the most capable administrator to investigate whatever it is that concerns you here on the Cape."

Again the spark of wariness flared. "Forgive me. It's not my intent to pry into your business, though as you might imagine, I have absorbed my share of confidences—confidences I will take to my grave."

Marmaduke shook his head slowly. "Certain admissions would raise the hairs on Satan's head. I'm afraid there is no end to man's secrets. Except at a minister's mouth."

He was relieved to see the man's brushing cease. He continued quickly. "A sad and terrible thing, all this death. I have presided over more funerals than any minister should. Each and every one is inestimably sad. Saddest of all when a child is taken by the sea."

Few men neglect the chance to show off what they know. "The wreck of the *Asia*," the designate said. "The girl's passing was indeed unfortunate."

It was like being a puppeteer. "God has his reasons for everything," said Marmaduke, "but to consign a child to the sea gives all but the hardest heart pause."

His own memories of the *Asia's* dead conjured only disappointment. It was a funeral he'd sorely wanted to attend. Daniel Cole had spoiled it. Now he had a chance to please Pomp and exact revenge.

"It's not a minister's place, but to perhaps aid you in your work, I will pass along a confidence. There are some who feel Keeper Cole and his men failed the *Asia*. Admittedly, this was the rarest instance. You know better than I, the man's record is nearly impeccable. But the *Asia* may be a blemish. Though Captain Cole did not allow it, there are some who believe the seas allowed for a boat rescue." Marmaduke let the accusation hang in the frosty air. "Not that I have any expertise in such matters, but I have spoken to those who do. They also tell me that Keeper Cole's failure to come to the aid of the *Asia* may have resulted in other misfortunes."

The designate gave his sleeve two quick pats. "What are you saying?"

Marmaduke knew he must proceed delicately, just as he knew time was running out. "May I speak plainly?"

"I demand it."

"Again, it is not my habit to divulge confidences, but I have been told that the *Asia* carried an item of some value. An item lost with the ship."

A fingertip touched a corner of the waxed mustache, lowered to briefly rest on a gold jacket button, and then fell to a rapier-sharp pant crease where it tapped twice.

"I tell you this only because you are a man of God, and I am certain I can trust your discretion without qualm," said Captain Daintree. "Something was lost."

The man's anxiety was so obvious Marmaduke nearly laughed. "Have you any additional information?"

"I'm afraid not."

When the designate spoke again, it took all of Marmaduke's reserve not to seize the man's shoulders and kiss him full on the lips.

"Some value is understating matters," said Captain Daintree. "We believe the item in question could alter the course of history. Again, I divulge this only because you are a man of God. I must also demand that should you be the beneficiary of any additional confidences, you report them directly to me. Who spoke of this matter?"

Marmaduke enjoyed giving the bureaucrat his own taste of mystery. "I'm afraid I must demure. My parishioners require the same vow of confidence you demand. I fear I've already divulged too much."

A cold wind eddied, biting through his trousers. The outhouse rose again in his mind. Pomp would be happy, but it would pay to make him happier still.

He made a final foray. "Captain Daintree, you are a man accustomed to inordinately heavy burdens, but there are times when life's burdens become too much for even the strongest man. During your visit, the door to my cottage will always be open, with the assurance that any confidence you offer remains between two men and one mighty God."

"I will consider your offer." The designate turned quickly, but not before Marmaduke Matthews saw another lie in another set of eyes.

10

Captain Daintree interviewed Hiram and Martin that afternoon in Cole's quarters, permitting Cole alone to be present. Cole had wanted Willie there too—Willie might catch something he missed—but Daintree had refused. Cole decided it was not a point worth arguing. He would listen carefully and enlist Willie later if he needed him.

Cole had considered telling Hiram and Martin about the interview beforehand, but in the end he decided against it. He knew they were hiding nothing, but surprise might loose something that would not otherwise come to light.

Again Captain Daintree wore dress blues. Four gold medals were pinned above his breast pocket. Papers were stacked neatly on Cole's desk, alongside a leather-bound folder.

The designate paced the floor, making precise turns. Hiram and Martin stood in the middle of the room.

"Gentlemen, you are being questioned regarding critical United States Lifesaving Service business. It is your solemn duty to be wholly forthright, volunteering everything you know of the *Asia's* demise to the fullest of your knowledge."

Hiram and Martin looked to Cole.

"Captain Daintree is aware I have already questioned you for my report," Cole said.

"I have read the report," said Daintree, cutting in, "but there are matters of which your keeper is unaware." The emissary fell silent, allowing this trump card to settle. "Given these gaps in Keeper Cole's knowledge, I believe there are questions he did not ask."

Cole wondered how much of this game was the work of Sumner Kimball, and how much was the work of Colin Daintree. Whoever was pulling the strings, he would learn nothing by being combative.

He nodded to Hiram and the Swede. "Cooperate fully."

Daintree began by repeating many of the questions Cole had asked. Now and again, he walked to the desk to make notes. He did not comment on the men's replies.

Finally, he said, "The girl died in your hands."

"No one could have saved her," Martin said. "We tried to set her legs, but she had already suffered severe blood loss, worsened by exposure to the cold."

Daintree paused, a finger balanced on the desk. "You are a doctor?"

"No, sir." Cole stepped away from the window.

"Surfman Nelson has saved more lives than some doctors."

"Belated congratulations," said Daintree, keeping his eyes on the Swede, "but he failed here, and I am not interested in diagnoses. I am interested in the girl's last moments, before his failure ended her hopes and possibly ours. Mr. Nelson, the report Keeper Cole filed states the girl was conscious. You spoke with her before she died."

"Yes." Martin felt the sadness seeping through him. "But only for a very short time."

"Much can be conferred in a short time. Tell me precisely what she said. Every word."

Martin saw the small mouth parting for the rolled cloth, the eyes swimming with fear. She had known what was coming.

"She was braver than most men," he said.

"I've no interest in opinions. Let me repeat. I need to know exactly what she said."

"She asked if she was far from New York. I told her it was a short trip by either boat or rail. She said she preferred rail."

"Did she say why she wished to go to New York?"

"No."

"Did she say if they were meeting anyone there?"

"No."

Cole saw Martin glance at Hiram.

"Did she say anything about her father?"

"No."

"Anything about their voyage?"

"No."

The failed questioning brought a rise in patting.

"Did she say anything to you that seemed odd?"

"People say many strange things when they are about to die."

"I am interested only in this girl. What else did she say?"

Martin said, "She said nothing more to me."

Daintree turned to Hiram.

"Surfman Paine. What did she say to you?"

Hiram heard the beating in his ears, his heart, the storm's buffeting winds, his failure arriving yet again on the black wings of memory. The girl watched him, as if she were in the room.

"Mr. Paine."

Hiram waited for the beating to rise above him, where it was not so loud. "She said she and her doll were going to be the talk of New York. She said she was going to ride in a steam elevator."

"And?"

"She said she was going to die. She said I was frightened."

Three of four men stood quietly.

"She said nothing more?" asked Daintree tersely.

"No."

"Search your memory."

"There was nothing else."

Daintree said, "Her name was Isabella."

The name echoed queerly. Daintree waited, but the boy said nothing.

"Did you ask her why she was going to be the talk of New York?"

"No."

"Did you ask her anything at all?"

"No."

"What *did* you say to her?"

Hiram stared past the designate. He could not imagine how it had been, tied to the mainmast, rolling in the heaving seas. Isabella. Mercy. He knew his own helplessness was pitiful.

"I said nothing."

After Martin and Hiram left, Daintree walked behind the desk. "Isabella Merton," he said. "Edwin Merton, her father, was the *Asia's* captain. The *Asia* was an Italian vessel with an Italian crew. Captain Merton, we have confirmed, was English. There is little love these days between the Italians and the English. We have reason to believe he was not the *Asia's* regular captain. We believe he assumed command for this one trip."

Daintree leaned forward, placing both palms on the desk. "The *Asia* was carrying lumber, as you surmised in your report. Why would a captain be specially conscripted to deliver such mundane cargo?"

"Tell me," said Cole.

"Captain Merton was an extremely capable man. He was enlisted to carry an item of the utmost value to our shores."

"I told you we recovered no valuables."

"That does not mean they do not exist."

"If they do, they likely belong to the sea."

"Perhaps," said Daintree. "But those who enlisted Captain Merton continue to have great faith in him. They are certain he made arrangements for the item in question to make its way to shore."

The ignorance of the land-bound forever surprised Cole. "Captain Merton was likely occupied with his sinking vessel," Cole said. "Do you know what this item is?"

The skinny man hesitated. "No."

"Does Superintendent Kimball know?"

"No."

Cole felt his irritation rising. Words so often led nowhere. "How was Superintendent Kimball apprised of this item?"

"He received a letter," said Daintree.

"From who?"

"I don't know. Powers beyond us are involved, Keeper Cole. They keep their secrets close."

Daintree forced himself to meet the dark eyes. The keeper himself resembled a storm. "We have been informed that two men aboard the *Asia* knew of the item. But you and I realize it's possible the girl was apprised in the last moments when the cause appeared lost."

Daintree thumbed a sheaf of paper from the pile and handed it to Cole. "The *Asia's* official manifest," he said.

Cole ran his eyes down the list.

"Nine names appear on the official manifest," said Daintree. "The captain, seven sailors, and the daughter. You buried eight men and the girl. This would lead one to believe that Captain Merton was among the men you buried."

Daintree reached for the leather-bound folder beside the papers. Removing the photograph, he handed it to Cole. "Captain Merton was an intensely private man, but even a private man cannot escape notice over a lifetime."

The photograph was grainy, made worse by the fact that the picnic had taken place on a gray day, but a glance was enough. Cole recognized the girl extending the buttercup, but the man sitting cross-legged on the blanket, smiling despite himself, was a stranger. For a moment, Cole wondered who had taken the picture and how they had cajoled the reticent father into posing.

"We did not bury this man," said Cole, returning the picture.

"So a captain is lost to the sea and a man without identity is buried in his stead. Have you any explanation?"

Cole saw the bald man on the frozen ground, the tips of his leather shoes pointing to the sky. A German on an Italian vessel captained by an Englishman. A seagoing Tower of Babel.

"No," Cole said.

Inserting the photograph carefully into the folder, Captain Daintree said, "Captain Merton was a lifelong sea captain, not a man of means. He lost his wife to tuberculosis six months ago. We believe he came to America to make a new life for his daughter."

Wishes, thought Cole, were often granted in pieces. "And the extra man," said Cole. "Have you any explanation?"

"No, but we believe he may be the crux of the puzzle."

"Does anyone else know of this item?"

Daintree felt a rush of guilt and remorse. Again, the cold wind eddied around the church steps. He had seen it clearly: greed in the eyes of a man of God.

He had made a mistake.

"No," he said.

Captain Daintree and Antone Lucas left for Wellfleet Station the next morning. After Daintree left, Cole sat at his desk. He picked up neither pen nor log book.

Cole had no doubt that Captain Merton had closely consulted the nautical charts. He was equally sure the captain knew, with an estimation better than most, where he was along the Cape when he faced his choice. Yet the man had discarded all he believed to be certain for what was almost certainly vaporous hope, and he was lured toward false harbor as easily as a moth to flame.

Cole saw again the grainy half-smile, the daughter, brow furrowed, peering intently at the buttercup beneath her father's chin. Cole had played the same game with Julia. He did not fault Edwin Merton for taking a hopeless chance.

11

It took Hiram two days to work up the courage to ask Willie about the goddess at the funeral. They were on the stable roof replacing worn shingles, Thoreau snorting protest below. With the weather continuing to be unseasonably warm, Cole had set the men to a fierce schedule of outdoor repairs. From the steeply pitched roof, Hiram could see the Atlantic running dark blue and smooth to the horizon.

To Hiram's joy, Willie knew precisely who had been sitting in the pew.

"Your angelic vision would be Hannah Lombard," Willie said, happy to set down his hammer. "Only child of Enos Lombard. Destined to be the loveliest spinster on the Cape. Woe to the man who would fall for her charms."

Hiram studiously examined the shingles at his feet.

Willie grinned. "Apparently that would be you, Master Paine."

Hiram surrendered entirely. "She is the most beautiful woman I've ever seen."

"Well your timeline is short, but I agree she's a fine specimen, a fact not lost on any breathing man, including her father. Rumor has it that any suitor of Hannah Lombard's would be better off wooing Medusa herself at the gates of hell."

Enos Lombard was one of the Cape's most accomplished shipmasters, his tirades at sea the fodder of legend. Still Hiram saw no reason for Willie's dark intimations.

"I don't believe in rumors or hell," he said, though he didn't believe himself.

"That must make life easier," said Willie. "Tell me, young Paine. Have you ever seen a shrunken head?"

"No."

The shriveled tokens were the rage on the Cape and the islands. The wealthy collected them like tea settings, from sailors on Cape and Nantucket vessels returning with the goods from various Pacific isles. The most aesthetically pleasing heads earned a tidy price. But Hiram was not wealthy; neither had he traveled any farther than Mashpee.

"Captain Lombard is an ardent admirer of the dark craft," Willie said, "collecting the heads wherever his voyages allow. They say he has shelf upon shelf of the prunish things—whole mute villages."

For a moment, Hiram forgot his pangs of yearning. "You've seen them?"

"Captain Lombard's personal collection, no. For some puzzling reason, the shipmaster has yet to invite me to tea. But I've seen them elsewhere, and I'm familiar with the art. There's no better testament to man's avarice and skill." He had the boy now. He pretended to reach for his hammer.

Hiram leaned so far forward, Willie feared the boy might roll off the roof. "What do the heads look like?"

"Queer things," said Willie, "and hypnotizing too. The skin is dry as fall's final leaf, and the inside of the skull is perfectly clean and smooth. If the work is done well, everything is preserved—nose, lips, ears, teeth, eyelids. The most prized heads possess fetching tattoos. Greed, it's said, has seen to the decimation of entire villages. The Pacific islanders are poor, and a comely head fetches a good price. Better still, I suppose, if it's attached to an annoying neighbor."

Willie let the sun warm his face, enjoying the pause before the *coup de grace*. "Of late, I'm told, Enos Lombard has immersed himself in the intricacies of the art. He sails the Pacific as we speak.

Under cover of night, heads are delivered to his ship's quarters, and a loyal deckhand mops up the mess by morning. Entirely possible that his daughter's bevy of suitors will provide him a steady supply of raw material, keeping his daughter forever chaste. Not the first time a man has lost his head on account of his willy. Not that you aren't pursuing a nobler cause."

Hiram was embarrassed by the ease with which Willie had unearthed his desires. "You don't have to be rude," he said, resuming his nailing. "And there's nothing funny about death."

"Life is easier to manage if one sees the lighter side of death." Willie considered the boy in front of him. "Truth be told, I'm a jealous old man. I squandered my own days of courtship by courting too many women. Which is how I came to be married to tedium and Daniel Cole."

Opportunity saw Hiram forget his indignation. "You understand women."

"If I knew anything at all, I'd be reclining in a soft bed with warm company instead of squatting on this shit-stained roof with you. If you're smart, you've already grasped my first lesson: men are not prone to monogamy, and women do not take kindly to being courted by the gaggle. One of the two parties has to give in, and it won't likely be women."

"I'm only interested in one woman."

"Well, that will make things easier, but not by much," said Willie. "And it's not me you have to convince."

The boy's hopeful look made Willie wish for the past.

"The odds of meeting Miss Lombard on this roof are long," he said, picking up his hammer. "Here's some advice. Before I discovered the whore house, I went to church." Willie drove a nail home. "Sunday's my day off. Now it's yours."

On Sunday, Hiram went into the kitchen before dawn. He boiled water and took the rusted iron off the shelf. After cleaning the iron's underside, he carefully pressed the wrinkles from his only dress shirt. His trousers were embarrassingly threadbare, but they were all he had.

He'd hoped to be gone before anyone woke, but he was buttoning his shirt when Ben stepped in to fix breakfast.

Hiram flushed, but Ben only smiled. "The Lord will be pleased. Say a prayer for my lapse in character."

As Hiram headed for the front door of the station, Willie stepped up to him and slapped his cheeks. A strange odor rose in Hiram's nose, like a medicine chest, but nicer.

"Women prefer a man who doesn't smell like low tide," said Willie.

Walking to Provincetown beneath a pewter sun, Hiram was nearly crippled with worry. With the exception of the funeral for the fishermen, he hadn't been to church since his father's death. When his father and his sister had been alive, their family had attended church every Sunday, he and Mercy rising, their long faces scrubbed clean with a scratchy rag before they were stuffed into stiff clothes and dragged off to the Presbyterian Church. Church was their mother's doing. Samuel Paine had suffered Reverend Matthews' services as reluctantly as his offspring, but he'd recognized the wisdom of keeping his pains quiet.

After his father's death, his mother had stopped going to church. She offered no explanation. She still kept a Bible on the bedside table. Hiram knew she read it because the silk thread moved about the pages. But their churchgoing days had ended.

Hiram wondered whether church had changed. He didn't want to make any mistakes. As children, he and Mercy had been intimidated by all the rituals. Now, he imagined himself responding to the Word when he should be listening, hopping up when he should be kneeling, and otherwise standing out as the lustful hypocrite he was.

By the time he arrived, an hour before the eight o'clock service, he was a wreck. He sat in the last pew at the back of the church and watched the congregation arrive. The older parishioners walked to their pews solemnly, with their heads down, as if approaching the guillotine, but he noticed that many of the churchgoers were young girls and, somewhat troubling, boys his age. Several boys shot him looks none too Christian.

Absorbed with the sudden dilemma of competition, Hiram didn't see Hannah Lombard until she was past, the faintest smell of peach trailing in her wake. This time, Hiram's heart was run through. A man held her pale arm. The man was square-shouldered, with fiery red hair that reached below his collar. As they walked, he leaned into her affectionately.

Hannah and her suitor sat in the pew she had graced during the funeral. The man leaned close, and the ivory shoulders shook with silent laughter.

Hiram experienced an un-Godlike rush of jealous anger, followed by an equally powerful urge to flee. He had one foot in the aisle when the doors at the rear of the church flew open and Reverend Matthews, tailed by the same two acolytes, strode for the pulpit. The choir burst into song.

Though it didn't seem possible, the service was longer than the memorial. Hiram stood and knelt and sat, and stood and knelt and sat again. He stole glances at the cursed suitor. The man no longer whispered hotly in Hannah's ear, but Hiram saw how, standing for hymns, Hannah Lombard leaned gently into him.

Outside of bitter disappointment and time's molasses unraveling, Hiram had little memory of the service. When it ended, he stepped from the pew so quickly he nearly collided with an old woman.

Mumbling apology, he made to move on, but fingers gripped his forearm in a painful pinch.

"You seek new quarters in your search for meaning," said Widow Mayhew. "Perhaps you'd better recognize me in my knickers."

Parishioners flowed about them. Hiram tried to mouth whatever words would provide him immediate escape, but, to his horror, the old lady only gripped his elbow harder.

"Then again," she said, "enlightenment may not be all that's on your mind. In that case, God's reward is the church social." Widow

Mayhew's nose crinkled. "Perhaps a cologne that smells a bit less like a pharmacy accident. At least your shoes match. Come along."

With a yank, she led him through the rear doors. Proceeding down two flights of stairs they stepped into a long, low-ceilinged room already reverberating with din. At the far end of the room, three silver tureens sat on a linen-draped table, alongside plates piled high with baked goods.

"The apple turnovers are sinfully delicious," the widow said. "I, for one, would not sit through Reverend Matthews' service without heavenly promise on the horizon. I believe you've already found someone you fancy, but I'll need your help from here."

Hiram felt helpless. His arm remained pinched in blacksmith tongs. His eyes betrayed him, straying to the amber glow in the center of the hall, gold among rusted pennies. The hateful red mane stood beside her.

Widow Mayhew gave a cluck. "You're not the first, but in matters of *amour*, one must always hold hope of being the last."

To Hiram's horror, Widow Mayhew yanked him forward. They bumped through a sea of fragrance, talcum powder and bad breath, Widow Mayhew muttering hellos, and then he was standing before Hannah Lombard. Placing a bony claw in the small of his back, Widow Mayhew provided a last push. The force surprised him. A hand too powerful to belong to Widow Mayhew grasped his forearm, saving him from lunging into Hannah Lombard's punch.

"Steady, lad. I don't believe she requires a refill just yet."

It was worse than dying, but he had to look, and when he did he saw the red-haired man was old. The face he stared into was boyish, light blue eyes floating above a sea of freckles, but the skin beneath the eyes sagged, and gray streaked the man's temples. He leaned on a cane, smiling warmly.

"This would be Paul Macy," said Widow Mayhew.

"I'm sorry." He was apologizing to Hannah while staring at the man. He felt as if he were burning alive, only burning alive would be more pleasant. "I must have stumbled."

"We all lose our way," said Paul Macy. "Why else would we be here?"

Hiram liked the man, partly because he was trying to put him at ease, but mostly because he was old.

"Miss Lombard. Mr. Macy. The young gentleman is Hiram Paine, winter man at Peaked Hill Bars."

He felt Hannah watching him. It was the easiest thing to turn his head an inch, but he stood as if his neck were forged in place. He was suffocating in peaches. He hated Willie. He hated the shirt squeezing his chest.

The angelic voice provided some relief. "Mr. Macy is also a man of the sea."

Mr. Macy chuckled. "You confuse your tenses, dear Hannah."

"Tell Mr. Paine of the bravery that saw you to this cane," said Hannah.

"More a matter of poor boat placement."

Hiram shook the offered hand.

"I was a boatsteerer," said Paul Macy. "A humorous title for a man who positioned his boat precisely above a surfacing sperm whale."

"That's the beginning of the story," said Hannah. "He saved three men from drowning. After his whaling days ended, Mr. Macy served on my father's ships as first mate until the dampness of the sea induced too much pain in his leg and he came to his senses. Now he tends to business matters here, while my father sails the same horrid seas gathering more of what he already has."

"It's called commerce," said Mr. Macy.

"I miss him."

Her heartbreak was so honest and open that Hiram lost the last of his heart.

"You're new to this church," said Hannah.

Hiram experienced his own small heartbreak. She hadn't noticed him at the funeral service. "We came to this church when I was a boy, but we stopped coming."

It sounded strange in his ears, but Hannah didn't ask any questions.

"We're new to this church ourselves," she said. "We come from an Episcopalian line, dating back to eternity, but Father decided that Episcopalians pass the plate too much, so here we are. Is your family with you?"

Hiram caught Widow Mayhew's look. Blushing turned Hannah Lombard's eyes greener.

Quickly, he said, "My father and sister passed away quite some time ago." He meant for it to sound off-handed, but it didn't. "My mother is healthy as an ox. She still reads the Bible, even though she no longer comes to church. I thought I'd try church again." He had no idea what he was saying. Was there no end to his idiocy?

"And how did you find it?" asked Widow Mayhew.

Hiram was stymied. If Hannah was devout, the truth would end his hopes before they started. But the alternative was a lie in the very bowels of the church.

"I find it long," smiled Hannah. "If it wasn't for my father's insistence and the persuasive Mr. Macy, my own attendance would be spotty."

Drunk with relief, Hiram blurted, "He doesn't even stop to breathe. Maybe that keeps him awake."

Everyone was quiet, though Mr. Macy appeared amused.

Hiram sensed the presence behind him, like the sepia outline of a great ship before it pushes through the fog.

"Reverend Matthews," said Widow Mayhew. "We were just discussing your sermon."

The minister accepted the widow's outstretched hand with a bow. "I'm pleased to see they merit discussion."

The man's voice rumbled in Hiram's chest. He was much bigger up close. It was like standing beside a great snow-draped tree.

"I believe you know Miss Lombard and Mr. Macy," said Widow Mayhew. "But today, a new face rejoins your flock."

The great ship came about.

"Another blessing from the Lord." The hand was soft and heavy with flesh, but the grip was powerful. "Hiram Paine. It's a joy to see your family return to the church."

"I came alone." Though he hadn't meant it to, it sounded brusque. Reverend Matthews continued smiling benignly.

Hiram felt terrible. Before he could stop himself, he said, "I enjoyed your sermon."

"Ah. What was it about the sermon that appealed to you?"

He had saved his lie for the minister of the church. Hiram readied to throw himself upon the man's mercy.

"The race is not to the swift," said Mr. Macy, "nor the battle to the strong. Neither yet bread to the wise, or yet riches to men of understanding, nor yet favor to men of skill; but time and chance happeneth to them all. Who could not admire Ecclesiastes' egalitarian outlook?"

The reverend turned to the whaler. "Two attentive parishioners. It will be difficult for me to retain the humility our Lord requires."

Hiram shot a grateful glance at Mr. Macy. To his horror, the whaler winked back.

Reverend Matthews was looking toward the table. A man gestured to one of the tureens.

Reverend Matthews gave a parting smile.

"Today's parishioners thirst for more than salvation. If you will excuse me."

Paul Macy barely waited for the last of the minister's robe to trail away. "He'd better not fill the bowl too high, or his parishioners might plunge their heads below the surface to enjoy the silence."

"Thank you," said Hiram. He felt weak. "I don't remember a word."

"You're not to be blamed. The man blows more wind than a wounded whale. Let's just hope your compliment doesn't fuel the fire."

"A compassionate lie followed by the truth," said Hannah. "I suspect God still views you with favor."

Hiram knew better.

That evening in his study, fresh torment joined Marmaduke Matthews, elbowing its way between the familiar hollowness and self-reproach. He had poured whisky until it brought animal numbness, but it didn't help.

The boy had shaken him more than he'd thought possible. Their meeting had required all his theatrical skills. He saw himself smiling and clasping the boy's hand in perfect servant-of-God fashion. Countenances were fog. He knew this as well as anyone.

Once, he'd been certain Nellie Paine would never leave his thoughts, but the ability to move on was one of man's greatest parlor tricks. With the passing years, she had retreated behind a hardened carapace that shielded him from the worst of the pain. Seeing the boy at the funeral service had cracked the shield as if it were hair's breadth ice. From the pulpit, he had allowed himself a quick look. It was enough to tell him the boy didn't know.

Seeing the boy in church had triggered painful memory and powerful curiosity. And so, though he felt himself half fighting each step, he had approached the boy at the social. The boy had been no more than a spindly limbed urchin then. He had thickened with muscle, and the softness was gone from his face, though it still possessed the familiar aquiline grace. The boy had lied about the sermon; he had seen it in the green eyes that nearly caused his collapse.

Slouched in the stuffed chair beside the fire, he felt his pudding lump of midsection. The years had turned him fat and sinful, but the aching never left. He poured that ache into his parishioners, a fiery tirade and promise of Godly retribution that left him drained, and, at times, oddly sated.

The cottage door banged open and shut. A grunt followed, a short woman straining for a coat peg, and then the clatter of footsteps. He had come to expect it, but the brash entry always startled and mildly annoyed him. Why not at least the façade of a visit? How hard was it to knock? The rude comfort was offensive, but he was too weak-willed to risk offending his guest.

Abby bustled into the study, beating her arms against her body. She gave him a happy nod and went to the whisky he always poured for her. He watched the whisky go down her white throat. It was true. She was not the sort of woman who set your heart racing at first glance, but a closer look revealed intelligent eyes and animal grace. There were the particulars too. When she took him in her mouth, the thick ringlets bobbed on her bare shoulders like flowers in a breeze. She had made him her prisoner.

Abby set down the tumbler with a contented sigh. "Temporary fire," she said. "I don't know how much longer I can stomach this cold. I read recently of a man named Henry Flagler who is laying out a railway in Florida, so that people might travel there to enjoy the climate. You can pick an orange in December and let the juice dribble down your front." The ringlets bobbed with the joy of the thought. "Whisky's no December orange. I'm still numb to the bone. But we'll remedy that soon enough."

Soon was not soon enough. Marmaduke crossed the study without a word, taking her where she stood. Even as he thrust beneath the folds of dress, his burst of pleasure was both elevated and extinguished by the vision of Nellie Paine.

Four miles to the east, Pomp inhaled the night's sting. The tepid afternoon had promised fog, but with the gloaming, winter's chill came instead. Night had arrived achingly clear. It was such a lovely night, he had to walk. He wandered absently through the dunes, lost to his surroundings, stopping only when he reached the cliff edge.

One hundred feet below, driftwood lay scattered like bones. Gulls, gray in the night, huddled at the water's edge, facing the sea. Pomp whistled a show tune and looked out at the glittering stars, the darkness behind them like a promise. Tonight was a loss, but how could he be disappointed? Nature would provide other opportunity.

Pomp smiled. Opportunity was a cagey mistress. She kept things interesting. Had the *Asia's* captain taken a little longer to die, he might have given up his secret. But the man had ended his life, and Pomp had buried him and started his walk home. A minute earlier, a minute later, and he would have missed the big surfman stumbling toward the day house, the bundle in his arms. Standing to the side of the window, he had watched the girl's last moments, the boy hovering over her.

The *Asia's* captain had thwarted him, departing without fully divulging his secrets. But now there were alternatives. Every puzzle had an answer. It was only a question of touching his finger to the proper piece.

Pomp balanced at the cliff edge like a diver, smelling the sea.

12

Several weeks passed without incident, an improbable run of serenity during a season that typically saw two shipwrecks a week off the Cape's shores. An almost festive air took hold of the men, as if they might escape winter altogether.

Two days before Thanksgiving, another bout of Indian summer descended. The sun beat down from the blue sky with a fever unprecedented for November. The men sweated like racehorses during the morning surfboat drill, and tended to afternoon repairs in their shirt sleeves. A light southeast wind ruffled the calm Atlantic with a sleeping child's breath.

When Antone came running from the day house shouting that a ship was aground, Martin, replacing the last of the stable shingles, sat up so quickly he nearly tumbled off the roof. Ben forgot the can of nails on his knee; the nails clattered across the porch as he leapt to his feet. Even Captain Cole, who had ushered Thoreau outside to enjoy the sun while he checked a shoe, stood frozen, foreleg in one hand.

Antone shouted again. To help the men along, he waved his arms overhead too. "Ship aground! One-half mile to the north!"

Releasing Thoreau, Cole said, "How far offshore?"

Antone was mildly embarrassed to be the bearer of such news. "She is stuck on the outermost shoal, Captain Cole. Two hundred yards."

"Is she in any immediate danger?"

"No, sir." Antone was at a loss. He felt he should say something more. "It is very odd."

Cole spoke to the dumbstruck men. "Collect the surfboat. The tide is dropping."

For the second time that day, they hauled the surfboat, perched on its own wagon, from the equipment room. Ben harnessed Thoreau, clucking reassurance as they made their way down the cliff path. Thoreau took high, reluctant steps, miffed by another go-round.

They heard the shouting as soon as they set foot on the beach; it was carried to their ears by the light onshore wind. Standing in the sand, the surfmen absorbed the strange scene. The schooner stood against the blue day, virtually every inch of canvas sagging. The Atlantic ringed the vessel in a slumbering puddle.

"I'll be damned," said Willie. "Here's a captain of considerable talent." Hiram could barely make out the letters on the forward quarterboard, but Willie said, "The *Tabor*. I'd drape the quarterboard if I were her crew."

Though it didn't seem possible, the shouting rose several decibels to a particularly vociferous tirade that filtered across the water.

"Not in a sociable mood," said Willie, "and I'll wager our arrival won't improve his afternoon. What the man lacks in navigational skills, he makes up for in wind. If he shouted into his sails, he might free himself and be gone."

Hiram wondered what orders a captain would be shouting in a situation like this. Whatever his demands, they were being responded to with haste. The wind wasn't strong enough to fill the sails, but several sailors climbed the rigging, and heads scurried about the deck.

Hiram had imagined all manner of rescues, but again, his imagination had been outdone.

"What can they do?" he whispered to Willie.

"Grounded in this sparse wind, nothing," said Willie. "I expect they'll run about like ninnies until we row out and present them with a more civilized option."

"Can't they just stay where they are until the tide floats them loose?"

"A possibility," said Willie, "but I suspect we won't stand here until that happens."

"The wind might rise," said Antone, "making them imperiled."

"And you might give the next commencement address at Harvard," said Willie.

"Enough," said Cole.

Cole turned to Hiram. "Take Surfman Nelson's oar."

Hiram was startled. He sometimes rowed during drills, but during rescues, it was his job to hold the bow into the waves while the men scrambled into the surfboat—not to man an oar.

"Get the boat in the water," Cole ordered. "There appears to be no immediate danger, other than the crew going deaf, but we need to push off."

Three men on a side, they pushed the surfboat into knee-deep water. Martin held the bow, which barely rose with the shin-high waves. Hiram had tied the legs of his oilskin tight around the outside of his boots, but frigid water still seeped in, producing a faint burn in his calves and feet.

Cole gave the signal. Moving as one, the men hopped smoothly over the gunnels and sat in their seats. There was a clacking as each man settled his oar in its lock; then, on Cole's order, six blades grabbed the water and the surfboat lurched forward. Cole used the forward momentum to vault over the stern, taking up the steering oar.

It felt as if they were rowing over glass. With no waves to impede their progress, each pull sent the surfboat leaping. The boat moved with preternatural speed.

Hiram felt a nervous excitement buzzing in his head and limbs. Occupied with the effort of the oars, the men fell silent. The world was reduced to the creak of wood, the labored grunts of the men, and, now and again, a softly issued correction from Captain Cole.

"More left. Fine. Now straightaway."

Hiram watched the beach recede faster than he thought possible. In less than a minute, Martin shrank to a smudge, dwarfed by the cliffs. Though he had seen it many times, the view of land from the water always struck Hiram with its fragility and beauty. There was another feeling, ominous even on a day as docile as this: out here, water assumed its rightful place, while the land shrunk away in defeat.

Lost in the hypnotic dip and tug of the oar, Hiram almost forgot the ship behind them. The bellow nearly saw him jump from his seat.

"What in hell's blazes?" The *Tabor's* captain was none too pleased, as Willie had forecast. They were fifty yards off the vessel's starboard side, but the captain did not wait to hail them.

"We're in no need of rescue!" he screamed. "Row yourselves and your boat straight to hell!"

A few more strokes brought the surfboat within ten yards of the schooner.

"Ship your oars," said Cole.

The voice roared again. "Damn you if you think I'll be ignored! I gave you an order. Lay off!"

The man's bellows were deafening and touched with madness. Hiram understood why the crew was scurrying so quickly.

The captain was now clearly visible. He stood at the railing, glaring down at them. Several of the crew also stood at the railing, a safe distance from the captain. Their faces were dark as maple syrup.

"By God! We need no aid!"

"One stroke," said Cole.

The surfboat glided away from the *Tabor's* captain.

"Stern to," said Cole.

Each man pushed with his oar. They now floated beneath the dark-skinned sailors.

Cole hailed the men. "Who is first mate?"

A white man with a tuft of hair perched on his head like a small animal presented himself meekly at the railing.

"First Mate Owen Bowley, sir."

"Mr. Bowley, order your men to lower a rope over the side and climb down one at a time," said Cole. "Stay to the center of the surfboat, and sit quietly."

The man hesitated and then disappeared.

It took the *Tabor's* captain a moment to grasp the order, but grasp it he did. He strode down the railing, the black sailors shrinking visibly at his approach.

"God damn you all! Have you no accounting of the laws of seamanship! I am the captain of this vessel! I give the orders!" He shook his head like a boxer shaking off a roundhouse punch. "No one leaves!"

Seaman Bowley reappeared. He stood a safe distance from his captain with a rope in his hand.

Cole spoke to the first mate. "Seaman Bowley, your vessel has run aground. You will take direction from me. Take in the sails."

The first mate whispered something. Three sailors turned on their heels.

The *Tabor's* captain began to leap up and down like a man afflicted. "A captain's word is above God's! The lot of you will be lashed! I'll smear the salt in myself!"

The rope unfurled slowly against the clear blue sky. The end fell into the surfboat. Seaman Bowley fixed his end to the railing and gave a nod. The first sailor climbed over the railing and lowered himself down the rope.

"Steady," Cole instructed, as the man's feet found the surfboat. "Move aft and sit quickly."

The man did as he was told. From overhead came the echo of canvas collapsing.

The captain roared. "No one abandons this ship!"

Cole turned to the captain. He did not raise his voice, but his words rang clear. "Sir, the tide is falling. There will be no opportunity to float your vessel before nightfall. I cannot allow you or your crew to remain aboard a stranded vessel overnight."

The captain seemed to consider this. In the interim, two more sailors slid nimbly down the rope, positioning themselves in the boat with downcast eyes.

The captain spluttered, and then, to Hiram's surprise, spat.

Cole took a half step to one side. The projectile landed precisely where he had been standing.

"The same unerring aim that saw him strike the bar," said Willie.

"Quiet," said Cole. "The man remains a captain."

A fifth sailor touched down in the surfboat. Losing his balance, the man leaned hard on the port gunwale. The surfboat dipped precipitously.

Cole pulled hard left on the steering oar, centering the boat. "Careful," he said.

The last two crewmen dropped aboard. The swaying rope dangled emptily. Alone on his ship, the *Tabor's* captain had gone silent.

He stared down at Cole. "I will not leave my ship."

Cole said, "Forward one stroke, Surfman Paine."

Hiram pulled. Cole was now directly beneath the rope. Reaching beneath the stern seat, the keeper tucked something inside his jacket. "Mr. Lucas. Take the steering oar and hold us steady."

Cole went up the rope and over the railing.

Even from the surfboat, it was obvious the *Tabor's* captain was an unusually large man. Cole approached him casually. The man appeared stunned to see him aboard. Hiram saw the thall pin before the *Tabor's* captain did. Stepping forward, Cole rapped the man just above his right ear. The captain disappeared from sight.

Cole hauled up the rope. He appeared a moment later, holding the captain in his arms. Leaning forward, Cole dropped the man over the side. He fell, spinning slowly like a rolling pin, the rope, attached to his waist, spooling out above him. He hit the water face first, sending up an icy spume of seawater. Using the ship's rail as a lever, Cole pulled hard on the rope so the captain didn't sink beneath the surface.

Antone ordered them to stern-to until they were beside the floating captain. On Antone's command, the surfmen shifted their weight to the landward side of the surfboat. Martin, leaning over the opposite side, grasped the captain under the arms and hauled him aboard.

To Hiram's astonishment, the man remained unconscious. Antone gave his legs an unnatural bend to fit him between the seats. He lay face up, countenance as placid as the sea.

The black sailors stared with focused intent toward shore.

"I hope his dreams are going his way," said Willie.

Cole shimmied down the rope, leaving it tied to the ship's rail. He took the steering oar from Antone. "Row for shore."

Cole had the sailors carry the captain to the day house. Hiram noticed the sailors deposited him on the floor none too gently. Captain Cole left the first mate and a small pile of firewood with the captain. Seaman Bowley made no complaint. Returning from the midnight patrol, Hiram saw firelight in the windows, but the day house remained quiet.

The following morning at full tide, wreckers from Truro floated the *Tabor* free, the pale captain wordlessly paying their hefty fee.

The surfmen rowed the sailors and their silent captain to the schooner. The wind had stiffened.

The *Tabor's* captain climbed from the surfboat first. Seaman Bowley followed, but not before giving Cole a nod of gratitude. The sailors followed, slipping over the railing and disappearing as if they had never existed. The last man untied the rope and tossed it down into the boat.

Cole ordered two dozen strokes.

Sitting in the surfboat, the surfmen watched the canvas rise. Slowly, the *Tabor* came about, her sails wallowing before the filling breeze. A figure stood alone on the foredeck, his back to the shore.

Not until the *Tabor* turned its wake to them did Hiram realize that not one of the sailors had looked back either. Hiram understood. Some men led and some men followed, and in the hands of the wrong leader, the followers were cursed.

A second surprise arrived two days later on an equally lovely morning. Hiram sat by the open window playing poker with Antone.

At first, he thought the voices belonged to the surfmen enjoying their rare holiday on the porch. Then a child's voice rang out. A return shout issued from the kitchen and Martin ran past, still holding a frying pan. Had Willie not pushed the screen door open, the Swede would have crashed right through it.

Antone put down his cards. "I lose anyhow," he said, and followed Martin out the door.

Willie held the door wide, letting in shouts and laughter.

"Best to scamper, Mr. Paine. They may already be out of prizes."

Out on the porch, Hiram nearly fell over the frying pan. A knot of women stood in the sand, holding cloth-covered dishes. Martin's daughter was already lost in his arms. Ben Maddocks crushed his wife in embrace, the petite woman holding her dish to one side. Hiram didn't feel the stairs or the sand under his feet. The smell of creamed corn enveloped him.

After a long moment, his mother stepped back, the green eyes amused. "You *are* surprised," she said. "Much to my dismay, I stand corrected. I assured your keeper even the most myopic men might expect something more than an extra nap on Thanksgiving, but apparently not." She cocked her head. "I see the man remains a socialite."

Hiram turned. Captain Cole stood on the porch, holding the frying pan.

His mother whispered, "Do I wait for the order to come in?" Raising the hem of her dress off the sand, she said, "I suppose I should make things easier on the man who arranged this fete. You can reintroduce me to your forgetful captain."

As they came up the stairs, Cole lifted the frying pan slightly and a last piece of burnt apple fell to the ground. "Mrs. Paine."

His mother's laugh drenched Hiram like warm rain.

"I hope that's not our pie," she said. "Happy Thanksgiving to you too, Daniel Cole. I suppose the both of us should be thankful, among other things, for a lifelong friendship, though now and again, you force me to wonder if I imagined the whole thing."

Cole gave a small smile. "I remember. And as you know, I'm not one for imagining." He looked at the brown lump. "I hope they're too full for pie."

Nellie Paine shocked both men by leaning forward and kissing Cole's cheek. "I'm so happy to see my son. I'm even thankful for your shortcomings. And I hold hope for you. You arranged for this celebration—out of character for a man reputed to be such a sourpuss. Perhaps, you're sliding into sentimentality in your dotage. Now, if you'll excuse me, the kitchen has fallen under new command."

Turning from the two slack-jawed men, Nellie clapped her hands. "Ladies! It will be a forgettable Thanksgiving if we don't warm these dishes."

The women made their way past, the screen door slapping. The surfmen followed, carrying the plates, ferrying the sweet smell of onion and candied potatoes.

In the ensuing silence, Cole and Hiram became aware of a patient presence.

Cole crouched. "You're bigger," he said.

"You're older."

"I suppose I am."

"It's been since last year." Martin's family lived all the way down in Falmouth. It was harder for them to visit the station. "I'm seven now. I tend my own garden. I like all flowers, but salt spray roses are my favorite. "

"You've become a beautiful young lady, Miss Helena."

"I suppose I am. Why are you holding a frying pan?"

"I'm not quite sure." Cole put the pan down. Reaching into his pocket, he produced a velvet sack, its end cinched with twine. "We missed Christmas," he said.

Helena's eyes grew big. "Can I open it?"

"Keeper's orders."

Helena carefully emptied the sack in her palm. The shiny jacks stayed, but the pink ball kept rolling. It bounced once. Before it could descend again, Helena snatched it from the air.

"You've played before," said Cole.

"It's my absolute favorite game." She bounced the ball, snatching it cleanly again. "Horse before carriage." The pale face suddenly fretted. "I forgot. Thank you." She placed her fingertips to a dark eyebrow.

"There's no need to salute me," Cole said.

"You're keeper."

"No."

"No?"

"Not today."

"Who is then?"

"Mrs. Paine."

"She's a lady."

"Does that make her any less able?"

Helena considered this solemnly. "No."

"Step forward, please." Cole pinned his keeper's pin to the bright red sweater. "You are assistant keeper."

Helena touched the pin. "I take orders from Mrs. Paine?"

"We all do," said Cole.

Into the early afternoon, the station breathed incapacitating aroma. The men escaped torment by fleeing outside. Ben brought Thoreau from the stable. He paraded Helena around the station, Thoreau plodding stoically beneath a rain of squeals and stroking, until the girl announced, "I have to go."

Helena Nelson climbed the porch steps to where Cole was watching.

For the next hour, Keeper Daniel Cole received a sound drubbing at jacks.

Dinner was a happy, rambunctious affair. Using confusion to her advantage, Helena spooned up as much cranberry preserves as she could stomach. The women caught up on news. The surfmen did their best to recall decorum gone rusty from eating among men. Still they ate as if the food on the table might sprout wings and soar off over the Atlantic. When everyone finally pushed back from the table, barely a scraping remained.

The single surfmen cleaned up. Martin and Ben sat on the porch with their wives. Helena slept in her father's lap, one hand on her stomach.

Cole was heading for the kitchen when Nellie stopped him. "May I speak with you, Daniel?"

They walked past the day house to the edge of the cliffs. The day remained so clear they could see the Gulf Stream on the horizon, an undulating procession of distant hummocks following one another like the cars of a train. Ocean cool caressed their faces. The softening afternoon, the bright ocean, his childhood friend by his side, they brought back pleasing memories. Cole gave himself up to the happy current.

Nellie touched his sleeve. "The day was a rousing success *and* a surprise," she said.

"Perhaps, I've drilled my myopic focus into them. I'm told I'm a trifle narrow-minded. A stubborn goat unable to see beyond the next coat of paint, to be exact."

"You'll get no sympathy from me, Daniel Cole. You *are* stubborn. Too stubborn to see the difference between loyalty and duty. They would follow you anywhere."

Nellie watched the sea. She spoke so quietly Cole almost didn't hear. "Its beauty doesn't make you forget," she said.

The happy current stilled.

"When we were little, we read about the Great Plains in school," said Nellie. "I wondered how those ranchers and homesteaders could live their entire lives without seeing the ocean. I pitied them. I don't pity them anymore."

Cole saw the twisting fingers. He wanted to take her hand, but he didn't.

"Do you think about the past, Daniel?"

He would have lied to anyone else. "Every day."

"It's not a pleasant occupation for either of us."

"I'm sorry."

"Stop. Everything's not your fault."

"Some things are," said Cole.

"That's the price for being alive."

Nellie traced a boot toe through the sand. The furrow began to fill in as soon as it appeared.

"We played tag in these dunes," she said.

"We played chase. You were too fast."

He remembered everything. The darting calves, the sunlight playing off the smooth brown skin, the bare feet scattering sand with each turn, the laughter, pure and victorious. He wanted to run now; his body actually tensed. The power of the urge shocked him, as did its childishness.

"The past never leaves me, Daniel. It's there from the moment I wake up until the moment I fall asleep, and then it comes to my dreams." The face that turned to him now was not victorious. It was broken. "Do you know why the past never leaves me, Daniel? Because my greatest fear is that the past will repeat itself. I have one thing left. If anything happens to Hiram, it will be more than I can bear."

The urge to mend turned him foolish. "We've never lost a man," he said.

"You of all people know that won't last."

"I'll do everything I can."

"I know you will, but even with the great Daniel Cole, the sea will eventually win. We understand each other, Daniel. Your sadness is my sadness. You sit in the cemetery. Mercy and Samuel walk with me every minute of every day." She could not look at him. "A child's touch, a warm body in your bed, and no horizon where it ends. It's a fool's belief, but we all grasp it."

Far below, the beach made its way north and south, thinning to nothing in the distance.

"How do you go on, Daniel?"

"I hope for times like these."

Nellie waited, but the man beside her stood still.

"I pray, Daniel. I pray every day for what I have left. I believe in God. How else can we look to the next day? But hope or prayer, they still leave you with fear."

It was poor timing, but he would have no other chance. "Hiram is attending church."

"Church?"

"He's not there strictly for religion. Willie tells me your son is smitten."

Nellie saw the last of her little boy drift away, dissolving into the far reaches of deepening blue sky. Always a new generation taking its first faltering steps toward their own unfathomable horizon.

She tried to keep her voice light. "I suppose everyone on the Cape but his mother knows the girl's name?"

"Hannah Lombard."

"Ah. It won't be an easy courtship with Enos Lombard standing sentry."

"It's possible the father may fail. Willie tells me Hannah Lombard and your son huddle together so happily at the Sunday social that all the wives and widows elbow each other for a glimpse."

She felt her heart, alone and heavy in her chest.

"You never raise a topic for conversation alone. Which church?"

"The Presbyterian church."

The ugliness rushed up so that her throat actually burned. They'd had a long and intimate relationship, she and this rank infection, yet it tasted just as foul every time.

"Does Hiram talk about the services?"

"I don't fraternize with the men, but I doubt it," Cole said. "With the exception of Surfman Maddocks and Surfman Lucas, ours is not a religious outfit."

"A world without God. Or, if there is a God, one disinclined to see justice triumph over hypocrisy. Why are we left with such bitter choices?"

Was it women, thought Cole, who always raised questions without answers? Or was it just that much of life was without answers, and women were particularly good at pointing this out?

"If his words are poisoning my son, I will see to God's justice myself," Nellie said.

Cole was startled by the force of the words. "My guess is Reverend Matthews is having no effect beyond his usual one," he said as casually as he dared. "From what Willie tells me, Hiram would join Hannah Lombard in a try pot if that was where she spent her Sunday mornings."

"Young love recognizes no barriers and possesses equal reserve. And how, pray tell, did Surfman Bangs become privy to my son's innermost feelings?"

"Hiram values his judgment regarding women."

"Then he is certainly lost."

"Hiram is an intelligent boy."

"You're not listening. Intellect has no place in matters of the heart." Nellie spoke again before she could change her mind. "Were you ever ruled by your heart, Daniel?"

Cole was surprised by the blunt question and his equally frank answer. "I loved Sara."

"That's not the question. I asked if you were ever ruled by your heart. Times when you threw that grave and stolid mind of yours to the wind. "

"Yes."

"I'm glad, Daniel. We both had our time."

Crying drifted from the station.

"Young Helena is paying for her own lack of reserve," said Nellie. "It's time to go."

When the wagons were loaded, Helena Nelson approached Cole. She stood staring at the ground.

"Here," she said. "I'm too sick to be in charge."

Cole took the pin.

"Soon enough you'll feel bright as a new penny," he said, but the girl had already turned away.

Cole watched as she crawled up into the wagon and wormed into the folds of her mother's dress. Settled, she stared vacantly toward a place no one could see. She didn't turn when her father hoisted himself up to kiss her cheek.

Martin lowered himself to the sand, his faltering smile falling away. Cole knew Martin's fear. No one knew what the world would bring.

That night, the midnight silence of the station was deeper. The smell of onions lingered. Martin slept with a drawing under his pillow; a letter rested between the pages of Ben's Bible.

Upstairs, Cole daydreamed, quill in hand, his mind leaving the logbook to chase a laughing girl through the dunes.

13

Hiram wondered if he was mad. Hannah consumed him. He measured time in Sundays, and between Sundays, torment clawed at him relentlessly. The pale, freckled shoulders, the hidden curves, the slight upturn of lips, they whispered to him everywhere, plunging him directly into sin's den. He had never slept with a woman, but this proved no obstacle to his imagination. Hannah's naked form rose in his thoughts, in scenarios that embarrassed him and made his loins boil. His will padded behind his genitals like a half-witted mongrel. Late at night, he walked far out into the dunes to relieve his desire. The instant he finished, he was filled with disgust and remorse. The next night he stood, performing his humiliating yanking again.

Finally, he went to Willie. He found the surfman in the equipment room squatting beside the Lyle gun, the faking box, with its intricately coiled rope, at his feet. Willie snaked the rope carefully back and forth between the wooden pegs; if the line didn't fly smoothly, the projectile at its end would never reach the foundering vessel.

Hiram waited by the shovels, pickaxes, and spare oars hung neatly along the wall. Usually the cavernous room, with its cathedral silence and incense of wood, iron, and oil, soothed him. He felt no serenity now. Impatience raged alongside his libido. He shuffled his feet and bumped into a bucket.

"Maybe you could further aid my concentration by snatching one of those shovels and swinging it against my head," said Willie. Carefully securing the last coil, Willie rose stiffly. "Christ, I hate that job. It makes my back scream and there's no one else to blame if it goes wrong. I'll kiss your lips if you're here to tell me it's your job now."

"I can't think of anything else."

"I'm told my kisses have that effect."

Hiram collapsed completely. "I think about Hannah all the time. I think ... " he paused, searching for the last words, "impure thoughts."

"Impure thoughts? Who are you, Whitman? You want to stick your willy in her."

Hiram wanted to leave, but Willie was his only hope. "I love her," he said, trying to sound offended.

"Maybe you do, but that's not the reason you're prancing around like a man with mites. First thing, stop whipping yourself. Lust is part of the human condition. Women have the same feelings. I'd say they're stronger."

The boy's shock was amusing, but Willie's mind had already slipped back to his first desire. The butcher's daughter had proved insatiable. Sadly, he had not. When, in short order, the act was finished, she had not been shy about addressing his shortcomings. Even now, the smell of pork made him maudlin.

"I'll admit it's unsettling," Willie said absently.

"What can I do?"

"Nothing."

Hiram did not want to imagine an eternity spent fumbling with his pant buttons. "There must be something."

The boy's desperation returned Willie to the present. "Too late to become a eunuch. Do you have any experience with women?"

"No."

"Your ignorance needs to be addressed. Women are far more than warm flesh, but it's also true that it's not ideal to enter into conjugal matters without some experience. Women expect much, even if they don't tell you so. Plus, it'll take some pressure off the pot."

"Whoring?" Hiram asked, trying not to sound nervous or hopeful.

"Best not to call it that."

"That's what it is. It's also a sin."

"So is lust, but we've covered that already. Miss Lombard doesn't need to know, and in the end she'll appreciate you for it. It won't provide every answer, though Lord knows I'm still hoping, but it will see you on your way. Think of it as trading. They have something you want and you have something they want. Nothing is a sin when both parties go home happy."

Willie congratulated himself on his persuasive skills, but the boy sagged helplessly again.

"What?" asked Willie, a trifle peeved.

"You gave me your day off. Sunday."

It took a moment. Willie tamped down a smile.

"Not everyone devotes Sunday to worship, Hiram. The Cork and Barrel opens its doors before church."

Hiram's first mistake was stealing the medicinal whisky flask locked in the medicine chest; Willie had trusted him with the location of the key. Walking through the dunes, strange moods swept over him. One moment, he was awash in dread; the next, anticipation saw him fairly float over the sand. Questions swirled. How did one engage a whore? Did you pay before or after? How much did it cost? Did you take your clothes off right away, or did you talk first? How much time did you get? If you were quick, did you get a second go?

Paramount in his mind was the confusion of the act itself. He had no idea how to proceed or what might happen. He had heard of a man, pinched at the proper moment, who had stuttered for the rest of his life. He didn't want to become a stutterer.

He arrived at the Cork and Barrel drunk and soaking wet. It started raining on the outskirts of Provincetown, a frigid rain that hammered in his ears. He stood in the rain beneath the ugly buffalo for a long time. Through the door came the sound of a harmonica and a noise like elephants crashing about.

Stepping through the door, he was nearly knocked back by the noise. It was Hiram's fault the flask was empty, but it was not his fault a whaling ship had put in the afternoon before. Though whaling was nearly finished in Nantucket, New Bedford still thrived; the mainland port, unlike its island cousin, could be reached by trains that transported the precious sperm oil across the country. The *Constellation* had sailed up from New Bedford to gather her last supplies before sailing for the Pacific whaling grounds, a trip that, given the dwindling supply of whales, could last several years.

Her whalers were reveling in a last fling. Masterfully drunk and happily self-absorbed, they shouted insults, spilled drinks, and bought more. The greasy smell of clothes ruined by whale fluids mingled with tobacco. The stench didn't bother Hiram. It smelled like life.

The sea of men parted as if he were royalty. Hiram found himself at the bar where, abruptly, a sallow man popped up in front of him like a carnival game.

The man glowered at him ferociously. "Order your grog, or stand away. I've no time to wait on idiots."

Hiram wanted to whisper, but he also wanted to be heard. When he spoke, he felt as if he had shouted his request to the entire pub. "I want to enlist a whore."

"I'll go notify the *Boston Herald*," the barkeep said, turning away.

A man thrust a glass into his hand. "To whores and whales! The meatier, the better!"

The man threw back his whisky. Hiram followed suit. This whisky set fire to his throat. He wanted to thank his friend, but through watery eyes he saw the man was gone.

In the far corner, a wild-haired whaler stood on a chair playing the harmonica. The floor was cleared of tables. The whalers danced madly, and when they fell into the cheering ring of onlookers they were absorbed and, with a collective shout, spat forth again. Several whores danced too, wheeling about a succession of stumbling men.

Hiram supposed he would have to enlist a whore himself.

Stepping from the bar, he gave himself to the milling current. A fortuitous eddy pushed him to the front of the circle. He stared at the dancing whores. They moved gracefully, like swans among pigs, and the way their hips swayed made the crotch of his pants rise. When they lifted their skirts, he saw their gartered thighs were white.

A young girl with a long ponytail that lashed about like rope high-stepped toward him. He focused his eyes happily on her just as she collided with him. He felt their teeth meet with a resounding clack. Hot breath filled his mouth and something warm slithered around his tongue, and then the girl was gone, back among the dancers, and he was left joyously gasping for breath.

He was still clapping when he realized the roaring had stopped. The girl with the hot breath approached him again. He prepared for another kiss, but she brushed angrily past. He wanted to stop her and apologize, or kiss her again, but before he could, someone shoved him hard from behind.

He stumbled into the middle of the nearly empty circle. No one was dancing. The harmonica player had stopped.

Hiram forced himself to focus. When he did, he saw an enormous man with a great hooked nose. The man extended his arm as if to shake Hiram's hand. The blade shone like a silver tooth.

Hiram stumbled back on his heels, the knife slicing the air where his stomach had been.

"You'll not kiss my whore," the man growled.

A voice shouted, "Show us his guts, Gnut!"

The hook-nosed man circled him now. Hiram focused on the knife, hearing his own panting in his ears. Fear sobered him like an unexpected draft.

He located his tongue. "She kissed me," he said.

The crowd roared, but the hooked-nosed man remained unamused. "The whore doesn't traffic in children," he said.

"Nor should you." Hiram was astonished. He was incapable of such cool threat. He wondered if he was so drunk that some brave newcomer inside him was in charge now. The pub was silent.

The whaler was surprised too. He stared at a spot to Hiram's right.

Keeping one eye on the knife, Hiram turned to the gray bowler.

The old man stepped past, elbowing him roughly back.

The whaler was twice the old man's size. "This is not your fight, Pomp."

The old man's voice was soft as a dove's cooing. "That is for me to decide. Truth is, I have no interest in the whelp. Your gutting him would neither please nor displease me. It's your implication that offends."

Confusion clouded about the hooked nose, but the whaler remained crouched, knife extended.

Pomp circled the whaler casually, like a man considering a purchase from every angle. The mottled hands hung loose, nearly brushing the bowed knees.

"You saw," said the whaler. "He tried to steal my whore."

"The lady is free to kiss whomever she pleases."

"He kissed her."

"And who here would blame him? I believe you were intending to do the same with that yawing mouth."

"I paid for her. She's mine." The whaler's eyes flicked to the crowd and hardened. "Stand aside. I mean to open him up."

The whaler brandished the knife.

"Your tongue reveals your stupidity," said Pomp, watching the knife with mild interest. "Your hand belies your wavering character."

Hiram's every nerve was fixed on the scene before him, but it made no sense. The whaler held the knife. Yet, the old man held the advantage.

The blade tipped forward.

"Go to hell, ape," hissed the whaler.

The man stopped in mid-lunge as if he had abruptly changed his mind. He took a half step to one side and went to his knees.

No one moved. Hiram's body felt numb. His head buzzed softly, as if it were filled with polite bees.

Hiram recognized the knife the old man had used to mark the blackfish, the pattern along the blade's upper edge like ripples on water. The blood was infinitely redder.

Pomp raised the man's chin with the knife tip. "So frail our fates. One moment carousing, the next balanced on the edge of Damascus steel."

Hiram saw the stain spreading down the seam of the man's tunic.

"From here, the blade can reach the brain, assuming there is one. Done precisely, you'll remain conscious. Odd to feel the delicate press of cold steel in such a strange place."

"Please, God."

"So easy to find religion." Pomp raised the knife tip so that the whaler was forced to straighten fully. The man's entire body shook at the end of the blade. "We own no one." Pomp sheathed the knife. "Remove this offal."

Two men stepped forward. They did not look at Pomp. Grasping the whaler beneath the arms, they began dragging him to the door, the man's legs smearing blood along the floor.

The whaler howled in pain, but the sallow bartender howled louder. "Imbeciles! Pick him up! Pick him up! Mother of God! Is the entire world endowed with the brains of a sow?"

Hiram felt a hand on his elbow.

"Not the entire world," said Pomp softly, "but enough of it to cause us concern."

Pomp turned to the harmonica player. "Play with all your heart and your drinks are free."

Before Pomp had ushered Hiram halfway across the room, the Cork and Barrel again shook on its foundations.

They made their way toward a table. As they approached, the man at the table rose. He was even bigger than the hawk-nosed whaler. His knit cap was pulled low. He finished his whisky, dropped the tumbler in his pocket, and walked for the door. Hiram wrestled for a moment with his memory, but the wildly unspooling circumstances fogged his mind.

Pomp sat him down in the man's chair, taking the chair beside him.

The old man smiled at the swaying sea, returned again to shouting and dancing. "The balm of forgetfulness, boon and curse to man. Still, I'd advise you not consort with any of these boisterous fellows again this morning. Loyalty is not their forte, but as you have witnessed, it takes little to ruffle their petticoats."

Hiram was nearly sober now, but it still felt like a dream. "Will he live?"

"Ship work will pain him for a time, but he'll be fine. You can run a man through with a thousand sharp instruments and not touch a vessel of import. The Babylonians were masters of the art. They didn't believe they were being cruel. They believed other races were lesser breeds, and so less sensitive to pain."

Two whiskeys arrived, carried by a plump woman with a great swell of breasts. Setting the drinks down, she regarded him candidly. "Can't say I blame Eileen for kissing you. If not for my age, I'd have a taste myself." She turned her smile on Pomp. "On the house, for defending our honor."

"My dear Abby, any gentleman would have done the same."

The woman shook her head. "You only confirm my belief that men are blind as worms. Believe what you will, Pomp, but there are times when I fear chivalry's days are numbered." Nudging a curl, she winked at Hiram. "Sadly, the same can be said of the days when men fight over you. On my way. No profit in dwelling in the past."

They both watched her forge through the crowd with a confident waddle.

"A lady or a whore, either way, you miss. She's right. Men are simple organisms. But women defy definition. Don't ever think you know them."

The old man leaned close. The nauseating smell was familiar. "You were in the day house. You tended to the girl."

The shock of it saw Hiram gag.

"It is not a question," said Pomp. "I set the scene so that you may complete the story. Do not disappoint me with fables."

Hiram spoke before courage deserted him. "The whaler knew you."

"Life, like this conversation, takes interesting turns. Yes, the man knew me, though fortunately our acquaintance is not personal. People like gossip. I am grist for the rumor mill."

Pomp leaned closer. Hiram remembered the smell; the wild dog's rotting chuffs.

"Troublesome aren't they, the yearnings of the flesh? The heights of pleasure paired with the depths of anguish. There are some who believe it's better to be free of such distress." Hiram felt the flat of the blade against his thigh, the firm press ending just short of his crotch. "I confess I am not among them. I believe the girl was conscious?"

The small figure reached for him, the edges of the dress curling upward in the dark green water. He couldn't fail again.

"This is not the time to hesitate," said Pomp.

Hiram felt a mild burning as the tip of the knife slid beneath the skin. He caught his breath. The blade stopped.

"A game for me, but I advise you take it seriously. Was she conscious?"

"Yes."

The blade made a small advance, this time rougher and the pain much worse. Hiram heard himself panting, foul whisky in his throat.

"I am interested in what she conveyed to you."

"Her legs were broken. She was in too much pain to speak." Hiram sat very still.

"Mmm. Is that so?"

"Yes."

"People find ways to speak through pain."

From some great distance, Hiram heard the pub's noise. He felt the blade, a horrible burrowing insect distracted for a moment under his skin. He saw Isabella's face set firmly.

"The pain was too much. She died when we tried to set her legs."

Pomp saw the half-truth. His was a half-truth too. Even he could not render the boy a eunuch in a public place. It was only a lesson, to take home and ponder.

Pomp moved the blade a last touch. The boy's eyes widened and his mouth fell open, but he kept quiet.

"Prometheus betrayed the gods," Pomp said. "He stole the sacred fire from Zeus and gave it to man. Are you familiar with his punishment?"

The boy barely moved his head.

"Zeus chained Prometheus for eternity. Each day, a great eagle ate his liver. Each day, the liver rejuvenated itself." Pomp slid the blade free. "A parable, of course. No one believes a man can be kept alive forever." Something passed across the old man's face. Softly, he said, "Fire was all we needed, but we are never content."

Hiram vomited. It surprised him more than anyone. One instant, his stomach was where it should be; the next, it had leapt into his mouth. He retched again. A viscous scum fanned across the table and spilled to the floor.

"Wasted whisky in bottomless supply," a man shouted to his companion.

The two men shared a great guffaw, but Hiram missed it. His stomach knotted, his eyes watered madly, and he puked again. He stood, coughing gibbous phlegm.

"Har!" shouted the man. "Who's lining up to kiss the pretty boy now?"

In the dunes, Hiram fell to his hands and knees. The world rang with retchings, fueled by the vision of his own blood, bright on Damascus steel.

After the boy left, Pomp walked to the end of the main wharf and stood regarding Cape Cod Bay. It was nearly noon. A northerly breeze flecked the water with whitecaps. It had stopped raining, but low clouds sent their shadows passing over the surface like the rippling silhouettes of fast-moving whales. Beneath his feet, the water made soft gurglings as it wandered about the pilings.

Shouts rang from the adjacent wharf, officers overseeing the loading of supplies aboard the *Constellation*. Pomp watched the sailors stutter step up the gangplank beneath heavy crates. High in the rigging, men checked stays and spars.

Pomp recalled his own whaling days fondly. On his first voyage, aboard the *Black Jack* out of Nantucket, the first mate had taken an immediate dislike to him. He had been assigned the lowly duty of cabin boy, and made to sleep and eat in the forecastle with the blacks. At the conclusion of that three-year journey, Pomp's assignment for the next voyage was as first mate, the *Black Jack's* original first mate having fallen overboard off the Falklands at night without a sound.

Pomp served as first mate aboard three subsequent whalers. Each of the three captains had come to prize his abilities to such a degree that it became known throughout the ship that the hump-backed ape was, to much intent and purpose, captain of the vessel. But he was never awarded the position officially. He had never been bitter about it, although ultimately he supposed he had exacted his revenge.

Pomp fingered the bills in his pocket. The bundle represented more money than a whaler would see in a lifetime, but it gave him no pleasure. Once you had money, it was of no interest. What kept him going was the chance to engage the few wits left on the Cape. The boy had lied, but this did not bother him. He could arrange another meeting.

Shouts came from across the water, a circle of men gathered around a fight. An officer hustled down the gangplank. A beaten man was damaged goods. Fighting and fucking. The interests of most men were short-term.

Pomp returned his mind to more uplifting thoughts. Daniel Cole was unlike other men. No doubt, the keeper knew of the treasure. If the mysterious item to which the imbecilic designate had alluded was of financial value, well and good. But it was the thrill of a grand contest that now warmed Pomp's veins, raising his spirits as he stood above the sloshing water and inhaled the burn of wind.

Pirouetting on a heel, he walked back down the wharf. He passed a kneeling whaler. The man retched. The fish fed.

"Heave ho, my friend," Pomp said. "Once on the scent, our untamed brethren rarely miss the prize."

14

When a crestfallen Hiram found him that afternoon, Willie knew something had gone sorely amiss. Smoking outside the day house, Willie watched the boy cross the sand as if he were dragging the Lyle gun.

Willie winced. "I'll pass on a draught of whatever you're breathing," he said. "Come to replace the medicine flask?"

Hiram hadn't thought it possible to retch so violently. He wondered if he had torn a hole in his stomach. His head throbbed. If he moved too quickly, sparks danced behind his eyes.

The boy looked so awful, Willie couldn't work up the enthusiasm to tease him. "Don't worry. I just finished restocking the supplies. Judging from the look on your face, I'd say your foray into womanhood wasn't pretty. I hope you stayed sober long enough to absorb at least some of the lesson."

"I didn't find a woman."

"I hope you shared the whisky with someone."

"I sat with Pomp."

Willie dropped the cigarette to the sand, grinding it out beneath a heel. "Christ almighty."

Hiram stepped into the soothing shadows under the eaves. "A whore kissed me. I didn't ask her to. She just did it." He heard his words, a child's excuses. "A whaler pulled a knife. He would have gutted me."

"Pomp saved you."

Hiram nodded slowly.

"He does nothing without reason," said Willie.

Hiram wished Willie would be furious. Hollow words were worse. "The whaler tried to stab him. Pomp hardly moved, and the man was on his knees bleeding."

"The whaler survived?"

Hiram tried not to forget the spreading stain. "Yes."

"And you?"

Hiram decided not to tell Willie about his own experience with the knife. He was about to give the surfman more than enough worry.

"Just sick," Hiram said.

"Well, there's one good thing." Willie saw the fear in the boy's eyes. He felt it in his own stomach too. "Is there something else you need to tell me?" he said.

"He was out in the storm. He saw us in the day house. He asked about Isabella. He wanted to know what she said."

Willie did not consider himself a brave man, although in his life he had rarely been afraid. He was afraid now. "What did you tell him, Hiram?"

"I told him she couldn't speak."

"Remarkably brave or remarkably stupid. Do you think he believed you?"

Hiram wanted to disappear in the shadows. "No. He knows, doesn't he Willie? He knows about the *Asia's* treasure."

"He does."

"How?"

"That I don't know."

It suddenly dawned on Hiram, though it had been in front of him the whole time. "Why would he be out in the storm?"

"He's a mooncusser, Hiram. Keeper Cole believes Pomp lured the *Asia* aground. I believe it too."

Something worse than sickness wormed inside Hiram. "Mooncussers don't exist."

"Why not?" said Willie, a trifle harshly. "You have fog, you have dark nights. You have opportunity and men without conscience."

"We patrol the entire shore." Even as he spoke, Hiram heard the old man's mocking words. *A vast and lovely shoreline. Yet it often seems too small for the both of us ...*

Every child on the Cape grew up with stories of mooncussers. He and Mercy had listened, hypnotized to their father's soft twanging voice, deliciously terrified by the specter of soulless men who walked the high ridgelines on stormy nights. It was the simplest exercise. A lantern or two displayed from shore, held in a hand or draped from the neck of a horse, a desperate captain, blinded by snow, sleet, or fog, who could mistake the swaying light for a ship at anchor and make for safe harbor. The wreckers took advantage of what natural misfortune brought them. The mooncussers molded misfortune to their aims, and cursed the clear, moonlit nights.

"The Cape is civilized," said Hiram.

"It comforts us to think so."

Willie pulled another smoke from his jacket. Steadying his hand, he lit a match. Exhaling, he said, "Recall Pomp's mark on the blackfish?"

"A circle."

"Or a full moon. Everyone knows mooncussers work the Outer Banks, but we choose to see North Carolina's barrier islands as a place where savagery and piracy still hold sway. But beasts will always be with us, and they don't care where they live. Only fools think differently." A little of the harshness left his voice. "Plenty of folks on the Cape will tell you mooncussing is a fairy tale, Hiram, but some are certain it's not. Pomp has been doing it for years. Rumor is the Provincelands are littered with ill-gotten spoils, dozens of caches buried among the dunes."

"Wouldn't he sell what he takes?"

Willie almost smiled. The boy's curiosity never winked out entirely. "It does seem pointless to expend such risk and effort without financial reward," Willie said. "But pointlessness suits Pomp."

You have fog, you have dark nights. You have opportunity and men without conscience.

"He's not alone," said Hiram.

Willie thought for a moment, trying to feel his way. As you grew older, so many foundations fell away. "Luring a vessel ashore is an enterprise of one, but stripping it of valuables before others arrive isn't, even for a man as energetic as Pomp," he said.

"Who works with him?"

In other circumstances, Willie might have told the boy, but matters were different now. That Pomp had sought Hiram out was deeply troubling. The boy required only enough knowledge to be wary. Knowing too much might place him even more in harm's way, though Willie wasn't sure this was possible.

"Who he works with doesn't matter."

"It does matter! If what you say is true, they killed Isabella! They killed the entire crew! It's murder. They should be brought to justice."

"They should be brought to justice, and possibly one day they will. But it won't be easy. No one has caught Pomp in the act yet, and not for lack of trying."

From where they stood, they could see for miles. Willie did not miss the irony, but he saw no humor in it. That Pomp was interested in Hiram was the worst news. That their encounter at the Cork and Barrel was largely his fault didn't make Willie feel better.

"Your rescue was child's play, Hiram. The whaler was lucky, and you were luckier still. Only Pomp himself knows how far he will go, but I'm certain it's a place few of us would want to imagine."

"The whaler knew him."

"I suppose he did."

"Pomp said he was grist for the rumor mill."

Now something worse than fear swept over Willie; a black despondency, bordering on conviction, which no amount of liquor, card-playing, or women could erase. He desperately wanted to have faith in the pure things in the world, but, mostly, it seemed to him that mankind was engaged in a downward spiral, without hope or end.

Pomp believed Hiram was of value, and blind innocence would no longer do.

"This is no rumor, Hiram. Three whalers saw it with their own eyes, though I wonder what sort of life they lived afterward. On Pomp's last whaling voyage, their ship went down suddenly in a squall off the Cook Islands. Those that didn't drown took to the whaleboats, four boats in all. Each boat had water and hardtack, but only meager supplies. Pomp and the ship's captain ended up in the same whaleboat, along with the three whalers. In the chaos of boarding, the captain's leg was crushed between the whaleboat and the ship."

The boy breathed stale whisky.

"They finished the last of the hardtack on the fifth day, the last of the water two days later. On the eighth day, the captain fell into delirium. Command of the boat fell to Pomp. That night, he ordered the men to row away from the other boats. They half protested, but Pomp persuaded them with a pistol. Pomp shot and prepared the captain himself. Everyone ate. They were rescued by another whaling ship two days later."

Hiram knew Willie wasn't finished. Such stories weren't unheard of. Men did what was required to survive.

Willie watched the horizon as if he expected the whaleboat to come crawling over the dark blue scrim. "Pomp was still eating when the whaler pulled alongside," he said.

Walking patrol that night, Willie considered his lies.

Among the whalers, Pomp's story had grown into something beyond myth. Like any unfathomable tale, it had changed with countless tellings. He himself had heard some wildly implausible versions, but he had kept his tongue during their telling.

He was among the few who had heard the story nearly firsthand. It had been told to him by a whore who had slept with one of the three whalers. Returning to Provincetown, the man had drunk and whored like no other. By the time he came to this particular woman's bed, he had already worn out a dozen whores. Perhaps by then, he realized no amount of pleasure and liquor would allow him escape.

He had broken down in her bed. When he finished telling the story, she had rocked him in her arms while they both wept.

There had been no pistol. At night, the three whalers had huddled in the stern, fists in their ears, the anguished screams rolling over the dark water. Eventually, the screaming dwindled, replaced by a queer gurgling.

When each dawn came, Pomp covered the body with a tarp. The three men never ate. Perhaps, after these unholy nights, they wanted to starve. That first dawn's light revealed the stains ringing the first mate's mouth.

They drifted for two more days and nights after that. Here, Willie had told Hiram the truth. The three men had stayed huddled in the stern. At night, over their shouted prayers, they heard the tarp rustle.

By the time their rescuers came alongside, the whalers were uncertain that rescue was what they wanted. Returning to Provincetown, two of them disappeared immediately. The third man departed within the month. Their story left with them. By now, no one knew what to believe.

But Willie knew what the whore had told him, crying again like a baby in his arms. After the whaleboat was hoisted up to the deck, a sailor pulled back the tarp. The body was open from throat to navel. Both calves were removed, along with most of the fat on the legs, the flow of blood adroitly staunched by tourniquets. As the sailors lifted the body, the captain gave a final sigh.

The three whalemen had refused to speak or deny guilt. Pomp had walked free.

Walking beneath the stars, Willie knew he had done the right thing. The boy knew enough. He was no longer blind. But there were some things the eyes should never see.

Silver clouds drifted among the stars. Willie tried to see their beauty.

With dawn, the silver clouds turned gray. When Pomp stepped from the Cork and Barrel, threads of mist rose from Bradford Street.

The sun was still below the horizon, but shouts rang from the distant wharf, the final preparations of the *Constellation* before she put to sea.

Pomp tipped his bowler in the wharf's direction. He was in a fine mood. His performance had been even better than he'd expected. Afterward, they had lain in bed, talking idly, Abby already descending into sleep. Pomp had almost missed her last drowsy murmuring. The words had produced a jolt of pleasure beyond that of his earlier release.

Turning his face toward the dawning sun, Pomp now heard Abby's voice again.

The minister tells me there is a girl.

Perhaps there were other means of helping the boy's memory along.

15

Two nights later, the first of three storms galloped in from the Atlantic, plunging into the Cape as if a crazed rider were astride.

Sleet lashed the station. The surfmen patrolled at a crawl, pulling their oilskins tight as frozen wetness pushed through the smallest openings.

The first storm doused them with misery, but spared them event. No ships ran aground along their shore, although two days later, they received word that a schooner had grounded to the south on Chatham Bars. During the surfboat rescue, as the surfboat came ashore, a Chatham surfman broke an arm, and a rescued sailor received a deep gash when a wave-tossed timber struck his face. The Peaked Hill Bars lifesavers absorbed the Chatham news quietly.

The second storm followed three nights later. Sleet became snow, whirling in off the ocean like a conglomeration of ghostly dust devils. The seas increased to an angrier boil.

Cole brought news of the wreck, spying the foundering ship just as she fetched onto the shoal. The men flew into their gear, sour anticipation in their throats. The seas were too rough for the surfboat. Thoreau was harnessed to the beach cart; breeches buoy, Lyle gun and faking line boxes already resting in the cart.

The vessel grounded a half mile south of the station. A brig, ninety feet in length, she had fixed herself seventy yards offshore, portside fully exposed to the sea. Leaping, white spumes marked the impact of the larger waves. When she flooded below deck, the weight would quickly her turn under. They had little time.

On the beach, the men waited for Cole's order. Standing in the beach cart, Cole gauged the elements. He did not rush. A single well-placed shot into the mast served them best. There, the line could be tied off by a crew member and, on the vessel's signal, the breeches buoy-- a cork lifesaving ring with pantaloon legs stitched to the underside—run out to the vessel to haul the men in. An errant shot increased everyone's troubles.

Cole observed the fuzzy progress of the lantern ascending the forward mast. The pinprick of light rose without pause, an admirable feat in frozen rigging that jerked wildly about. The man knew his business.

Cole grabbed a pick. Leaping from the wagon, he shouted to Willie to light a flare. Swinging the pick, Cole broke the sand's ice coating. In two minutes, he had a hole deep enough for the sand anchor. Each surfman knew his task; tedious drilling served its purpose. The instant Cole finished the hole, the men filled it in, burying the sand anchor firmly. Willie placed the faking box carefully in the sand, performing a last quick check of the coiled line affixed now to the shell inside the cannon.

The men watched Cole raise the cannon slightly. Turning his back to the wind, he pulled the lanyard to ignite the powder. The muzzle flashed. Shell and trailing line disappeared over the water.

Then followed the agonizing moments during which all they could do was wait. It was said that Daniel Cole could knock a thimble from under a sparrow with the eighteen-pound shot, but the men knew full well that, even in the most skilled hands, every shot remained an exercise in hope.

To aid hope, Ben prayed. The other men watched the lantern in the rigging. It swayed nonsensically in the snow-blown sky. Then it bobbed three times.

In an instant, the surfmen attached the shore end of the line to the sand anchor and raised the fifteen-foot wooden crotch, so that the line between ship and shore draped above the waves. Willie fastened the traveler block, the breeches buoy dangling beneath it, to the suspended line. The men put their backs to hauling at the line. The breeches buoy disappeared out over the ocean.

The signal man was the first to come ashore, still holding the lantern. This was odd. The man should have left the lantern with his mates, now waiting their turn in the rigging. When the man's feet touched the sand, he remained rigid inside the breeches buoy. Hiram and Martin each grabbed an arm and yanked the man free. When they released him, he stood still on the beach, holding the lantern up before him, his eyes searching the darkness.

Hiram shouted in the man's ear. "How many aboard?!"

The man regarded him serenely.

There was no time to wait for an answer. Hiram shouted again. "Make to the shelter of the cliffs!"

The man stared at the snow as if each flake housed a face. Slowly he turned and walked for the cliffs.

Hiram's world pinched to running the line, again and again, up the beach. Coated with frozen sand, the rope cut through his gloves and into his palms and fingers, but his hands were so cold he barely felt the sting. He willed his fingers tight. His calves burned. He forgot time. He was resigned to pulling forever.

Six more sailors rode ashore, materializing out of the snowy swirl like wingless angels. These men were decidedly more animated. Clawing free of the breeches buoy, several fell to their knees and prayed. One man hugged Hiram with a ferocity that threatened to crack his ribs. Each sailor was directed to the cliffs and the waiting wagon, blankets tucked beneath the tarp.

"That is the last!"

Hiram heard Keeper Cole's muffled shout. He dropped the rope and collapsed to his knees, panting at the sand.

Keeper Cole shouted again. It made no sense. Hiram reached for the rope at his feet, but the line was slack. Looking up, he saw the keeper running for the water.

The silent man still held the lantern. He walked into the frothing water, wading out toward the breaking waves, lantern thrust forward as if seeking some treasure in a dark grotto. An enormous wave looped forward. Man and lantern disappeared.

Cole had just reached the berm when the wave broke. The keeper stopped, using the high ground to try to find the sailor in the chaotic foaming.

Something slammed into Hiram's side. Hiram heard a grunt, his own or someone else's, he couldn't tell. A pale form ran along the beach toward the keeper, the arms again wind-milling comically. Stripped to his long johns, Ben ran past the keeper without stopping. Vaulting off the berm, he staggered slightly as his legs plunged into the soft, steeply angled sand. Regaining his balance, he ran down the slope and dove into the churning water.

Cole was running back up the beach toward the cliffs. Leaping into the back of the wagon, he shoved at the huddled men. Yanking something from under the tarp, he leapt down from the wagon. With one hand he shed his oilskin as he ran; his other hand clutched the coil of rope.

Fifty yards south of where Ben had disappeared, Cole vaulted the berm. Wading into waist-deep water, he stopped. A wave broke, toppling forward like a crumbling building. Its rush wrapped the keeper to his chest. The water coiled about him and drew for the sea. Cole staggered forward and Hiram's heart stopped, but the keeper kept his footing. Hiram saw Willie standing at the top of the berm, holding the opposite end of the Heaving Stick, the other men gathered about him.

Hiram ran to the men. They all stood, eyes boring into the foamy tumult, the black ocean behind it. If Ben were swept out past the waves, there would be no rescue.

A hand shook his shoulder so hard, his jaw clacked. Martin shouted and pointed south. One man appeared, a dark speck amid the white leaping, a pebble in a snow bank. Hiram watched with horror as a dark wall rose. Curving forward, the wave wiped the pebble away.

The men ran south, each holding a portion of rope. Hiram saw Captain Cole, half swimming, half stumbling, dragged alongshore by the current. Fighting to get to his feet, Cole drew his arm back. Another frail line disappeared into the dark.

This time, two pebbles appeared. They spun together in the field of white. Cole waved an arm.

Antone shouted. "Men on!"

Again, Hiram clamped down with deadened hands and ran for the cliffs. For an instant, the running was easy; then the rope jerked taut. Driving with their legs, the men leaned out over the sand, the clawing ocean fighting their every step.

Hiram pulled until he fell over Antone. The surfman was kneeling in the sand, the slack rope at his side.

By the time Hiram clambered to his feet, Cole was coming over the berm, supporting a slumping figure. Willie walked behind Cole, propping up a stockier form.

When the keeper reached them, Martin swept Ben up as if he were a child.

The surfmen gave their cots to the rescued sailors who slept as if they were dead, except for the captain of the *Phineas E. Sprague*, a Scotsman in his sixties, who stayed up through the night drinking and playing cards with Willie.

Martin returned from the last patrol of the night carrying a surprise. Within the hour, the luscious risings of fat and salt drifted in from the kitchen. The ham hock was no worse for its swim, though slightly oversalted.

The smells woke even the half-dead, and when the ham came out of the kitchen, the surfmen and the sailors fell on it with gusto and an understandable sense of celebration. Hiram sat beside the captain during the meal. The man heartily forked and belched ham, and when his mouth was unoccupied, he bellowed bawdy jokes that made the men roar. The sailor who had walked into the sea sat alone in a chair near the stairs. Hiram saw the *Sprague's* captain take the man a plate and sit with him until the sailor began eating.

Ben sat across from Hiram. His appetite was also unaffected. His skin remained candle-colored, and he sported a vivid purple bruise above his left eye where a wave had tossed the Heaving Stick against his brow. But he ate and laughed with abandon, although his ears still turned red with the captain's language.

Hiram ate with a lump in his throat. He was awestruck by Ben's bravery. All three men baffled him. One man had walked into the sea; another had plunged in without thought. The third acted as if neither event had taken place.

After the ham was reduced to bone, Willie produced a harmonica, and the captain of the *Phineas E. Sprague*, endowed with a lovely baritone, sang an assortment of Scottish ballads.

When the man stopped, Hiram followed him outside. Hiram waited discretely while the *Sprague's* captain, still humming, relieved himself against the station. When he finished, the captain turned and gave Hiram a broad grin.

"I thought glorious Scotland had cornered the market on miserable cold," he said. "A relief to see my pecker still performs. Now, lad, either you're mightily polite and waiting your turn, or you'd like a word."

"The sailor, sir. He walked back into the water."

The captain zipped himself. A hint of sobriety crept across his face. "He did. How old are you, son?"

"Seventeen."

"Have you a lady?"

"Yes, sir," he said, although the fact he hadn't consulted Hannah about the matter made him flush.

"I am sure she is upstanding and loyal."

"Yes, sir."

"Not every man is so fortunate. Three weeks ago, the sailor you speak of received correspondence from home. His wife gave birth to a son. Happy news in most instances, but we have been at sea for eleven months." The captain smoothed his front. "He taught me those ballads. Sang like a bird all the time. He was good company and a fine sailor, but I fear he is now a liability on any ship. He jeopardized the life of your friend, but I would ask you understand."

"I'm sorry for him."

The captain winked, but there was no joy in it. "I know you are. But now it's both gift and curse to possess a sensitive heart."

"You lost your ship, sir."

"Yes, it appears I have."

Hiram wondered how to phrase the question without insulting the man. "Doesn't it bother you?"

"Like this cold?"

"I'm sorry, sir. You're right."

Hiram started to turn, but the captain of the *Phineas E. Sprague* raised a hand.

"An honest question deserves an honest answer. All my crew is accounted for, and we've ham and coffee making a merry stew in our stomachs. I've lost a few trifles, it's true. There'll be teeth gnashing and scoldings from my superiors and others who don't understand the sea. But, excepting this fearsome cold, all's well and good."

Cinching his belt, he stepped past Hiram. "Always remember, son. After the clouds comes fair weather."

Captain and crew of the *Phineas E. Sprague* left the next afternoon for the Wellfleet Station, where they boarded a train to Boston and onto New York. Just outside Groton, the heartbroken sailor made his way to a juncture between cars and stepped quietly beneath the wheels. The rest of the crew continued onto New York where, by week's end, their shipping company had made the necessary arrangements to see them all back to sea, and the opportunity to face death again.

Hiram had one last man to question.

When he finally got Ben alone, the two of them in the kitchen cleaning up the following evening's supper, he said, "You could have died."

It embarrassed him how he'd misjudged Ben. He'd seen him as stiff and humorless. He'd been frightened by his fervent belief too. To cover his own fear, he'd mocked Ben. He hadn't made fun of him openly, but it was just as bad to mock someone in your mind. Worse, actually. That's what cowards did.

Now Ben had proved himself a hero.

"You risked your life. It was the bravest thing I've ever seen."

Ben stared at the dishrag in his hand. "No," he said.

"I don't understand."

Ben didn't look up. "We're friends now, aren't we?" He smiled slightly. "Turd sniffer."

"We're friends," Hiram said, though he felt he didn't deserve Ben's friendship.

"Good. Friends are honest with each other." Ben looked up, the smile gone. "It wasn't brave, Hiram. I still don't know why I did it. I was standing on the beach, and the next thing I knew I was in the water, clinging to the sailor and screaming for help. I wanted to push him away, but I was too terrified to let go. I only wanted to save myself."

Ben picked up a pot. "Don't make me a hero," he said.

Late that night, Hiram lay in his cot, listening to the wind's accusing whisper. He had watched the sailor walk into the sea. He was closest. Ben had run right past him. Ben could say whatever he wanted, but in his mind it was simple. Ben was brave, and he had faltered again. He was a coward.

Again, he felt the heat of the summer sun, the pond's last gentle eddies tapping against the waterline of the drifting dory. Mercy had clenched the rod so tight, her tiny forearms swelled. Sitting on the stern seat, he had stared at the familiar unfoldings, the tremors running up her body to shake her head, the dark eyes rolling back as if to ascertain the cause of the shaking inside her skull. He was eight, she was five, but the seizures were already an accepted part of their lives.

This time, though, she stood abruptly, jerked one last time, and fell over the side.

Even as he looked down into the water, upon Mercy's pale blue dress spreading like a beautiful lily, he had believed everything would be fine. He wanted to tell her this, for he saw the question on her face, gloomy white just beneath the surface, despair and hope swimming together in her dark eyes. But then his certainty and his sister disappeared, a curtain of green closing over hope and despair.

Sitting again, he had stared at the shore, the whispering marsh grasses already sharing their terrible secret.

16

The letter arrived the following afternoon, delivered by an annoyed Obed Shiverick, who shoved the envelope into Cole's hands with a harrumph and departed. It was not the day for mail delivery.

Cole opened the letter at his desk, noting the Pennsylvania postmark. His eye went to the signature, and he experienced a small start.

The letter was direct, the sort of missive Cole would have expected.

Dear Captain Cole:

I have been apprised of the failed visit of Captain Daintree. I have little knowledge of the man, which in retrospect is only fair as he was offered no knowledge of me and but the scantest information regarding the matter which sees this letter to you.

Time is of the essence. I will not waste time explaining. The Asia did carry an important item. Not even Superintendent Kimball is aware of the exact nature of the item and its value. Given all hope lies with you, I tell you alone that this item is small, and seemingly inconsequential; no more than a few sheaves of paper. No doubt, this makes you even more skeptical. It certainly makes your task more difficult. But I know what good men can do, and I am told you are a good man.

I would not presume to overestimate my importance in world events, but I do believe this item is an important stepping stone in our great nation's ascendancy to world dominion. With Europe fast approaching turmoil, the bolstering of our own nation's strength could not come at a better time. I must allow, this item will make me wealthy. Though I once held this above all but one God, it matters little to me now. What does matter is advancing our nation's collective future, in the hope that every man, woman, and child might enjoy a better life.

The Asia's *demise proved the worst of luck, but one must see the fortunate in even the worst circumstance. In conversations with Superintendent Kimball, I have learned that you are a man of uncommon character and ability. That the securing of this item has fallen to you is a stroke of good fortune in an otherwise difficult setback. I trust you will make every effort you can. You must make every effort you can.*

I can tell you no more. I sincerely apologize for my secrecy. As a leader of men, you understand why I do not divulge specifics to you or Superintendent Kimball. A secret is safest when it rests on the fewest tongues. Should this item fall into the wrong hands, it could do significant harm, and quite possibly alter the course of history to history's detriment.

I have enclosed telephone instructions. I am available to you day and night.

With high regards

The signature, like the letter, was without flourishes.

Cole rose and went to the window. The day was already darkening, mist crawling about the dunes. No doubt, Obed Shiverick was cursing his way home. Cole wondered who had convinced the postman to deliver the letter.

The letter confirmed what Cole already knew. America was firmly set on a path hailed as the dawn of a glorious age. He felt inconsequential in the great current. Though there was no point in it, he often wondered what sort of world Julia would have grown old in. It was a parent's aim to make the world a better place for his children, a place where they would experience new opportunity, advanced ideals, security, and happiness. Assured of this, a parent could go content to his grave. But even the most glorious beginning could end badly. Cradling his newborn daughter, Cole had felt joy he had never known. Though Edwin Merton's face had been sober, Cole had seen the light in his eyes—eyes wholly absorbed by a girl extending a buttercup. He had watched the same light fade from Martin's face as the Swede had stared helplessly at his daughter sitting in the wagon. Watching Helena Nelson, he had known it too. It was the same thing every time you looked on your child. On any child. Hope and fear.

He wondered what sort of future mankind was crafting.

Returning to his desk, Cole removed the keepsake box from the bottom drawer. He ignored the items inside. The present was paramount now. Slipping the letter into the box, he closed the lid.

He was about to return the box when there was a knock on the door.

Willie stepped in. The surfman's eyes went to the box, and then lifted to him. "Have you seen the fog?"

17

The two men stood near the edge of the Provincelands' cliffs, a quarter mile south of Race Point Station. They had watched the fog arrive, the first vapors, ghost scouts of an advancing army, galloping in on the afternoon's incoming tide. Now, night fully settled, the fog was impenetrable.

Icarus snorted. The white mare stood just behind the men, her great form waxing and waning. The light from the lantern fused with the mist, throwing a fuzzy halo about her.

John Kilbride peered east, presumably at the Atlantic. "Shit me a biscuit," he said. "This fog's thicker than a whaler's skull."

Pomp was pleasantly surprised. He had sensed the fog's arrival early in the afternoon, the first faint touch of moisture on his pores. He had sent for Kilbride, dispatching the Provincetown urchin who ran his errands. The boy was fleet-footed and mute, which was all Pomp required.

"Heaven dispatches buttermilk clouds to aid our cause," said Pomp.

"I'd prefer buttermilk," said Kilbride. "You had to send that circus freak before supper."

Pomp let the irksome comment slide. His own belly was full—he had treated himself to fresh mutton—but more than creature comforts were responsible for his buoyant mood. Fog cast a spell on him, its countless forms yet another testament to nature's versatility.

It rolled in from the sea in great waves. It advanced in probing fingers, seeping through the dunes like spilled milk. Sometimes, it bounded ashore in great billowing balls, spectral tumbleweeds given airy flight. Tonight it simply hunkered in place, making the world its own. Had he been a prayerful man, tonight's fog would be his prayer's answer.

As a boy, he had loved the fog. On foggy days, he had slipped from the orphanage and walked the mile to Wellfleet Bay, borrowing a dinghy from the docks and rowing out into the bay. Far from shore, he would plant one oar and pull with the other, spinning the dinghy in wild circles until he finally allowed it to settle. Robbed of compass points, he tested his senses, straining for sounds from shore, turning his cheek slowly until it was kissed by the hint of land breeze. One morning, one of the orphanage bullies followed him. Part of a group that tormented him mercilessly, the boy collared Pomp on the dock, forcing his way into the dinghy. Pomp had rowed sullenly until he saw the boy slouch and go silent as the fog crawled around them. Pretending to be lost, Pomp had rowed aimlessly in the fog while the boy wept.

Now fog was a boon to larger enterprise, but the child in him found it no less stimulating. The world was charged. The air hung saltier, sounds pressed closer. In the absence of sight, other senses sprang to life. He felt the dampness settling delicately on his skin as if he were a flower receiving dew's caress.

Below, on the invisible beach, the waves made the sound of rolling thunder. The third storm was on its way. The groundswell was already appreciable. The meat of the storm still brewed at sea, but the required elements were already in place.

Exhilaration rose in Pomp's breast. "I have a fine feeling about this night," he said.

Kilbride's fear of heights, healthy enough on a clear day, made his stomach hurt.

"We'll be lucky to see a ship, if we don't fall to our death first," he said. "How can we find ships we can't see?"

A portion of Pomp's fine feeling evaporated. In the early years of their partnership, John Kilbride had possessed a capacity for violence that was inspiring. Now all the man did was whine.

"They find us," said Pomp, taking up the mare's reins. "By now, I'd think you'd remember."

They walked slowly south. Icarus shuddered, agitation rippling her flanks. Pomp smiled. She knew. Man considered himself above the beasts, but this was conceit and folly. If not for a few happy discoveries—fire, gunpowder, shelter—Pomp had no doubt who would rule. Fang, claw, and indomitable spirit were most suited to the world.

Pomp gave the mare a tender stroke. "Patience," he said.

Kilbride walked a safe distance behind the horse and the old man, stewing. Icarus tolerated Pomp and hated the rest of mankind, but she reserved a special loathing for Kilbride. Over the years, the mare had bitten and kicked him at every opportunity. Once, when he'd forgotten himself and knelt to tie a boot, she had dealt him a blow that saw his head ring for three days. He wished horse and man a vault into the void.

When Pomp spoke, Kilbride's skin chilled.

"Some believe Icarus can fly. A fey horse, I'm told, bred on graveyard grass. It pleases me to confirm, yet again, that the depth of man's ignorance knows no bottom." Pomp nudged the lantern beneath the mare's neck.

The tide was nearing its peak, drawn to pregnant fullness by the cloaked full moon. Enemies could become friends. Courtesy of the fat tide, a ship would pass over the outer bars unaware, the full waters beneath her keel like a harbor channel. When she ran ashore, the thundering waves would do their work.

Pomp did not let the happy circumstances blind him. There were always sticking points, even on a night as perfect as this. On rare occasions, the more industrious wreckers were afoot. One black winter night, idly watching the destruction of a misguided schooner from the berm, he was nearly revealed by Barnabas and Watkins. The two men would have come on him unannounced had the fat man not laughed. Pomp had already extinguished the lantern, but in an unusual display of sloppiness, he had left it hanging beneath the mare's neck. He had barely had time to cut the fastening and shove the lantern under the seat of the wagon.

Pomp knew that some, Barnabas and Watkins included, suspected him of mooncussing, but suspicion did not bring conviction. Conviction, for Pomp, was inconceivable. Imprisonment raised the one specter he feared.

The greater flies in the ointment were the surfmen. That they stupidly hove to scheduled patrols made them a bit easier to avoid. On dark nights, his sharp eyes spied them long before they saw him. Fog bore more risk. Light carried far in a fog; it was as easy for a surfman to spot a swaying lantern as a ship's captain. The Race Point surfmen could be counted on to look away, but the men from Peaked Hill Bars and High Head were not beholden to John Kilbride. Foggy nights elevated the game.

There was a last troublesome matter, one he regarded with equal parts annoyance and disquiet. There were nights when Pomp felt he was being watched. Not once had he seen any sign, not a whisper of noise, not a trace of track; employing his own considerable senses, he had discerned nothing. Yet on certain nights, walking the ridgeline with Icarus and the swaying lantern, warning rang clear as a ship's bell.

The thought aggravated him now. He snatched at his pocket watch. Plenty of time. At the pace they were walking, they wouldn't intersect the patrol from Peaked Hill Bars for at least two hours. He felt a little better.

Ships, of course, were no guarantee either, but on this night, tantalizing possibility was afoot. Two days earlier, Abby had entertained a banker who carried the lien on a schooner, which, at this moment was making her way north from New Bedford to Boston. Although he had benefited from the same weakness time and time again, Pomp never ceased to be amazed how men were reduced to fools by a woman's favors. Trousers about his ankles, already fully inflated on one front, the banker had felt the need to inflate his importance too, informing the always inquisitive Abby that the vessel in question carried both conventional cargo and a gift to be delivered to a society matron who would no doubt be equally surprised to know her husband was cavorting with a woman one-third his age. A few additional noodlings and Abby had extracted the trinket's nature and location.

On some fronts, it was a seamless operation; on others, less so. Pomp looked back at the big man shuffling like a four-year-old through the sand.

"Wrest your eyes from my horse's ass, and toss a glance to sea," said Pomp. "I'm not paying you to engage in animal fantasy."

Kilbride was fantasizing about the mare, but the fantasy involved the animal being served as steaks, hot on a fire.

"All I see is fog," said Kilbride.

"Men see what they want to see, until reality kicks them in the teeth."

Following the old man and the hellion horse, Kilbride's mood grew darker still. His stomach churned. Dampness made the night colder. Back at the station, a fire burned and whisky flowed.

He had come to despise the entire process, the mute boy arriving at the station in all weather and at all times, his own meek assent, the old man's mockery. He could quit, but quitting was complicated. He had heard the tall tales of the drunken sailors and the religious cranks, but he had seen things the drunkest storytellers couldn't conjure. These spectacles were their bond. Many nights, Kilbride wished for conventional nightmares.

There were agreeable reasons for staying too. Over the years, he had reaped substantial benefit. They sold most of the collected goods to chandlers willing to buy without question, splitting the profits evenly. The profits were tidy. There were other enticing matters. What many thought to be rumor, Kilbride knew to be fact. Pomp had treasure buried throughout the Provincelands, spoils collected in the days before their partnership and during their years together, choice items ferreted aside. The old man buried these caches in secret. There was a time when Kilbride believed Pomp might reward him with a cache or two, but their relationship had gone sour. He held no hope of inheritance now. No doubt, the humped gnome would be pleased to see the treasures concealed forever. But he could be ruthless and cunning too. He might reap treasure yet. He might give the storytellers a spectacle.

The thought restored his bravado. "Here's to Daniel Cole and his men breaking their necks in this soup," he said.

Pomp's voice drifted back through the fog. "Daniel Cole sees more than you ever will. Stay out of humping range, and sit on your tongue."

Kilbride slipped back into vengeful reverie, aided by the hypnotic swinging light. In the process, he nearly walked into the mare's backside.

"Christ," he said, scrabbling back.

Pomp and the mare stood still, a perverse statue bathed in smoky half-light.

Kilbride heard the drum of surf. Slowly, other sounds rose, shouts coming from the south. Several gauzy lights appeared, drifting eerily in the air. The shouting grew louder. There was a tremendous grinding, followed by a giant's guttural groan, the protest of a vessel abruptly denied momentum. Timber splintered, the sound like rifle shots.

Pomp extinguished the lantern. "They have found safe haven," he said.

The two men descended a path just north of the vessel. From the foot of the cliffs, the ship remained invisible, but the panicked shouts of sailors and the basso thunder of wave upon wood were amplified by the fog.

Crackling reached Kilbride's ears, followed by a piteous scream. A fireball appeared in midair. It staggered wildly about the deck. The screaming stopped when the fireball fell into the sea. A sharp thump followed. Flames leapt into the sky. These screams went on and on, their owners trapped in the hold.

The old man swayed, eyes closed, simian brow slick with wetness.

They waited in the fog. There were more explosions and many shouts; shouts that were commands, shouts that were screams, shouts that sounded hope's end. Slowly, the shouts faded, leaving only the booming waves and the crackle of flame.

Pomp consulted his watch. "Time to see ourselves aboard. We have an hour before the northward patrol arrives. Probably less time before the fire ruins our chances. I suspect the survivors have fled inland, but stay alert."

Kilbride tried to sound calm. "The ship's still burning."

Trotting along the beach, Pomp did not turn. "More reason to move quickly."

A rope ladder dangled over the side. Pomp shimmied up. Banging his way up, Kilbride passed the ship's quarterboard. The *Amaretta*.

The deck was thick with black smoke. Clambering over the railing, Kilbride felt the oily draught pour into his lungs. Pomp was gone. Overhead, fire raged in the sails. Flaming bits of canvas fell to the deck like defeated stars.

Kilbride stood paralyzed. Self-preservation screamed at him to flee, but fleeing would infuriate the old man. He scanned the ship. Flames consumed the forward deck; flame and smoke leapt and roiled from the forward hold.

Kilbride ran aft. The smoke stung his eyes. Tufts of flame sprouted on the deck like bright shrubs, thrusting their heat against his legs. Heat, too, coiled about him. He ran gasping, his panicked breaths keeping pace with his pounding footfalls.

The cabin door was open.

Inside, it was suddenly clear. Pomp stood behind a large desk, his hands feeling along its beveled edges. In the fireplace, flames burned in civilized confinement.

"The ax," Pomp said.

Kilbride retrieved the hand ax secured beside the fireplace.

Pomp snatched the ax and raised it overhead. "It seems finesse will not do."

A wave struck the ship as Pomp's first blow fell. The ship listed violently. Kilbride grabbed at a shelf, fingers pinching the edge. The cabin filled with clattering. Kilbride's eyes followed the glowing embers to where the fireplace logs had stopped against the captain's bunk. The edges of a wool blanket flared.

The ship settled back with a great creaking. The flaming logs hesitated, and then rolled again. Crashing against the wall, they fired a jacket lying in a heap on the floor.

The heat was like drowning.

Kilbride managed a shout. "We have to go!"

Pomp paused in his blows. "A stubborn piece of craftsmanship. The captain had fine taste."

The flames ran up a bookcase. The books ignited in domino fashion, culminating in a rectangular wall of flame. Kilbride felt himself burning, claws raking his skin. The heat punched down his throat.

Gagging, he staggered for the door. "Wait." To Kilbride's surprise, his feet obeyed.

Pomp stood, ax overhead. In the hellish inferno, the gray eyes watched him curiously. "How much is treasure worth to you?"

Kilbride could find no thought.

Pomp swung the ax and the desktop split. He jerked the ax back and forth. Then tossing the ax aside, he plunged his hand into the narrow opening. Before Kilbride could react, the old man was out the door.

Kilbride ran. Something exploded, and a furnace wind nearly blew him off his feet. He ran through flames. Black smoke danced about him. Somehow, he found the ladder. He went over the railing with his own screams in his ears. His hand slipped. He fell in a dreamy toppling, the breeze pleasantly cool against his skin. His reverie ended with an impact that drove the wind from him and set a fire raging in his right shoulder. He lay in a few inches of water. A flaming shape the size of three men whirligigged through the air. Striking an arm's length away, it sprayed him with hot ash and frigid water. The burning drove him to his feet.

On the dry sand, he fell to his hands and knees. He coughed up something that looked like flesh. The sand in front of his nose flickered with light and shadow.

Above him, the old man spoke. "The fates continue to smile. A cargo of kerosene will erase our efforts."

"God damn you to hell."

"You're a little late."

"We almost died."

"You never grasped the thrill of the hunt. You are more the fool for it."

Kilbride was beyond insult. Lights popped behind his eyes. Ash burned in his throat. The pain in his shoulder made his eyes water.

"To infidelity," said Pomp.

The satisfaction in Pomp's voice saw Kilbride lift his head.

The old man let the stone fall. Kilbride wanted to save it, this beautiful green orb descending to the ugly earth, but the orb saved itself, stopping with a small hop before his eyes.

Swinging on its silver chain, the emerald's surface made the fire its own.

Pomp left Kilbride on the beach. He had one more task. He rarely rode Icarus. Although she tolerated him, she remained a skittish ride at best, apt to throw him as easily as anyone else. But he rode her now. The night was passing quickly.

Ezekiel Donne waited in the fog-sheathed dunes, precisely where Pomp had instructed. Still, Pomp nearly rode past him. Motionless as death and clad in gray long johns, he might have been a patch of fog.

Holes in the long johns showed blackened skin, ruined by cold. The man was a survivor.

Ezekiel held the sack in his hand.

Pomp smiled, relieved. "You listen," Pomp said.

"I do."

It was true. No word escaped him. At times, Ezekiel's memory surprised Pomp, but the man was still insane. Pomp had considered having Abby deliver the item, but in the end he'd decided to enlist Ezekiel. Best if the night's errand were shared only between him and the addled who dwelled invisible on society's periphery. Trusting Ezekiel with the delivery had been a risk.

Ezekiel thrust the blood-stained sack forward.

Icarus shied, but she settled quickly enough.

"I found it where you said," said Ezekiel.

"Well done," said Pomp.

Ezekiel formed a crooked smile, and gave the bloody sack a playful bob.

"A man's?"

"Not this time," said Pomp, taking the sack.

"Oh."

Ezekiel hated men. He knew they mocked him. When he was a boy, bullies had tied him to a tree until he'd drunk his own piss. He remembered. Disappointment tasted like piss. Just wearing man's trappings made his skin crawl.

He loved the old man's stories. Even bullies screamed like babies. He hated men enough to do those things to them too.

Excitement saw him jingle the coin purse at his side. "Another time?" he asked.

"Should opportunity present itself." Pomp held something out.

Ezekiel extended his hand cautiously. He didn't like to get his hopes up. The object was cold and hard in his fist. His heart hammered. He wanted to do a jig, but that had not worked out so well before. He had not forgotten how Pomp had quieted him when the church bells sang the fishermen's end.

"You can look," said Pomp.

The shiny green stone erased his disappointment. He hated men, but he liked pretty things more. "Mine?"

"Yours. A faithful steward is hard to find."

Ezekiel watched the old man ride away. He placed the stone gently in the coin purse. He turned the contents slowly with his fingers. The purse held pretty things: smooth bits of sea glass, coins, a child's brass ring, lovingly polished. His prizes made a muted tinkling against the stone, so quiet you had to strain to hear it. He wasn't sure which pleased him more, the straining or the soft jingling.

Later, he remembered it was Pomp's words.

An hour later, Pomp stood outside the mansion. For a time, the matter had caused him small debate. The shipmaster was too moral for his taste, but he remained a hard man who accepted the circumstances and forged on, closer to the wolves than the lambs. In the end, respect for the shipmaster saw Pomp compromise. It would just be a warning, a sign that ghosts indeed walked among the living and that further betrayal would not be tolerated.

Pomp scanned the windows. Only one held a lit candle.

At dawn, the lifesavers buried the blackened bodies on the beach. The wreckers came and salvaged what they could from the smoldering ship.

Daniel Cole walked the ridgeline in a gray mist. There had been no wind. The footprints and hoof marks were clear. He was certain the *Amaretta's* survivors, once collected from their various homes of refuge, would report seeing a light ashore.

It was still not proof enough for conviction, but it was proof enough for him.

As he turned for the station, the last of the fog furled up like a sail.

19

The fog had reason to flee. The third storm was approaching with promise to outshine the rest. By midmorning, the skyline was dark, fitful lightning striking the distant sea. By noon, the horizon's clouds pressed low over the station like a blanket, coal black and unbroken. The waves grew by the hour. They marched shoreward with the solemn piety of monks, their advances marked by the hiss of liquid cutting through air.

Cole canceled the afternoon chores and sent Mayo and the Swede on patrol. Stretched on his cot, Hiram tried to occupy his mind. For once, he would have preferred chores. Time slow-boiled. Ben laid two cots away, reading his Bible. Antone made a flurry of trips to the outhouse; nervousness gave him a skittish stomach that overrode his own Godly inclinations. Willie worked on a scrimshaw carving. In the nearly dark station, the curved whale tooth glowed in his hands. Hiram wished Willie would insult Antone or tell a story he had heard a hundred times, or that someone would suggest a game of poker, but the men were lost in themselves.

Hiram rose and went to the window. The clouds were unlike anything he had seen. Their bloated undersides distended and retreated as if breathing; tendrils reached down, the tattered ends moving like inquisitive fingers. Worse than the hypnotic clouds, the world had assumed a graveyard hush. While the clouds cavorted overhead, the dune grass hung limp.

The outhouse door clacked shut. Hiram watched Antone walk bow-legged across the sand. Hiram felt a hand on his shoulder.

"That man's gone and chafed himself," said Willie. "Follow me. I want to show you something."

Hiram followed Willie upstairs. Cole's door was shut. As they passed, they heard paper shuffling.

"Scratching away in his precious log book," whispered Willie, continuing along the landing. "Little need for a barometric reading this time around. A corpse could forecast this storm." Willie stopped at the door at the end of the landing. "Antone shits himself to a chafe. Our keeper dips a quill in ink. Ben memorizes the Bible. We each face insignificance in our own fashion."

Willie opened the door. Cold spilled around them. As they climbed the steel steps, rising in a loop to the lookout, their footfalls made a hollow clanging. At the top of the steps, Hiram squeezed through the trapdoor opening.

The lookout was little bigger than a closet. Four windows faced north, south, east, and west.

Willie went to the east-facing window. "There's beauty in this," he said.

The lookout smelled of creosote and dust. Hiram stepped up beside Willie. The sky was blacker, as if the short climb had put them closer to hell.

Willie's voice echoed slightly. "That sky reminds me of your cooking," he said.

"How can it be so quiet?"

"The wind will drop down to entertain us soon enough. Whoever orchestrates this world is only having a little fun on high before he moves his brushstrokes down here. Maybe it's God's way of sneaking up on those unwilling to look to the heavens."

Hiram had never heard Willie talk about God before.

"Do you believe in God?" he asked.

"Depends. I'm not much for prayer under normal circumstances, but I've said my share of prayers at times like these when it got convenient. If there is a God, I hope he'll start by forgiving the hypocrites."

"Do you think he looks out for us?"

"No."

Turning up his collar, Willie nodded at the Atlantic. "Good thing Antone couldn't see that from the outhouse."

The waves rolled forward in walls that seemed to stretch the length of the Cape. Hiram had never seen waves so far out to sea.

"Terrifying, isn't it?" said Willie.

Hiram felt his chest squeeze. He wished Willie hadn't brought him here.

"Have a look," said Willie. "There are three other windows."

Hiram went to each window. He didn't know what he was supposed to see. From every direction, threat rushed in. He returned to the first window where Willie still looked at the ocean.

"I once asked a man I greatly admire how he manages fear," Willie said. "He told me he examined it closely from every side, so there weren't any imaginings."

Hiram didn't know if he felt any better, but he did know that standing in the lookout was better than staring at the ceiling. "You should watch me cook," he said.

"That's the spirit."

Cold pushed through a crack. Outside, the dune grasses moved.

"And so it begins," said Willie.

The skies ruptured at six o'clock. For most of the afternoon, the rising wind had buffeted the station, rattling the windows and driving sand through the cracks, where it rested on the floor in quiet veins. Now hail joined the buffeting, propelled by the raging wind.

Hiram woke to the clattering yowl in a sweat. He was surprised he had slept. He changed into his gear and waited. Mayo returned from patrol, then Martin. Both men went immediately to the stove, becoming bulky shadows in the lantern light. Martin gave Hiram a thin smile.

Hiram imagined walking around the lookout tower. It didn't help. He thought he might be sick. The wind kept howling without once catching its breath.

Stepping into the frozen night, Hiram saw the dune grass jerking to and fro as if trying to uproot itself and run.

By half past midnight, they knew Hiram was missing. Men rarely returned from patrol to the minute, especially in foul weather. Certain keepers, in fact, discarded schedules entirely during storms, but Captain Cole was not among them. At Peaked Hill Bars, the rule was clear: forty minutes overdue and search parties were dispatched.

When Cole came downstairs, the men were already in their oilskins. Now the shrieking wind waxed and waned, as if, at intervals, packs of howling demons were galloping past the station.

Cole timed his words. "Mr. Bangs and Mr. Lucas will proceed north along the beach to the halfway house. If Surfman Paine was injured, it's possible the Race Point patrol found him and took him there. Surfman Mayo and I will walk north along the ridge. He might have gone up to the cliffs to avoid flooding on the beach. Surfman Maddocks will stay here, in the event that Mr. Paine returns."

Cole felt his hands shaking. He had decided to send Hiram out on patrol alone; there could be no more protecting the boy. This decision was no easier. "Our first responsibility is to the ships along our coast. If someone must wait for aid, it will be one of ours."

Stepping outside the station, Hiram felt the cold crushing the air from his lungs. When he gasped, the wind stuffed his mouth with grit and wetness. In that first terrifying instant, he thought he would drown on dry land.

It was worse on the beach. The wind tore the tops from the waves, hurling balls of sleet and foam across the sand, turning air to water. Hiram tucked his chin into his armpit, siphoning air from a tiny pocket. When he turned to the ocean, he saw nothing but the shorebreak, a cauldron of black waves and white explosions.

Patrolling was futile, but the other men had walked and he would too. He kept to the middle of the beach, now and again glancing pointlessly seaward. His legs dragged. Looking down, he was surprised to see water churned to a milky white, hopping about his calves. Soon shin-deep water reached all the way up the beach, leaping at the base of the cliffs.

When the ground disappeared under his feet, Hiram thought its withdrawal, and his own short slide, odd. Milky water wrapped his chest, curling about him with disinterest. For a moment, he felt the drawing as a slight tug; then he was yanked off his feet and dragged under. The cold was like a punch. He fought to the surface, spitting and coughing. He felt himself accelerating. The retreating waters had gouged a cut that was sweeping him to the sea. He was pulled under again.

He clawed back to the surface. His lungs snatched air, and then hands grabbed his ankles and yanked him down again. He remembered his boots. Somehow his fingers found their rubber edge. Spinning in darkness, he wrestled off one, then the other.

He thrashed back to the surface. He was out among the waves. The withdrawing water ran into the incoming waves like a river, standing them upright and delaying their breaking. He rode over the waves in a roller coaster gallop, swooping up steep faces and down sloping backs, swallowing water and shouting.

A wave broke, its leading edge thick as the underside of the surfboat. The instant before impact, the world took a peaceful breath, and then Hiram was crushed down and spun with a concussive violence so strong he wondered if his arms and legs would tear loose.

He rose to the surface on someone else's accord. Floating on his back, he admired the way the foamy ocean gave ghostly light to the sky. He was a leaf now, spinning easily. A breeze insinuated itself beneath him, lifting him gently above the earth. It was soothing, this placid rising, but then the breeze stopped and he was pitched forward into unholy turbulence. Light, brighter than any flare, erupted behind his eyes. He waited for the light to dim, but it never did. It burned bright without showing him the way.

When Cole and Frank Mayo arrived at the small shack between Peaked Hill Bars and Race Point Station, one surfman was present. The man's name was William Cook. Slumped in a chair beside the potbelly stove, he was well past drunk.

A frigid draft alerted William Cook to his company. He lifted his chin from his chest. His bleary eyes focused quickly enough.

Cole strode forward. "How long have you been here?"

"I just arrived."

The man's wool socks, hanging by the stove, were nearly dry.

Cole took a slow breath. "Your negligence has placed a man in jeopardy. If he comes to any harm, you will pay."

Drunk or sober, William Cook was not partial to threats. He knew enough of Daniel Cole not to trifle with the man, but the whisky warming his mind made the keeper appear small and almost boyish.

"If he's come to harm, it's his own damn fault. Only an idiot would stay out in this storm." The man's throat rose and fell; a vein in his neck pulsed.

Cole felt something fall away. His body relaxed, wires springing loose. It was such a pleasant sensation that he stood for a moment, savoring it. "Leave now."

In different circumstances, William Cook would have laughed. But even drunk, he sensed a clock ticking. Standing with as much insolence as he could muster, he reached for his oilskin.

"No," Cole said.

Both Mayo and Cook stared at the keeper, but only Cook spoke.

"It's storming like the devil."

"I require you feel his bite," Cole said.

In the face of the loose smile, William Cook did not protest. When he opened the door, he made a choking sound.

"Mr. Cook," the keeper said.

Cook turned, pathetic hope on his face.

"Tell John Kilbride I will be by to see him."

In the silence of William Cook's departure, Cole felt the wires assembling. Turning to Mayo he said, "We need to search the beach."

At the moment Daniel Cole experienced his release, Willie and Antone found Hiram at the foot of the cliffs directly below the halfway house. The waters had retreated slightly. With their retreat, a portion of the undermined cliff had collapsed, leaving a raised bank of sand. Willie spied the dark shape, curled as if on a pyre.

When Cole and Mayo reached the top of the path, Willie and Antone were ascending, the sagging body between them. Hiram's feet were bare. His shirt was gone. His torso was salt white.

Cole felt something slipping away. This time it was not pleasant.

Willie shouted in his ear. "He's alive, Daniel!"

To the south, the milling waters scoured away the sand. The torn body lifted and spun slowly, and the patient ocean claimed Edwin Merton for good.

20

The dream of the crows came to Hiram again, only this time the dream was different. The crows didn't lift from Mercy's eyes, clasping their jiggling bits. Instead, they covered his eyes, a black cloud that refused to dissipate. The strangeness of the dream had no end. The crows cried out, but there was no victory in their noises. They sounded defeated and bone-weary. He wondered if, at long last, they were giving up.

A tired sound rose again, infused with something that made Hiram want to shout with joy. He ignored the crows and concentrated on the voice.

"The fire needs wood."

Another voice answered, farther away. Perhaps someone was coming down the path. He did not want to be found. He hunched his shoulders and pressed low to the soupy muck, hiding in the marsh grass.

The distant voice came close. A man's voice. Familiar.

"You should eat."

He was so puzzled, he forgot he was hiding. He lifted his head.

He felt the silence, and then warm hands clasped his face, the fingers gripping painfully at his cheeks. The hands shook, and so his head did too, and he remembered how the light had exploded behind his eyes, but he welcomed this shaking and the pain with all his heart.

Nellie Paine held her son and laughed and cried.

Behind her, Daniel Cole silently said a word of thanks to the person who deserved it most.

The men had stripped off Hiram's clothes and stoked the fire, staying in the halfway house, massaging and warming Hiram until the peak of the storm passed. An hour before dawn, Cole carried the boy back to Peaked Hill Bars. Settling Hiram in the library, Cole had continued onto Provincetown to fetch Doc Bloomer. After examining Hiram, the taciturn physician told Cole the boy would die. He had been exposed to the elements for too long.

Cole kept the news from the men. Returning Doc Bloomer to Provincetown, he turned the wagon to Truro. The hail had turned to sleet, and the winds had eased. In the sitting room of the tidy cottage, virtually unchanged since his long-ago visits, he told Nellie Paine the truth.

He had braced himself for the worst, receiving instead the first in a succession of lessons. Nellie had absorbed the news without expression. She went to kitchen, gathered up a sack of supplies and left the cottage without a word. Cole had fetched a winter coat and a rain slicker from the hall closet. Sitting in the wagon, Nellie took the coat and slicker without interest.

"Go," she said.

Heading for the station, she grilled him on every detail of Hiram's ordeal, questioning him again and again on the same points until Cole wondered if she had come unhinged.

Standing over her unconscious son in the library, she had shed no tears. Cole had waited, for what he didn't know, and when she went downstairs he followed her.

Removing blankets from three of the cots, she addressed the men. "He will not die," she said.

Cole placed a second cot in the library, but Nellie Paine didn't sleep. All that first night Cole heard her voice through the wall. At midnight, he had gone to the library to see if she required anything. The look she gave him returned him to his quarters without a word. The talking stopped, replaced by footsteps. The steps beat a parade ground-march. Eventually, he fell asleep to the monotonous beat. When he woke the feet were still marching.

Nellie had given each surfman a single task, as if, in focusing on one duty, each man could perfect it. Mayo was assigned to boiling water. Martin chopped the dried vegetables she had brought in the sack. The few times she left the library to tend to her toiletry, Antone or Willie took her place, sitting on a stool beside the cot, talking without pause, as ordered, choosing subjects Hiram enjoyed. In this way, Nellie Paine discovered the depth of her son's feelings for Hannah Lombard.

Cole's duty was firewood. Often, when he brought in an armload of wood, she demanded more. The first time this happened, he made the mistake of pointing out that firewood was already spilling across the floor. He offered no additional observations. He lost track of the number of trips he made to the woodpile beside the stable. Nellie stoked the fire until the stove pipe glowed. Soon he worried she might burn down the station.

Nellie sat on the stool and talked to her son. She spoke casually, as if she and Hiram were seated at the breakfast table. Cole fought against it, but when he came into the room he eavesdropped anyhow. Nellie talked of family picnics, about what a mess Hiram had made picking berries, and recollected how he had carved a three-winged osprey for her when he was eight. She spoke of her dreams for his future, and how one day she would take his children blueberry picking and let them stain themselves terribly because it would be Hiram's job to clean them up. Other times, she addressed broader topics. Once, Cole listened in on a discourse on the collapse of the Roman Empire, the Romans undone by greed and egotism. On another occasion, Cole pushed wood about and listened, fascinated, as Nellie described the building of the Brooklyn Bridge in New York City, the construction of the seemingly impossible suspension bridge designed by the deceased engineering genius John Roebling and now carried on by his son.

Hiram breathed quietly.

Cole had never witnessed such focus. Sara had been the finest mother, caring and protective, but this determination was something else, something unbending and almost dangerous. Each time he entered the room, no matter how soft his tread, Nellie spun on him as if he were a grave robber, then promptly relegated him to invisibility. Her first night, he had brought her beef broth. The next morning, he removed the congealed bowl. He made hot biscuits with maple syrup. After that, he knew not to waste food. The cot lay unruffled. Nellie talked and walked.

And her son did not die.

On the day Hiram regained consciousness, Nellie Paine allowed each surfman a brief visit. It was easy for the men to be quiet; they were made sheepish by the woman standing sentry beside the cot. They were also slightly off-kilter. After Nellie's announcement, Cole had told them Doc Bloomer's prognosis. All of them, with the exception of Ben, had expected Hiram to die.

Standing beside the cot, they struggled to express their joy and relief. Martin squeezed Hiram's hand so hard, Hiram thought his knuckles would pop. Antone made a mumbling gift of a pack of cards. Ben gave Hiram his Bible and fairly ran from the room. Only Willie was at ease.

"I said to examine the world from every side, not jump in for a swim," he said. "I'd hope you won't hold me responsible."

Hiram felt as if someone had poured syrup into his skull. The syrup dulled the throbbing, but it slowed his thoughts and his smile. "I don't listen to everything you say."

"I'll take that for absolution," said Willie. "While you're in a lenient mood, I'll also confess that I once pinched two loaves of bread from Mrs. Crockett's windowsill and her undergarments from the line to keep the bread warm. Also, your mother now knows more about Hannah Lombard than you might prefer."

Hiram wrestled the words to his tongue. "Does Hannah know?"

Willie reached across to straighten the blanket.

"Not yet," Willie said.

"Do you think she might visit?"

His mother laid a cool palm on his forehead. "Hannah left the Cape," she said. "She took a trip with Mr. Macy."

"Why?"

His mother looked away.

Willie stood. "Not everyone regards our home as a garden spot," he said.

That night, Cole took the eight to midnight patrol, relieving a surprised and grateful Mayo. The night was bitter, the ocean granite smooth beneath a clear sky. Walking beside the sea had always helped him think, but on this night it proved useless. Cole felt he could walk to the Outer Banks and back and still return without answers.

Back in his quarters, he again considered his problems. He had plenty of them, and in each instance, he needed to assess his options with cold impartiality.

His most immediate problem was, on the surface, simple. The Race Point crew had again disobeyed United States Lifesaving Service regulations. When Hiram hadn't appeared at the halfway house, William Cook's duty was to search for him. He could write Washington, but Washington would react slowly or, more likely, do nothing again. Here he had already decided on a course of action, though the outcome was anybody's guess.

Outside the window, a full moon ladled silver on the sands. The tide was just now assuming its full swell. The tides, the seasons, the great flocks of migratory birds, each came and went in their time. People saw nature as ferociously unpredictable, but in Cole's mind, the natural world was often an orderly place. It was man who came with an unfathomable set of complications.

His mind returned to Hiram. A man in his position could not play favorites, but he couldn't change what he felt. Hiram's brush with death had shaken him profoundly. His heart was now involved in matters of duty. It was weakness, pure and simple. Worse, if he was wholly honest with himself, the deeper truth was more damning still. He had favored the boy before he had set foot in the station. The truth was, when he looked at Hiram, an uncomfortable number of times he saw a young Nellie Paine. The boy's quick movements, the way he absently fingered a lock of hair, the alert green eyes, each was a rekindling of his childhood friend.

Most damning, not all his emotions hearkened back to childhood. During Hiram's convalescence, he had gone to the library far more often than necessary. Nor was there any rational reason to stand in the dark and listen to a woman's footfalls. He had loved and lost a wife and a daughter. His obligations now were to his duties as keeper. With the wreck of the *Asia*, and now the delivery of the letter, his duties had assumed added importance. Yet he was undermined by distraction. Even now, ostensibly addressing his problems, he was acutely aware of Nellie Paine in the next room.

Only when his mind had settled on the last problem, did he forget her. That Pomp knew of the *Asia* was no surprise; that he had seen Hiram in the day house with the girl was dark news. Whether Hiram harbored any clues regarding the missing treasure, Cole didn't know, but he did know that Pomp was intent on finding out. Blind luck had seen the boy escape Pomp at the Cork and Barrel. The incident with Hannah Lombard had shown that blind luck could not be counted on twice. For ten years, he had waged a losing battle with an adversary of near-supernatural ability. It didn't seem possible, but now that the stakes had risen, so had Pomp's skills.

Nellie knocked a third time to be heard.

She noticed how Daniel Cole rose quickly, a hand smoothing the blue jacket. Brow slightly furrowed, he looked like a small boy summoned unexpectedly to the front of the class.

Nervousness nearly saw her laugh. "I'm sorry, Daniel. I know it's late, but I saw your light. I thought this would be a good time." She concentrated on her breathing, slowing her words to match its pace. "I'm leaving in the morning. I know I shouldn't stay any longer. I wanted to thank you for everything you did. " It was a small smile, constructed in pieces. "I also want to apologize for my behavior. I was afraid for my son."

Cole still stood silently behind the desk.

"Honest to God, Daniel, must you always stand like an undertaker in my presence?"

"I'm afraid my faults are becoming even more firmly entrenched."

"Your list of faults is shorter than most. It is certainly shorter than you hold it to be."

Daniel Cole pieced together his own smile. "My life involves assessing others," he said. "I should also turn a critical eye on myself."

"Shouldn't it be an honest eye? You're not as fault-ridden as you think. You even have qualities I fancy."

The moon pushed a silver finger into the room. Nellie went to the window to fill the pause. Drawing back slightly allowed her to see his reflection. He had stepped out from behind the desk.

She spoke to the window pane. "I remember far more about you than you imagine, Daniel Cole. Not many of those memories involve flaws."

"Memories are imperfect. More so at our age."

Nellie smiled at her reflection. "Now that I'm Methuselah? I recall that the inability to offer petty flattery is one of your faults."

"It seems I am creating new memories with old faults."

Holding her smile in place, she turned. "Coming to get me ran counter to your duties, Daniel. I'll always be grateful for what you did."

"You saved his life."

"We saved his life."

"No," said Cole. "I collected firewood and listened in on you." It felt good, for once, to be certain. "I've never seen anything like it."

"I did what any mother would do."

"Most mothers would have succumbed to sleep."

"Sleep, as you might point out, is for the young."

So many things, thought Nellie, had slipped through her grasp. Things she had held to be certain—a husband to grow old with, a daughter who would stand over her grave—they had lifted away. So many opportunities gone. She had fought for her son out of love, but she had also fought with rage and fear.

She wished she weren't shaking. "I can't do it again," she said.

She watched, detached, as he came forward and took her in his arms. She was mildly surprised by the heat of his hands.

The kiss contained all the pleasure of her imaginings, but even as Daniel Cole pressed into her, she saw her son in the reeds beside the pond. Numbed by her own shock, she had watched him leave the cottage at dawn. Samuel had convinced her that the body wouldn't surface for at least two days, but he was wrong. They found Hiram at dusk, kneeling over his sister in the mud, his voice a croak. She could not imagine how he had managed to keep the crows off for all those hours. She had rocked her son, telling him it wasn't his fault, that a little boy wasn't expected to save his sister, that time would make things better. Even as she spoke, his arms had brandished behind her, the crows settling on their prize.

A young girl has dreams. A woman has memories and nightmares.

Nellie stepped away. Dark eyes watched her quietly.

"A flaw," said Cole. "I remember us young."

"Were we so different?"

"Yes."

She touched his cheek and left. One could do worse than an honest man.

That afternoon, Cole told Hiram what the rest of the Cape already knew. The news had carried almost as swiftly as the girl's screams, Paul Macy crashing into the room, reaching for Hannah Lombard, the girl clawing madly at the bed sheets, the half-eaten goat liver on the bed beside her, its blood-veined glistening illuminated by a room ablaze with candles, themselves like a fire.

Hiram understood. Prometheus had betrayed the gods. The message was for him.

21

Saturday came two days later. Cole left Peaked Hill Bars at noon. When his first stop proved unfruitful, he turned Thoreau toward Provincetown.

Stoic man and animal traveled beneath a spitting rain. Cole barely noticed his surroundings. He felt profoundly tired and oddly disembodied, as if he were watching another man pass through the dunes. His drowsiness annoyed him. His task required focus. It was not the best plan, but it was right in its action.

Cole nearly rode past the Cork and Barrel. After Sara and Julia's death, he had visited the pub several times with Willie. He had gone to forget, but liquor and people had made his sorrow worse and so he had stopped going. Riding down the sodden slash of Bradford Street, Thoreau's steaming breaths rising into the rain, he wondered if he was lost. He scanned the storefronts. They stared back like strange faces. He passed a new grocery and a livery, and then he saw a boarding stable he had never seen. Idly, his mind took in the sign in the window: "Carriages for all Occasions. We furnish careful drivers to accompany tourists to the life-saving stations and all other points of interest."

Tourists were visiting the Cape in increasing numbers, and great hotels were rising from the sand: the Chequesset in Wellfleet, the Cotocheset at Wianno, the Chequaquet at Craigville. In the summer, when he was alone at the station, he saw families wandering through the dunes, searching for a place to picnic or a path to lead them to the beach. More than once, he had looked up from some repair to see an entire family staring at him as if he were a circus animal. One man had asked for a surfboat ride. Cole knew he should see the humor in it, but the truth was, he saw something insidious in the tourists. They were like water rising behind a dam.

He gave up looking to the storefronts for help. He knew the pub was near the main wharf. A half mile ahead, masts rose above ramshackle rooftops.

He reined up in front of the buffalo. Snow, rain, and freeze had given the beast an embattled appearance. It looked as though it were the last of its race, head bent beneath a weight of wounds, readying for a last wobbly charge. Cole recalled the miserly owner. Securing Thoreau to the hitching post, he searched his mind halfheartedly for the man's name.

Stepping into the pub, Cole allowed his eyes a moment to adjust. He smelled tobacco and the sour stink of spilled ale. Only three tables were occupied, two of them by a half dozen women who stopped talking to stare at him.

Apathy was still on him, but something else was rising to take its place. This time, he did not push it away. As he passed the table of women, a young girl stood. Smoothing her dress, she put on a pretty smile that fell away.

Cole caught a movement, followed by the tinkling of glass. A man had popped up behind the bar. Cole recognized the pasty-faced owner. The man watched him, a bottle in one hand.

Cole walked to the farthest table. He ignored Pomp. John Kilbride shifted back in his seat to rise. Cole stepped so close he nearly stood on Kilbride's boots.

Cole spoke in a mild tone, but his words cut through the quiet tavern. "My man nearly died."

Kilbride had expected Daniel Cole to come looking for him. When the delirious and frostbitten William Cook had staggered into the station, Kilbride had experienced a pleasant rise of blood lust. Daniel Cole was a righteous bastard. Kilbride knew righteousness would drive the man to make amends. But he had expected Cole to come to the station, not to the pub. Occupied with whittling, he hadn't even bothered to look to the door when the whores had tittered.

Surprise had cost him the advantage. He sat with the penknife in his hand as Cole stood nearly on top of him. He couldn't rise without bumping the man. He could only wait to see what unfolded. This infuriated him. It was always better to take the offensive.

He reined in his temper. "Last I looked, our job was to come to the rescue of failing vessels, not boys who can't watch their step. And in case you've forgotten, I'm not the man you sent out into the storm half-naked."

Cole recognized the foolishness of talk, but something in him felt the need to see talk through to its end. He spoke slowly, as if gradually recalling the facts. "William Cook should have looked for him. As station keeper, you are responsible for your men and their actions."

"You might shepherd children, but I don't," said Kilbride. "My men answer to themselves. Perhaps Surfman Cook was wise to stay put. It was quite a storm."

"It was for those who were out in it."

Cole spoke almost sleepily, and to Kilbride's practiced eye, the man appeared inattentive. His own knife, however, was tucked inside his boot. With Cole so close, it was impossible to snatch it. The penknife would work in a clinch, but he preferred a meatier weapon.

All he needed was a half step. He glanced at Pomp for help, but the old man simply sat, twirling his tumbler with a content look.

Kilbride felt a warning bump of unease, like a current humping over a telltale rock in a river, but the whisky helped sweep him past.

Reaching slowly into his jacket he retrieved his pocket watch. "I have chores to tend to," he said. "I'm sure you understand."

Cole stood quiet as a grave. The man's stillness was unnerving. Men were predictable. They acted quickly, out of fear or anger. Most men approached him in fear, backpedaling before the first blow was struck. The few men who took the offensive were as handily defeated;

fighter's reflexes and bloodlust had seen him nearly kill several men with his bare hands. But the way this man just stared at him was puzzling.

"I'd appreciate it if you didn't sit in my lap. Only the ladies get this close." Kilbride felt the whores watching him. The thought of these women whom he had mistreated restored some equilibrium.

"Well Daniel, you've never been much of a conversationalist. If you've got nothing more to say, I'll be leaving."

"Your negligence nearly cost a good man his life."

Kilbride's laugh was genuine. "I'm not deaf. You might have to repeat yourself at your station, but you're dealing with sharper minds here."

"Seeing as you came all this way, I'll do you the courtesy of repeating myself." Kilbride heard himself talking fast and loud. He recognized his own bluff, but he could do nothing else. He gripped the penknife. "Surfman Cook is the man you want to see. He had his orders to patrol, and he ignored them."

Kilbride meant to continue—he was just getting around to telling the gathering that William Cook would stop by later in the day—but an anvil struck him in the face. He landed on his back, his skull cracking against wood. He wanted to lie still, but he knew he must stand. Rolling over, he pushed his palms against the floor, but his viscous limbs floundered.

A hand snatched his hair, nearly tearing it from his scalp. His eyes filled with tears. The hand yanked. He followed its lead. Scrabbling across the floorboards, he felt the bump of his palms and knees.

The hand stopped yanking. The world filled with his panting.

The hand pushed him against something. Its smooth surface was comforting. Kilbride rested his cheek against it, hoping to clear his head.

Neither Rummy nor the whores had seen the first blow. It were as if John Kilbride had simply fallen back in his chair and the Peaked Hill Bars keeper had moved quickly to help him up. In a matter of seconds, Cole had dragged Kilbride across the floor and pushed his face against the potbelly stove.

Kilbride's head canted slightly, as if he were straining to hear some faintly whispered secret. The whisper assumed the horror of truth. The big man's face contorted and his lips peeled back. There was no sound. Then the screams came, bursting through the gates just behind truth's dawning.

Kilbride's hands went to the stove first. Jerking away, they clawed at the forearm overhead. Deep furrows appeared, white, pink, and then running red. The grip did not waver. Head pinned, Kilbride's body flopped and twisted, as if run through by opposing orders. Liquid seeped from a pant cuff. Kilbride issued an odd mewling.

A woman screamed.

Cole released his grip. Kilbride's face skidded down the stove. Skeins of skin turned black and furled inward. Kilbride curled into his own ball, his stink warring with the sweet smell of burning flesh.

Cole returned to the table.

"Leave the boy alone," Cole said.

Pomp sat impassive. "We shall see."

The whores held each other and cried.

"Mother of God," said one.

Cole looked through them. "No God would have created this world," he said and walked out the door.

Cole took no satisfaction in the beating. Stepping outside, he felt a hollow loss. There was no turning back.

Thoreau waited in the drizzle. A small crowd stood across the street. Cole could think of no reason for people to stand out in the rain, but there they were. His eyes went to a little girl. She wore a bow in her hair. He smiled faintly. The girl began to cry. Her mother shot him a poisonous glare and pushed the girl behind her.

Not until he was beyond town did he remember. He glanced at his forearm. In places, Kilbride had raked it to the muscle. His trousers were wet with rain and blood.

He brought Thoreau to a stop. Climbing into the back of the wagon, he found a cloth sack. Placing one foot on the sack, he used his good arm to tear off a strip. The effort made his head swim.

He wrapped his forearm. He gave a cluck and Thoreau plodded forward. The last scattered homes gave way to rolling dunes.

He had done what was required. John Kilbride's negligence could go unpunished no longer. There had been no alternative. Yet, as he bumped along, a voice chided him. Cole let the voice speak.

Entering the Cork and Barrel, he had only planned on teaching Kilbride a lesson, but when the man's nose had gone soft beneath his fist, something had rushed up inside him. Striding for the stove, he had barely felt Kilbride's weight in his fingers. Pressing the man's face to the stove, he had experienced an almost reverential awe, as if a will far more powerful than his own held sway, orchestrating not retribution, but destruction. Holding the mewling man, confusion had fallen away. In that moment, his life possessed clarity and purpose.

The woman's scream had saved Kilbride, not for its piercing noise, but for its humanity. The thing that had consumed Cole fell away like cannon smoke before a heavy wind. In its absence, only ugly brutality and the lie of violence remained.

At the cemetery, Cole dismounted, holding his arm close. The bandage was serving its purpose; the blood had congealed. He had lost more blood than was good, but not enough to matter. The rain had stopped. Chill rose from the earth. The familiar headstones grinned at him like misaligned teeth.

Movement made him nauseous. He focused on the muddy earth. At the two small headstones, he went to his knees; crouching was too much effort. Already, the headstones were mottled with lichen and moss. A crack extended from one of the few letters. Ornish Helms had offered to carve epitaphs for free, but Cole had declined. Words seemed pointless.

A fit of shaking seized him. He closed his eyes. Sara lay on their bed, her hair drifting across her smooth back as she moved. He felt her warmth. He wanted to lie down beside her, but they no longer belonged to the same world, and the world he inhabited had profoundly altered. He had surprised himself, but he had meant to kiss Nellie Paine. Yet, even as he felt her reciprocate, noting with cautious joy her anxious press, he was aware of his folly. Already he had decided on retribution.

It was a civilized world. He would be punished for beating John Kilbride; certainly jail time, and likely dismissal from the Lifesaving Service. When he was released, he would return to fishing. But he would not allow Nellie Paine to associate with a man dishonored.

Sara and Julia had died in a fire while he was fishing. By punishing John Kilbride, he had betrayed Nellie Paine. He had done what he'd wanted, in his selfishness, failing the three women he loved.

"I'm sorry," he said.

Rising to his feet, he felt the dead tugging him down. His wife and his daughter, the girl with the doll, the man in the shoes, he had failed them all. He was a hapless man in an empty cemetery, unable to see the past to its end even as the present slipped away.

That night, Nellie Paine fell asleep in the armchair facing the black woods. It was the chair Daniel Cole always sat in when he came to visit after her husband's death, the two of them drinking tea in silence. Another man would have spilled words into her anger and hurt. Daniel Cole had filled the room with silence and the comfort of friendship.

For a time, she slept peacefully, folded in the chair, lulled by the sound of the rain. Men's faces rose before her, men she had known well, men she had only glimpsed in passing. The stern face of her Quaker father, the keening of possibility in a handsome dockworker's eyes, the impish grin of her husband before his joy inexplicably died away, tenderness and hope in Daniel Cole's dark gaze.

Another face came to her, convulsed with lust. She woke in a panic, alone again, without solace.

22

John Kilbride drank what he needed, and then he drank more. Lifting the hand mirror, he looked at his face again. He tilted the mirror so that it flared with lantern light, making his face disappear. Laughter drifted up from downstairs.

He had stayed in his quarters for six days. His men had left him alone, setting his meals outside the door. When he shouted for whisky, they sat that outside too.

Kilbride turned the mirror slowly. His flesh was the purple of winter nightfall. Skin dripped like wax from his left temple to his jaw, where it joined a fibrous latticework of tendrils that resembled a seine net resting on a dark ocean bottom.

"Fetching," he said.

He put the mirror down. He ran two fingers gently over the latticework. He still felt pain. He wondered if it was infected. He had done nothing more than pour whisky over the wounds, stifling his own screams with a cloth stuffed in his mouth.

He stared past the lantern into the darkness. He knew now what he had seen in the keeper's sleepy eyes. He wished he had recognized it then, but there was no going back. Most people didn't have the nerve to kill another human being. They knew this, and it was precisely why civilized man, despite condescending actions to the contrary, respected, even exalted, killers. The killer controlled his life and the lives of others. The weak paid homage.

He hated Daniel Cole, but he had to give him his due. Kilbride was a killer, and now the keeper had made him a fool. By now, word of his beating had spread across the docks. He was not liked. He knew this. No doubt, the cowards had toasted his comeuppance. He cared nothing for them. For six days, but one man had consumed his thoughts.

The lantern light hurt his head. As he pushed the lantern away, light rose and wavered on the whisky bottle. Kilbride stared at the bottle. He felt the old happiness return. The world righted itself, the predator back in control.

He picked up the mirror, watching himself tip the bottle to his ruined face.

"To you, Daniel Cole. For one of us, the night is improving."

By the time Kilbride reached Peaked Hill Bars, he was half sober and wholly miserable. His head pounded, and the wind slashed his raw face. He reminded himself of the satisfaction he was about to enjoy, but the aching cold undermined his enthusiasm.

Inhaling, he forced himself to focus. Save for the single light upstairs, the station was dark. No doubt, the lap dog was tending to lifesaving business. He would have enjoyed climbing through Daniel Cole's window and punishing him, but he knew the other men were downstairs, and he was still too drunk to perform anything more than the simple task at hand.

This would be a taste.

He took out his pocket watch. One o'clock. His timing was perfect. The midnight patrols were gone, the returned men slumbering soundly.

The horse snorted as Kilbride eased the tarp off the woodpile. The oil-doused rags made for quick work. Flames emerged from the woodpile as if they had been waiting there. He stood watching their eager wagging, overcome with warmth and reverence, and then he ran.

Cole heard the whinnying first. Running down the stairs, he was out the door before his shouts fully woke the surfmen.

Hiram sat up. Something was terribly wrong. The men were yanking on their pants and yelling. There was a roaring, as if waves were breaking outside the door. A shrieking rode over the roar. Hiram didn't know the sound, but it filled him with a sickness so foul he prayed he was dreaming.

Outside, night had turned to day. The light was so bright Hiram pinched his eyes shut. He wished he could shut his ears. Dark shapes dashed about the flaming stable. A ball of flame burst from the inferno. The fiery orb crossed the sand, trailing a shower of sparks. It continued beyond the cliff without pause, galloping into frozen space.

Someone else ran for the cliffs.

Just short of the edge, Ben went to his knees. As he prayed, sparks settled to the sand about him like perished fireflies.

23

Kilbride banged on the door of Pomp's cabin in the dead of night, delirious and largely frozen. He had stumbled through the sands in a dream. Whores stared at him with mocking eyes and fires roared in his brain, and once, when he had stopped and bent double to ease his burning lungs, a hand, soft and gentle, had swept over his cheek, erasing his scars. As he lurched across the splintered porch, a gray ball darted past, banging hard against his knee. Only when Pomp opened the door did Kilbride remember the bleat.

Pomp registered neither surprise nor welcome. The old man sat a chair beside the dark fireplace and fetched a bottle of whisky.

Kilbride slumped in the chair. Three shots of whisky restored a portion of his senses. The cabin was freezing. He eyed the fireplace longingly.

To his surprise, Pomp built a fire. For the second time, flames brought Kilbride solace. A blanket settled across his shoulders. Kilbride watched the flames, half aware of the squatting silhouette, silently waiting.

"I burned Daniel Cole's stable to the ground."

The silhouette remained still. "The horse?"

"A fireball," said Kilbride. "Galloped off the cliff with hell riding on its back." The poetry pleased him. "I'm not done with Daniel

Cole. A man burns as easily as a horse. I might burn a few lifesavers too, to see how they gallop."

"Did anyone see you?"

"Vanished like a ghost," he said, with a smugness he didn't quite feel.

Pomp rose. "Why did you come here?"

Kilbride fidgeted, searching the corners of his mind for a fact he should know. He reached for the bottle. The whisky did not jog his memory.

"Without proof, they have nothing," he said.

"You have a motive. The law will come to see you. The lifesaving service too. This is an unexpected setback."

Kilbride touched three fingers to the tendriled cheek.

"Let them come," he said, but Pomp saw his hand shake.

Watching the faltering man made Pomp a little sad. He thought of the captain of the *Asia*. For a time, the man had bellowed to the heavens, embracing his punishment, but in the end everyone capitulated. How strong was the soul?

Pomp set to work.

Kilbride stared at the fire. He was warm. The blanket rested on his shoulders like an approving arm. Pomp came and went in shadow, but once Kilbride thought he saw a smile of approval. Closing his eyes, he conjured previous conquests performed under Pomp's eye. The old man would appreciate what he had planned for Daniel Cole. He would suffer agonies far beyond the horse.

Kilbride chuckled. Outside, the wind rose.

Pomp placed a plate of cold mutton stew on the table. "Best to look forward," said Pomp.

Kilbride ate ravenously. He had never tasted anything so good. Pomp placed a second bottle of whisky on the table. Kilbride helped himself. Stew fell from his mouth onto his front. He wiped his numb mouth with a sleeve.

"The bureaucrats are afraid of me," he said.

"It's possible, though we can no longer rely on it."

Kilbride felt as if the things he knew were slipping away from him. Pomp moved about. Kilbride watched the flames twist. He might have slept. If he did, his dreams were empty. The stew troubled his stomach.

Pomp thrust the candle close to Kilbride's face. The finger of flame was so much smaller than the one that had kissed the heavens. The old man studied the wounds. Kilbride felt the callused fingers move down the scars. The candle flame hurt his eyes, and his stomach clenched, but he recoiled before no man. He leaned forward, so Pomp could have a better look.

"Such intricacy makes you believe there is a God," the old man said.

To Kilbride's relief, Pomp put the candle on the table. Though the flame still rose, darkness crawled in. Kilbride shook his head, but the darkness did not retreat. He wished for the flame again.

The blanket left his shoulders. "I don't know what to do," he said.

Pomp helped him up.

"Time again for revenge."

The words returned him to the world. He was going to punish someone, but he couldn't remember who.

"Revenge?"

"Yes, my blemished friend. Revenge for trifles and troubles. Revenge for plans foiled, and ships and salvage escaped. Revenge against those who would steal our moonless nights and turn our home into a place of sameness and light. Revenge against the sheep, and the few misguided wolves who choose to protect them."

Kilbride stood up straight, a child on his best behavior. His head jerked slightly. Pomp imagined the poison making its slow touches, a fastidious artist dabbing an imperfect canvas. The vial was one of his more unique acquisitions, removed from an unfortunate vessel that never returned to its Uruguayan home. The keeper would be dead before dawn. His stomach would rupture, dousing his organs in bilious juices and whisky. It would not kill him instantly, however, providing time for reflection and a final lesson.

Taking Kilbride's elbow, Pomp led him into the night.

The shock of cold briefly bestowed the keeper's wits. "Where am I going?"

"Walk with me."

They walked. Kilbride's mind wandered. The old man led him by the elbow. The stars smiled. Kilbride smiled.

"The buried treasures," he said.

"A king's fortune," said Pomp. "Riches beyond compare."

Already, Kilbride felt their weight in his hands. It was just as he had imagined.

"Thank you," Kilbride said.

"Your just due."

Kilbride was surprised to see they had reached the road. It stretched away into the dark, toward Wellfleet. It was genius to bury the treasures right under their hoof beats.

"Just ahead," said Pomp.

Kilbride walked. The road looked the same. He wondered what clues he was looking for. He turned. The world was inhabited only by stars.

He searched until his stomach burst. The rupturing made him cry out. When he opened his mouth, sand poured in. He tried to sit up. Things spilled inside him. In the silence between his moans, he heard breathing that was not his own.

Pomp squatted a few yards away. He was curious about the poison's effects. He was pleased too. The keeper had covered a surprising distance on his own. At the last, the man had accommodated him nicely. He wouldn't even have to move the body. It wasn't a heavily traveled road. It would take time, but eventually someone would find him. Again, there would be one clear suspect.

Kilbride had closed his eyes to the pain, but he opened them with the first slash, the furrow like the brightest red ribbon. When he saw the knife, his bladder and bowels loosed as one.

"Please," he said.

These cuts were not neat. It was a rash crime of retribution. Finally, Pomp stood. "We choose our own fortunes," he said, not without sadness.

Just before dawn, the stars receded. The foot prodded. And the remains of John Kilbride shifted in the sand, dimly aware of a happy jingling.

24

Using a tarp and ropes, at dawn the men dragged Thoreau's blackened body from the foot of the cliffs to the sea. They watched wordlessly as the water slowly drew the horse away.

At noon, they held a brief ceremony beside the charred foundations of the stable. The day was the color of steel. Ben had fashioned a wooden cross. Only Captain Cole was absent as Ben pushed the cross into the ground.

Ben held another piece of wood. He had wanted to carve an epitaph to hang on the cross. He had struggled for words all morning.

He stared at the blank grain. "He put his trust in us," Ben said and began to cry.

The men stood awkwardly.

"There aren't words for something as senseless as this," Willie said.

Willie was surprised by the depth of his feeling. During their years together, the horse had done nothing but try to kick him. What weighed on him wasn't so much sadness for Thoreau's passing, though he was deeply sorry for the horse's suffering. What crushed down on him was a despair for mankind. It was a hopeless malaise that settled in his bones. The burning of an innocent animal was brutality that was hard to fathom, and yet Willie knew such senseless brutality would repeat itself again and again, in his lifetime and beyond.

The men knew who was responsible. John Kilbride had dropped his pocket watch at the top of the closest dune. Cole had recognized it from the Cork and Barrel.

Willie spat in the sand. "Goddamn if it's not a mixed up world," he said. "Times like these, I believe putting man in charge was a grievous mistake."

Ben turned to Willie as if seeing him for the first time. "The Lord God made man keeper of the beasts," Ben said.

"Well, we've botched the job mightily," said Willie. "If I was God, I'd wipe the slate clean and start fresh. We're a piss poor example of how life should be lived."

Martin looked toward the station. "Is Keeper Cole coming?"

"Can't you schoolboys do anything without him?" said Willie. "No, he's not coming. He's too practical to attend a horse's funeral. And probably too disgusted."

"There is nothing different in paying your respects to an animal," said Martin slowly. He did not want to offend the captain directly.

"I suspect Captain Cole would agree with you," said Willie, "but I'm certain our keeper is focused on more practical matters, like how we'll get the Lyle gun to the beach. If none of you wordsmiths can think of anything to say, I'm getting the hell out of here."

To everyone's surprise, Mayo spoke. "And in that day, I will make a covenant for them with the beasts of the field, and with the birds of the heavens, and with the creeping things of the ground. And I will break the bow and the sword and the battle out of the land, and will make them to lie down safely."

Cold filled the silence. Ben stared at the wood in his hand. One by one, the surfmen left, until only Ben remained.

When Willie returned at dusk, the board hung from the cross. Squatting, Willie read the words: "Lifesaver and Noble Friend. Example to Man."

Cole summoned Willie to his quarters that evening. "How are the men?"

"As well as can be expected," said Willie. "It's a sad blow that makes you question our future."

Cole was surprised by Willie's words. It was exactly how he felt. He was suddenly grateful to have Willie as a friend.

Willie undermined Cole's gratitude immediately. "No doubt, you've been berating yourself all day, Daniel, ascertaining that you alone are responsible for another of this world's lightning strikes."

"We both know I might as well have set the match."

"I'll allow that you might have been a bit too thorough, but you gave John Kilbride the punishment he's long deserved. You couldn't predict what would happen next. I'll bet Kilbride wasn't even certain until he struck the match."

"I appreciate what you're trying to do, but I know where fault lies."

"While you're heaping bodies on your conscience, why don't you toss in Gettysburg and the Inquisition? Daniel, it's a confused and troubled world, and it proceeds in the direction it chooses."

"That doesn't mean we walk through it with our eyes closed."

"You can predict the future? Maybe you'll tell me there's hope for us."

Cole was too tired to argue. He was also too tired to trust his own judgment, which was why he had decided to get Willie's counsel before making his decision. Now he wondered if this decision was poor judgment too.

Before he could change his mind, he said, "What should I do?"

Willie rarely felt sorry for Daniel Cole, but he felt sorry for him now. "For starters, I wouldn't go off and play vigilante again," Willie said. "Beating a man once has likely troubled the law enough. Hunting him down and punishing him again will force even the reluctant Constable Winslow's hand. The man worships you, but should you take matters into your own hands again, even Elkanah Winslow will be obligated to toss you in the coop. I doubt you'd keep this job either."

Willie knew his friend had already considered these unfoldings. "We both know you may already be on your way to dismissal," he continued. "Your record is the only thing that might save you. Justifiable as your action was, it was outside the law. You know it, I know it, and if Washington doesn't already know it, they'll know it soon enough.

"I don't expect an explanation for what you did, although I'm happy you did it. I expect you yourself don't have an explanation that satisfies you. But since you're asking my opinion, I'd advise you go directly to Sumner Kimball. He's an intelligent and reasonable man. John Kilbride has committed a crime against the Lifesaving Service and its property. No one can ignore that. You have evidence. I can't say how the Lifesaving Service views your initial pursuit of justice, but I do know that continuing to pursue the matter yourself will just bring more trouble down on your stubborn head."

Cole gave no indication he had heard anything. He stared at the door. Willie wondered if the keeper was still in the room.

"Let me also point out that your removal would put me in charge," said Willie. "Even you can't predict the outcome of that."

"I suspect the world would manage."

Willie studied his friend. He had never seen him so tired and beaten. He spoke as much to cheer himself. "Kilbride deserved punishment. If you see that as your mistake, fine. But I'll remind you again that everyone makes mistakes, Daniel. Look at us. You offered me this job, and I accepted it."

"I appreciate your advice."

Willie waited, but it was clear there would be nothing more. "I'll dismiss myself then," he said.

Willie paused at the door. "You might like to know we held a brief ceremony for Thoreau," he said. "That horse was smarter than the lot of us. If we ever needed proof, today's the day."

Cole nodded. Proof and proof again was exactly what they needed.

25

John Kilbride was a simple man. Cole knew whose help the Race Point keeper would seek.

Cole left the station the following morning before breakfast, slipping out the back door. He left a brief note for Willie on his desk, telling him to manage the station in his stead.

It was a fine morning, cold and clear, lazy wisps of white cloud napping in the sky. Cole walked northwest along the dirt track to Provincetown before turning off into the dunes. He had never had reason to visit Pomp's cabin before, but he had come across it several times while walking among the dunes for pleasure as he sometimes did. He knew this struck the men as odd, given they saw plenty of empty sand in the course of duty, but Cole found that walking among the dunes bestowed a sense of perspective and often lifted his spirits. The sun made the sand glitter, glacial moraine sparking thousandfold, the hummocked dunes rolling away in every direction. It was like sailing on a great, still sea, but it wasn't still at all. The sands were creeping westward, sneaking away beneath their feet. For ten years now, he had measured their movement. It was his secret game, pacing off the distance from the station to the cliff edge on the first of each month, notching the small retreat in the logbook. By his measure, the great cliffs were retreating westward at nearly three feet a year. Eventually, they would march right beneath the station.

One day, another man would walk the sands wholly ignorant of the lifesavers' presence.

Most men found their own insignificance unsettling. He was not among them. The sands' erasure pleased him. In nature, nothing stood still. Stillness brought failure, decay, and death. Nature understood this. He, too, preferred action.

Cole found Pomp's cabin just before noon. From a distance, the sagging, patchwork structure at the foot of the towering dune resembled a pebble at the toe of a boot, waiting to be scuffed aside. Pomp sat outside.

Cole approached from the south, his eyes on the old man. The cabin faced a flat swath of sand that ran for eighty yards before merging with the first dunes. Three goats basked in the sun in the lee of a dune. As Cole passed, the largest goat pawed the sand and bleated, shaking its beard.

Pomp sat on a crate fifty yards from the cabin. His head remained down, the top of the bowler directed at Cole like a solitary eye.

The old man stayed bent to his whittling until Cole was in front of him.

The bowler tilted back, flaked lips parting over white teeth. "A fine day is enhanced by pleasant surprise."

The deep voice was sleepy, but the eyes alertly walked Cole's length. Cole had decided against bringing his knife. He wanted no more violence. Now he wondered if his decision was foolish.

"I'm unarmed."

Pomp returned to whittling. "One would expect nothing less of a guest."

"I've come for John Kilbride."

"Again?"

"Yes."

"Am I his keeper? A strange surmise."

"Not so strange, given what we both know."

"Ah. I enjoy a good riddle." Pomp stood. Several crates were scattered about the cabin. Pomp fetched one and set it beside his own.

"Please join me. Perhaps between the two of us, we can decipher a riddle or two."

Cole sat. Pomp's whittling hand was inches away. Tufts of white hair sprouted below each knuckle.

"So many years, and now your first visit."

"I'm not much for visits."

"So I've come to learn, though you make exceptions. The Provincetown Cemetery comes to mind. I favor cemeteries myself. They remind me that time is not to be squandered. You and I, Keeper Cole, we have not squandered our time." Pomp balanced the knife on his knee. Producing a flask from his jacket pocket, he uncorked it. "A toast to the lives we've led."

"I didn't come to drink."

"A shame. It's fine whisky."

"John Kilbride burned our stable and killed our horse."

Pomp chuckled. "Not one for small talk. If I tell you where John Kilbride is, what will you do?"

"See to justice."

"Your justice?"

"No. I'll report it to the authorities."

"You have proof of his guilt?"

"He dropped his pocket watch."

Pomp took a swig and wiped his mouth. "He was a fine horse," he said. "Samuel Mullet was a fool to part with him. It's the rare man who sees the nobility in an animal. I am truly sorry."

Pomp turned the flask. The amber liquid bent the rays of the sun. "Your thorough beating broke him."

"That wasn't my intent," Cole said.

"Wasn't it?" Pomp closed his eyes and lifted his face to the sun. "John Kilbride, as we know, was a vain man. I will be honest with you, Captain Cole, though you are not honest with me. There are times I wish I had come to this world winsome. Life would have been easier. I might have become a whaling captain, pursuing the world's greatest quarry before retiring to comfort, admiration, and a passel of grandchildren bored to stone by my stories. Though it is impossible to predict such matters, I might even have discovered love. There is no telling where different physical gifts may have led. But the gods declined to bestow beauty upon me, and in this, I have been graced. Had I been born with advantages, I would have made less of myself. From this realization, I draw supreme contentment. Ugliness, at least as man defines it, is my prize."

Threat hummed about him, but Cole felt drowsy, a child slipping away before the last refrain of a bedtime story.

Pomp put the flask away and returned to whittling. "Most men are not content, are they, my good captain? There is always something more to yearn for. Riches, of course, another woman to covet, another life to consider. And so the days pass, not in living, but in dreaming. Yearning is unique to our species, our distinctive downfall. Does a wolf pine for matters beyond its control? You and I are most like the animals. We know our place in this world, and we have made the most of it. But we are imperfect."

Cole focused on the knife's scrapings. "Where is John Kilbride?"

"What makes you think I know the whereabouts of Race Point's keeper?"

"He's your partner."

"Partner? In what enterprise, pray tell?"

"Mooncussing."

"An impolite accusation."

"I am being honest."

"It is a start," said Pomp.

The first clouds, nudged by the sea breeze, tumbled in from the east like wrestling children.

Pomp stopped whittling. "What if I told you I have drawn ships ashore? What if I told you I have taken what I wanted, that I've drawn this very knife down a soft belly? Do you know that a woman who refuses to swallow her husband's ejaculate, will, upon the deck of a sinking ship, choke down a platter of jewels? What if I admit to you that I have killed for the game alone? What good does this knowledge do you? It only confirms what you already know. But knowledge is not proof. Civilization won't condemn me until I pull my blade from its heart."

Scorn filled the gray eyes.

"My tenacious captain, civilization is steering us both to our end. We both know you have no proof of my crimes, and in the civilized world, without proof, there is no crime. Ignorance and confusion render man indecisive. The line between good and evil fogs. And as we become more civilized, the fog will become worse. In years to come, men will commit acts that render my works infantile. Daniel, if I am correct, means 'God is judge,' but he isn't interested."

The men sat in silence.

"I merely do what I am compelled to do," said Pomp, smiling slightly. "You are among the few who understand."

"You will make a mistake," Cole said. "I won't miss the opportunity when you do."

"Should the opportunity present itself, I have no doubt you will capitalize on it. I admire your abilities, Captain Cole, putting you again among a distinct minority. You and I are from a different place, a place not long for this world. We are warriors. And the time for warriors is passing."

"You are a murderer."

Pomp shrugged. "I may kill, and you, no doubt, save. We have chosen different sides of the chessboard. But as the game proceeds, the pieces mix, and their intent can change. And now our game has taken an intriguing turn."

"You were on the beach," said Cole.

"I found the *Asia's* captain. You found the girl. Two chess pieces, perhaps of equal value, perhaps not."

In the distance, a goat bleated.

"You killed them both," Cole said.

"However you see it, they both arrived on our shore with life in them."

"The girl divulged nothing," Cole said.

"You were by her side?"

Cole said nothing.

"The boy interests me greatly," said Pomp.

Cole knew why he had come. He cared nothing for the treasure or John Kilbride. He wanted no more heartbreak for Nellie Paine. He would do whatever was required.

"I told you to stay away from him."

"No idle threat. Whether I choose to heed your advice, Captain Cole, depends on my whims and yours."

Cole felt the quieting. Again, its advance was not gentle, as something lulled to sleep, but swift, pointed, and poised. Cole welcomed it. It surged through him until it beat behind his eyes and fought to leap through his fingers. He saw the coil in the old man's slouch, the still hand on the knife, the steel like an answer.

Pomp shifted, the faint rustle of garment a shout.

The quiet rose until it wobbled precariously, liquid in a brimming goblet.

"We might solve the puzzle with the right clues," Pomp said.

Remembering turned Cole away. "There are no clues. The boy knows nothing. I questioned him at length. So did the designate."

"A silly man," said Pomp, "but no doubt efficient in his fashion. I'm sure each of us was painstakingly thorough, but this does not always guarantee success. Sadly, the *Asia's* captain proved a warrior, departing this world with his secret and leaving us two pertinent questions. How did this item come ashore and where is it now?"

Cole heard again the shrieking winds. "You think it survived the wreck," he said.

"I'm certain of it," Pomp said. "Though it makes ours an uneven exchange, I will tell you that forces nearly as great as nature are afoot."

Cole tried to hide what he knew, but it was too late in life to acquire new talents.

"You are not surprised," said Pomp.

"No."

"Then perhaps we stand upon the same page. I will be blunt, Captain Cole, for bluntness is what we know. If this item is as valuable as we believe, it will easily profit us both. You who will otherwise grow old on a surfman's meager savings, and I who have grown tired of commonplace baubles."

"I don't consort with murderers."

"Perhaps you do. It is only a matter of where restraint ends. I believe you understand." Pomp gestured to the three goats. "There is one less than before. I chose to use his liver as an allegorical message, sacrificing one innocent with the hope of sparing another."

Pomp whistled. Lifting their heads as one, the goats trotted toward them.

"See how they come? One day, I will make stew of all of them, but there is not a trifle of hesitation in their step. Only man sees his future."

Pomp smiled at the approaching goats with fatherly affection. "Murderer? I have openly declared it. But you, Keeper Cole, are not so honest. Freed of moral constraint, you would have killed John Kilbride with your bare hands. That is your strength. But it is also mine."

The goats stood close, bearded and staring.

"Silly creatures," said Pomp. "Always hungry."

The surfmen were repairing rope on the porch, enjoying the last of the fading afternoon, when the captain strode past them, proceeding through the door and up the stairs without a word.

That evening, Pomp removed a yellowlegs from one of the cages. Unwelcome agitation made it difficult to still his hands. The small bird almost squirmed loose as Pomp pinned it to the table.

After Daniel Cole's departure, he had remained on the crate. Their meeting had provided them both understanding, and it had been pleasant watching the keeper falter. The man understood himself better than most.

The game was not over yet. But their conversation had shed no new light on the *Asia*, and this soured Pomp's good feelings. Since the night on the beach when the entertainment had turned, with the shout of a single name, into something of untoward promise, he had devoted substantial thought to the puzzle. His effort had brought nothing. Answers continued to evade him, savvy jackrabbits making perfect use of cover. His faltering made him question his abilities. This made him angry.

He applied the knife abruptly, nearly losing the bird to the first penetration. Calming himself, he mustered steadiness in his disobedient hand. Opening a tidy cavity in the small swell of breast, he probed delicately. The yellowlegs made no sound, but its eyes flicked about with disjointed purpose, and its wings pushed against his hand. Pomp admired the bird's soundless struggle. Pain was the truest measure of man and animal. Most men screamed so that you could hear them in Boston. When they weren't screaming, they were weeping, panting, spitting up fluids and promises, and offering him things he didn't want and they could no longer offer. There were exceptions, however, and these were what kept him interested. Yet, at the last, even these men came unhinged. Or, perhaps, they became themselves.

Pomp maneuvered among the seamless clustering of organs. Selecting the one he wanted, he worked patiently. He withdrew the knife slowly. Balanced on the tip of the blade, the heart trailed gossamer webbing more slender than anything man could contrive, as fragile as eggshells, as functional as steel. The bird pushed beneath his hand.

Soothing balm and illumination arrived at the same instant. He saw again the wild eyes of the *Asia's* captain and listened as the man spit blood, cursing Andrew Carnegie and crying out for his daughter. Pomp felt his spirit soar. Foolish to think the man's entreaties were founded on love alone.

He heard his own self-absorbed voice. *Do you know that a woman who refuses to swallow her husband's ejaculate will, upon the deck of a sinking ship, choke down a platter's worth of jewels?*

Pomp celebrated his epiphany by removing additional organs. He had not lost his touch. The eyes remained wide for an exceedingly long time.

26

When Marmaduke Matthews opened the door to the brash knocking, the sight of the mute boy sent cold into his bones. The boy stared through him. He never handed over the note. Marmaduke wondered what might happen if he didn't take the note from his hand. When he did, the boy spun and shot into the dark like a sparrow.

Pomp's summons were always short. Even in its brevity, this note made the night swim.

When Marmaduke arrived, Pomp was waiting, a shadow beneath the oak. The old man didn't acknowledge him. Pomp stood looking down at Provincetown, the lights like fading matchsticks. The oak's boughs creaked.

"A paltry foothold," said Pomp. "Night reveals us."

Marmaduke saw the shovels. The sickness in his stomach spilled into his heart.

"Let's play out a hunch," Pomp said.

It was hard digging. They chipped away at the frozen till. Within minutes, Marmaduke's back screamed. Quickly, the remainder of his body joined in lament. Striking the ground with his shovel, he heard his rasping gasps.

Marmaduke dug at the foot of the girl's grave. After pulling up the cross, Pomp shoveled at the head. The old man worked with abandon, his shovel never pausing. After thirty minutes, Pomp reached soft earth. They switched places.

They uncovered the top of the casket. Marmaduke barely felt the crowbar in his hands. They both pried until the pine shrieked protest and split with a crack.

Pomp raised the lid. The smell was like a stockyard.

"Hello child," he said.

Marmaduke pleaded with himself, but his eyes acted on their own accord. The sunken face was impassive, but the slight cock of the head pronounced judgment. The bare arms, bent at the elbow so they could hold the doll, were as thin as chicken bones. A moist sliver crawled from the girl's nose. Another inched along the edge of an ear.

Marmaduke clung to his wits until Pomp began cutting, and then he ran. He plunged into the woods without account for a path. Branches slashed his face and tore his clothes. He fell, scrabbled forward, rose, ran, and fell again. He did not feel the falls or the slashing branches. He might have prayed, he didn't know.

In the boughs of the black trees, the wind sang like a choir, merciless and damning.

The abdominal flesh parted in a furrow. Pomp probed patiently, his fingers meandering through the slushy fishings like someone walking through a bog. He walked his fingers up and down the girl's stomach. He cut open the lungs and the rectum too.

He stepped out of the grave. Wiping his hands on a cloth, he had a brief smoke, consulting the night sky. The reverend's abrupt departure was unexpected but amusing. The sight of the burly minister crashing into the woods took part of the sting from the night's failure, although now it meant more work for him.

Back in the grave, Pomp considered the girl, the yawning cavity like a laugh. He was wrong, but he was not defeated. He would return to the boy.

He arranged the dress so the girl was covered. He had not meant for a child to die. His eye went to the doll in the garish dress. It had fallen to the side. It was an ungainly thing, fashioned roughly of wood, but a child didn't care. As he picked it up to place it back in the girl's arms, he recognized victory. He laughed, the doll oddly light in his hands.

The doll smiled up at him, a laudatory smile it seemed, and he was not surprised to see the smile was slightly askance. A man of the sea would be competent with woodwork. He might lovingly craft a shape adequate to meet his daughter's approval, but his hand might not be so deft with a fine brush. Still, the work was impressive. Cricking the doll's neck back slightly, Pomp peered at the smile with appreciation. Pressed back in the mouth, only close inspection revealed the teeth were painted on cork. A watertight vessel.

Touching the tip of the fishing knife to the doll's chest, he applied gentle pressure. The wood resisted, and then the blade pushed through. Pomp worked the blade carefully down the torso, just deep enough to part the wood; a swim to shore and time in the grave had turned the wood supple. Pomp wormed two fingers through the incision. Wax caressed a fingertip. Carefully, he worked the cloth cylinder, roughly two thumb lengths' long and sewn at both ends, through the opening.

Gently twisting, Pomp cracked the wax coating. Taking the knife, he cut away a stitched end. The cloth beneath the wax was dry, as were the sheaves of tightly rolled paper inside. Pomp did not unroll them; the night was already bluing. There would be time later.

Pomp slid the lid in place and bowed his head. "You did not die in vain."

An hour before dawn, Pomp finished smoothing the grave. As he walked through the Provincelands, the first snowflakes touched his face with a lover's caress.

The first flakes swirled through the cemetery and danced about the oak. Then settling upon the freshly dug soil, they waned. Their followers, however, fell undaunted. Slowly, they took hold, white lilies disguising a dark plain.

27

Pomp gave Captain Edwin Merton a nod for his foresight. The man had foolishly sailed toward a vapor, but he had prepared for the possibility of his demise. The brief instructions to his daughter, written on cheap stationary, were clear, as was Andrew Carnegie's name. No doubt, at the last, the father had repeated his instructions. The girl had placed her trust in no one; the boy had told him the truth.

Pomp separated the instructions from the remaining sheaves. That the accompanying papers were penned in German provided only a minor setback.

It took all of his self-control, but Pomp waited until late the following night. He did not want to be spotted by a nosy parishioner seeking God's solace.

Snow had turned to hard rain. The brick pathway glistened. The minister's cottage sat behind the church at the top of a hill. The steep path always made Pomp smile—a deterrent to the elderly and the infirm, those apt to trouble a minister most. Pomp thought of Abby. She was likely panting before the minister fell on her. Man of God, vessel of sin. Life was entertaining.

When the sleepy-eyed minister opened the door, Pomp said, "I require your expertise."

The minister closed his eyes. His jowls worked silently. He opened his eyes again. Nothing in his manner had changed. A deep scratch ran across his right cheek, narrowly skirting the eye.

"Perhaps, God did play a hand," said Pomp, pushing past, "but we can thank him later."

Trundling into the study, the minister sat without question at the large desk. It was not like the man to be silent or patient.

The study was unnaturally bright. Lanterns burned on three mantles, as well as on the desk and two tables. There was a fire in the fireplace. A stack of books rested on the table closest to the fire.

Pomp placed the papers on the desk. "I need you to decipher this," he said.

Marmaduke took up the four sheaves. He ticked through them and then looked up.

"They were inside the doll," said Pomp. "As you recall, there was a misstep first." Pomp caught the slight tic.

Marmaduke Matthews looked down at the papers. "German," he said. "I recognize the pedigree."

Marmaduke felt the old man's impatient gaze, but he was already absorbed by the writing. The penmanship was elegant. He took a moment to appreciate it; no hesitation, no redirection in the flowing script. The instructions had been penned by a confident man. He ran a fingertip along the edge of a page. The paper was constructed of superb stock.

"If you're finished fondling, I'd welcome your getting to the act," said Pomp. "I understand that has never been a hurdle in the past."

"Of course." The old man no longer terrified him. It was not courage that bolstered him. It was more an immeasurable weariness, stretching beyond any horizon his dulled mind could see. Returning from the cemetery, he had slept through the day, a deep sleep, untroubled by dreams. He woke deadened. He had eaten nothing, but he was not hungry. He had dressed and gone to the bookshelves. Collecting what he required, he had begun reading.

With fear gone, he felt an odd empowerment, but he was not foolish enough to delay. Moving a lantern close, he read.

When he finished, he was mildly surprised to see the cowled form standing before him, a storybook figure from a dusty tale in the past. He placed his hands on the desk. They felt heavy, the flesh between the fingers moist.

Briefly, the familiar Marmaduke Matthews resurfaced. His mind unspooled options in rapid-fire succession. It would not do to trick the old man. Fooling him was unlikely. Marmaduke knew the old man had examined the papers closely. Pomp knew they were of value. At the least, the old man had recognized the name that leapt from the foreign prattle. It was their greatest find, a votive candle in a dark passage.

"God does traffic in irony," said Pomp. "When at last I want to hear from you, you are rendered speechless."

"It is astonishing. A harbinger of a new world."

"Poetic, but I require something more tangible."

Marmaduke felt the sheaves in his fingers, light as butterflies. They had traveled from a distant continent, spurned a hungry sea, and rested within the earth. They were almost as durable as the product they promised.

"Allow me to share in your astonishment," said Pomp.

Marmaduke heard his throat clear. A figurine of Jesus regarded him kindly from a nearby bookcase, arms outstretched.

"The French economist Michel Chevalier claims we Americans have a perfect passion for railroads. I believe Monsieur Chevalier is blinded to our true character. The railroad is merely the means. Our real passion is money." Marmaduke almost smiled. It sounded like a sermon. Profit. The one true God.

"Save your wind for rutting and get to the point."

Marmaduke looked to Jesus. *Why would I be troubled by whoring, when I have resurrected the dead?*

"The papers contain word of a discovery from Germany, a discovery that was to be delivered to Mr. Andrew Carnegie. Mr. Carnegie employs a retinue of laboratory technicians to research the mysteries of steel manufacture. Though steel is now the foundation of our society, the steel masters still know nothing of what unfolds inside the blast furnace. Their creation remains an imperfect alchemy, although people still scramble to buy it, mystery or no. In a nation starved for steel, imperfection is easily swallowed."

Marmaduke allowed his mind to wander for a moment, to a new world, far from this one. "Mr. Carnegie, however, appears to be a man of singular focus, able to see beyond immediate gain. He wishes to ferret out the weaknesses of his product and eliminate them. And so he operates his laboratories, at least one of them, apparently in Germany."

"The tide has turned," said Pomp.

"Yes."

The import turned both men silent.

Marmaduke looked to the bookcase. "It's not just the railroads," he said. "Steel is being turned to raising America up. In Chicago and New York, work is underway on great, steel-girded buildings. They say that, one day, America will be a land of sprawling cities that scrape the heavens."

The beneficent Jesus gave neither approval nor disapproval. "Steel that is both stronger and cheaper than the product offered by the competition is of fathomless value. These papers outline a formula for such a steel. Steel that will bury Mr. Carnegie's competitors."

Marmaduke tapped a forefinger to the last sheaf of paper. "The plans are beyond value, but they have been assigned value. These are the contractual arrangements. Had the *Asia's* captain succeeded in delivering this formula, he would have received five thousand dollars. Plus an additional thousand if Mr. Carnegie had considered the information delivered in timely fashion."

The study was quiet but for the pop of the fire and the drum of rain, both men absorbing the absurdity of the sum and a world of capitalism beyond their ken.

"Perhaps you should have your prayers ready," Pomp said. "With such largesse at stake, the *Asia's* captain might defy the flames of hell and return for his prize."

Marmaduke wondered whether his prayers were any longer of value. He stared at the mottled hand.

"I'll take them," said Pomp, "and you may return to your communion with God."

Marmaduke felt the soft rush through his fingers, opportunity spilling away. He was surprised by how easy it was to give the papers up. The first step in atonement was to reject your demons.

The fire burned itself out. Wind and rain moved the trees. The church bell tolled, and tolled again. Marmaduke Matthews admired the majestic white steeple, made gray, but no less regal, by the night and the rain. He bent his head. God had provided him chance for redemption.

He began to write. At first he wrote slowly, with hesitation, struggling with the words. Then he forgot himself. He bent to the paper, words pouring to the page. When he finished, a smile touched his lips. It was a sermon, really, the words graced finally with truth. Sliding the letter into an envelope, he sealed it. He placed the envelope in the box just inside the door. Obed Shiverick came twice a week. By happy coincidence, the postman would arrive in the morning, no doubt cursing the rain. Curmudgeonly messenger delivering the words to the one man who mattered.

He took care in dressing. He strode swiftly through the rain, white vestments flowing behind him. His hands shook only once, searching for a candle on the shelf in the sacristy.

From the pulpit, the candle threw reluctant light to the first three pews. Beyond that, night reigned. In his imagination, the dark reaches upon which he gazed unrolled like waves in a sea, pew upon pew of souls, hopeful and waiting.

The first words were awkward. The echo of the empty room rang in his ears, and he knew he was a sad man, alone in a dark church. Slowly, though, self-consciousness left him. The words became a hymn. Smiling faces appeared in the pews. His mother and father, Abby, the little girl from the *Asia,* and finally Nellie Paine. Nellie Paine did not smile. Seeing this, he faltered, but as he peered with all his heart, he saw in her angelic visage contentment, and, though not love, acceptance. It was everything a flawed man could hope for.

His heart swelled, providing wings to the words, raw, bereft of hesitation or subterfuge, a painful bleating of hypocrisy and mockery and wanton lust. The congregation listened in rapt silence. It was his greatest sermon ever.

When he finished, he thought briefly of the old man. Even in his epiphany, he knew he was still afraid. He picked up the pistol beside the candle. Angel of mercy, quick as a flash.

Outside, the rain drummed its approval.

28

The downpour that applauded Reverend Matthews' sermon turned to snow with the dawn. The snow fell heavily for two days. On the third morning, it stopped, replaced by a bright sun. The Cape radiated a fairytale glistening.

Marmaduke Matthews' letter and the news of his suicide reached Cole at noon, delivered by Obed Shiverick, who, irked by the snow's delays, addressed the minister's passing in two terse sentences, turned his horse, and left.

Cole read the letter in his quarters. The letter was divided into two parts. The first was confessional. This Cole read just once, absorbing the breadth of the reverend's transgressions with brief pause. When he came to Nellie's name, he felt the familiar press of anger and self-reproach. Ghosts that never left, they had hovered over him even as he'd kissed her. He deserved their haunting. His oversight was unforgivable.

In his visits following Samuel Paine's death, he had seen how Nellie resided with one foot in her husband's grave. Fixing tea, accepting the food he brought, sitting by the window filled with quiet woods, she would suddenly start, as if surprised to find herself in the world of the living. Her helplessness had shouted in his face, but his preoccupation with his duties had made him blind.

When Marmaduke Matthews had come to the cottage, her abject lassitude was no match for his lust. Cole had arrived several hours later. Pressed against a bedroom dresser, Nellie had struck at him wildly and then gone to bed like a child. He had cleaned up the cottage—a table overturned, broken reading glasses, a Bible face down on the floor—and then sat in a chair outside her door. For the second time in his life, he had had no idea what to do. When Hiram came home from school, he had told the young boy his mother had taken ill. The boy had accepted this and gone off to play with friends.

When Nellie came out of the bedroom, she had dressed and straightened herself, but something was not quite right with her eyes. She asked first for her son. Then she extracted a promise of secrecy and asked him to leave.

He would never know if the minister had come to the cabin with immoral intent; though it hung between them always, he and Nellie never discussed the incident again. It served no point, but he had never stopped debating—intended rape or dark alchemy fired by animal spark. The letter in his hands insinuated the latter, but the discovery brought no closure. The reverend's confession only confirmed their shared sin. His self-absorption had permitted the minister's lust. His hatred of the minister had its roots in two sinners.

Folding the confessional, he held it over the candle flame.

Though Reverend Matthews was uncharacteristically plain, Cole read the second part of the letter twice. The details of the minister's collusion with Pomp were clear. Marmaduke Matthews was a sinner, but he was an organized and intelligent man. The letter laid out Pomp's mooncussing clearly, and the machinations that made it work: the whore who relayed the confidences of clients, the minister who betrayed the trust of parishioners, the keeper who worked beside Pomp. Marmaduke Matthews was thorough, listing dates, ships, and, in some instances, spoils, in ledger-like detail. The letter spelled Pomp's end. Even civilization could not ignore him now.

Reverend Matthews had described the *Asia's* circumstances in equal detail. Cole had been wrong. Edwin Merton had thwarted the sea. Conceit had rendered him unbending. Now, the girl lay mutilated, and stakes beyond his imaginings rested in Pomp's hands. Cole cared little for one, and everything for the other.

Cole placed the second half of the letter in the bottom drawer of his desk, sliding it under the keepsake box.

He extinguished the candle, the smoke making a last reedy ascent. For a moment, his thoughts turned to the bald man, real as death, though not on the manifest; hand burnt by some laboratory mishap, laid out on the frozen earth in expensive shoes, perhaps his first extravagant purchase. It was not hard for Cole to imagine the steel master's last moments—painstaking work, dreams of wealth and fame, all wrenched from his grasp by an uncaring tempest.

Cole stood. He could not linger in daydream. By now, Pomp knew of the minister's suicide. Word of such an event would have reached Boston. But the old man would remain unaware of the reverend's letter and his own jeopardized position. Then again, Pomp had had the formula for three days. It was probably already too late. Whatever his intentions, the old man had likely executed them already.

Cole went downstairs and issued orders.

He waited until evening. Bending, he opened the bottom drawer. The bowie knife rested at the back of the drawer, behind the keepsake box. He carried the knife during rescues; more than once, it had cut through lines and fallen rigging. He kept the blade sharp. Before he took the knife, he let his fingers rest on the box.

Standing at the window, Cole heard the protest of banging pots. The law would not move quickly enough. No more lives could be risked. He looked to the day house, smoke furling from the blackened stovepipe. He imagined the strong-limbed boy inside. Retreating sands and log books were not the only markers of passing time, or opportunity missed. He wondered how things might have been if he had caught the girl at the last.

Snow, thick as lamb's wool, began to fall. Cole raised the window. Shuffling down the sloped shingles, he reached the edge of the roof and dropped to the snow.

29

P omp, too, was hamstrung by debate. For two days now they had conferred in the cabin, and they had not confined themselves strictly to debate. Their shared pleasure was finer than it had ever been. He was not naïve. Abby was trying to persuade him with word and deed. Between couplings, Abby pasted and sewed. When she was done, her deft fingers working miracles, she returned to convincing him, and when she tired of that, she sat and looked out at the snow. He read poetry, but even the loveliness of Keats and the honesty of Byron failed to aid his divided mind.

He sat sipping whisky in the gloom, watching the snow, pleased how its silence made no attempt to influence him. Abby dozed on the cot near the fire, full curve of a hip adding its shape to the shifting shadows. Pomp would have preferred cold, but Abby had provided invaluable service, and, with time, friendship. The warmth turned the yellowlegs active. Their twitterings and scratchings mingled with the fire's snappings. The formula rested on his lap.

Pomp turned his mind to Andrew Carnegie again. Marmaduke Matthews had spoken to him as if he were a child. It was true, he took little interest in the world's events, but he kept abreast of items that interested him. Regarding the robber barons, he had read as much as he could. Carnegie, Cornelius Vanderbilt, the railroad millionaires Jim Fisk and Jay Gould, they both fascinated and disgusted him. They were as ruthless as any wild animal, wolves with ledgers and fob watches; Pomp admired the broken lives and destruction they scattered in their uncaring wake. But they harnessed powers primitive man once worshipped and feared, and they harnessed those powers with foolish nonchalance.

Pomp saw man's path. Generations more clever and conceited would follow. The day would come when man controlled much of the world, although it was possible this very control might provoke the greatest disasters of all. The thought made Pomp smile. Man was arrogant, and arrogance inevitably wrought downfall. Outside, the snow wept confirmation.

Now, he had opportunity to play a small role in the grand pageant. Yet he remained at a crossroad, delayed by the very avarice that had seduced the robber barons. Abby was clear in what they should do. She had calculated a sum, shocking even to Pomp, to which she was certain Andrew Carnegie would accede. Her figuring was nothing short of a marvel. Again, he had admired her rapier intellect. Wealthier than either of them had ever imagined, they would be free to do whatever they chose. As for criminal guilt, there was none. Many would find his methods distasteful, but there was no guilt in his unearthing of the plans. He had simply outwitted the sheep.

Abby snored. The world waited.

Pomp saw the shadow moving through the snow. It was the greatest pleasure savored so far.

Raising his tumbler, he swallowed the remaining whisky. "To men of decision," he said. Removing his bowler, he woke Abby.

Willie discovered Cole's disappearance. Cole had told him he would be occupied with paperwork, but when Willie finally climbed the stairs and knocked on the keeper's door to announce supper, silence told him he had been duped.

Martin and Antone had just returned from patrol. Standing inside the door, the two men swatted snow from their oilskins.

"Keep them on," said Willie. "Keeper Cole is gone."

Martin froze in his swatting. "Gone? He did not tell us?"

"No."

"Why would he leave without telling us?"

In other circumstances, the Swede's bewilderment would have been amusing.

Willie worked to tame his windmilling thoughts. "When was the last time anyone saw the captain?"

In the flurry of discussion, it was decided the keeper last appeared late in the afternoon, coming downstairs to send Mayo to the equipment room and Willie to the kitchen to start supper.

For a moment, Willie forgot the gravity of the situation. Martin and Antone were dispatched to patrol; Hiram assigned to lookout in the day house. At the last, Cole had dispatched Mayo to the equipment room to inspect their readiness, while he himself had gone obediently to the kitchen. They were all children.

"It is snowing," Martin said. "He left the station when vessels might be jeopardized."

The rest of the men were silent.

Willie ticked through what he knew. The day had started as dull and predictable as any. They had eaten breakfast, forced as always to wait while Antone droned the Lord's Prayer over congealing beans. They had cleaned up. To everyone's relief, the snow had seen to the cancellation of the surfboat drill. Obed Shiverick had grumpily delivered the mail.

Willie ran up the stairs. He went right to the bottom drawer. Daniel Cole was a creature of habit.

When he returned, Willie carried a curious acceptance, as if someone had held a mirror up to the world he knew and turned it just so, revealing the hidden corners. The neatly made cots with their threadbare blankets, the scuffed floor, the squat stove with its bent pipe, his own playing cards fanned across the table—Willie was struck with the peculiar feeling that he was seeing, not their lives in that moment, but a carefully arranged museum display in some distant time. A new world was dawning. It would not reach back.

He told the men what he had read. He ended with the only possible conclusion. "Captain Cole has gone after Pomp."

Within minutes, the men were moving quickly through the snow. Willie left no one behind to man the station. No one questioned his decision. Pomp was one man, but he was like no other.

30

Cole never saw the harpoon. He had crouched behind a snowy pile of lobster traps, watching the dusky figure in the window. The bowler hadn't moved.

Slipping out the back window, Pomp came up from behind. The oak handle struck Cole first in the back of the head, knocking him face first into the snow. As the world tipped toward blackness, hands turned him on his back. The second and third blows turned his legs to water, the water saturated with excruciating pain. The world receded. Cole welcomed the savior darkness.

When Cole regained consciousness, he was bound to a chair. He tried to move. Fire raged up his legs. He cried out.

A hand gently pressed his shoulder. "Stay still."

Cole tasted blood and bile. The cabin was nearly dark. He faced the remains of a failing fire, a last charred log glowing with firefly embers. Pomp squatted before him.

Something pulsed behind his eyes, performing a steady drumbeat. Slowly, he lowered his chin. He looked at his legs. Nausea rushed into his throat. He shut his eyes and concentrated on the drumbeat.

The old man spoke at his feet. "I am truly sorry."

When Cole opened his eyes again, the old man was leaning forward, examining the blood-soaked bandages. He was hatless.

Beneath the downy hairs, the liver-spotted pate resembled stained earth.

"Your shins are broken. I want you to know I am a capable man when it comes to applying a splint. You will walk again, though not, I'm afraid, without a pronounced limp. It marks the end of your lifesaving days." The old man looked up at him with regret. "You left me no choice. They are clean breaks. I soaped the wounds. I want no chance of infection."

Pomp disappeared. When he returned, Cole took the tin cup. The water, cold in his mouth, dried before it reached his parched throat.

The old man disappeared again. Cole heard the sound of water pouring and a single soft admonishment. A horse whinnied. The sound made Cole sad.

Returning with a chair, Pomp sat before him, leaning close. Cole smelled stale sweat and the faintest drift of something pleasant, like roses after a rain.

"I am nearly as saddened by the circumstances as you are, Captain Cole. Now, here we sit, if not undamaged, at least alive."

Pomp's voice arrived in waves, tumbling forward one moment, receding the next. A doll rested in the old man's lap. Long fingers gently stroked the doll's hair. Cole knew the doll, but his aching head balked.

"Reverend Matthews wrote a letter," Cole said. "He confessed everything."

The words stuck to his tongue, joining blood and bile. He swallowed and prepared to be sick.

Pomp handed him the cup. Cole wanted to drink it down, but he knew if he did, it would come right back up. He took several sips.

The great brow bobbed. "A man of moderation. There are few of us left. The good reverend, as you now likely know, did not grasp moderation in any form."

Cole felt no satisfaction. "His letter finishes you."

"Damning, is it?"

"You will go to prison."

"Perhaps. And the repentant reverend?"

"He shot himself."

"Ah. Do you think he sitteth on the right hand already?"

Cole fought the drowsiness fogging his mind. Delay was all he had, though he had no idea what delay might accomplish. He remembered the old man's question, a small victory nearly drummed away by the pulsing in his head.

"He's dead," Cole said.

"You realize this puny man's death, and his damning letter, sees the two of us to a meeting beside the road. Life continues on, no matter who takes leave of the stage or where they go."

Cole watched the stroking of the snowy fingers. He recognized the smiling doll. She had hair and a new dress, but the smile was still lopsided.

Pomp looked down at the doll. "Silent and unreadable, and bereft of yearning," he said. "The perfect keeper of secrets. The reverend wrote of her resurrection?"

"I know everything."

"Does it make any difference?"

Cole didn't know. He heard a whisper of cloth behind him, a dress sweeping across a pivoting calf. Pomp's eyes flicked to the sound and then returned to him. Cole yearned to see what the old man had seen. He wanted summer's breeze to run through the dunes again. He had neglected the small things, and they were not small at all. But he could only look forward at the gray eyes.

"Tell me, Keeper Cole, are these plans something you truly want? Are they something your very soul desires? Or, are they merely something tiresome duty demands?"

"The plans belong to a world beyond us." The words slushed in his head.

"We both see the truth," said Pomp.

Pomp's hand stopped its stroking. He gave Cole great consideration. "You realize, Captain Cole, that, distasteful as it may be to you, in the end we are brothers. I will speak honestly. I have not yet reached a decision regarding these papers. You might influence me."

After a brief silence, Cole spoke. "I doubt that."

"Only truly great men underestimate their influence."

The fiery pain beat in waves. Cole contemplated unconsciousness, but unconsciousness was failure.

"What do you think Andrew Carnegie would think of us, Captain Cole?"

Cole pushed his head up. It was impossibly heavy. "We are of no concern to him."

"Triflings, are we not? Dust motes lodged briefly on the great wheels of change. In the end, even the Andrew Carnegies are swept away. It is foolish of anyone to overestimate their importance, and yet most everyone does. You and I, Captain Cole, are among the few exceptions. We have been educated by the sea. The sea does not recognize good or evil, fool or genius, man or child. The dispassionate waters seize them all. The sea has provided us opportunity to flare brightly on history's stage. How we shall act? Would you alter, if only for a time, the great current's course?"

The smell of stale sweat choked him. Cole reached for the wet roses. Fertile spring. The promise of hope.

"Our greedy friend, John Kilbride," Pomp said, "would have run to Andrew Carnegie as fast as his oversized boots could fly, but choice is beyond him now."

Cole fought to recall the man. The pulsing continued, waves breaking, but the silence between the waves was deeper than anything Cole had ever heard, and soothing too. Cole forced himself to listen.

"A king's ransom in reward," said Pomp, "or perhaps something better. Destroying the plans would strike a blow against a civilization we both hold in contempt."

There was something beautiful in the old man's face, but Cole did not share in it. He felt a helplessness, terrible and heavy. He controlled neither sea nor land. Mothers and daughters died in fires. Widows were raped. Men harvested land and sea with mad thoughtlessness and died for the whisper of money, taking their children with them.

"Give me the plans," he said.

"For once, Captain Cole, you do not operate from a position of power."

"We can work together."

Beauty spilled into the gray eyes.

"Give me the formula," Cole said, "and I'll destroy the letter."

Sadness swept away the beauty.

"You offer me freedom," said Pomp. "But if I return the plans to you, Andrew Carnegie and his ilk will wall us all inside a prison."

In the silence between the waves, Cole worked to complete this one thing. "They will accomplish that whether you return the plans or not."

Pomp knew now why the blackfish had come ashore. He sat back.

Cole no longer saw the old man. Blood clots travel where they will, swimming in their fashion until they lodge and swim no more. Now, he stood by the glittering water, watching the beating waves, a warm wind blowing back their feathered tops as they tossed themselves playfully against the shore. A woman watched the waves beside him, her head light against his shoulder. The woman said nothing, but her gossamer touch told him how the world should be. It was pleasant to look at the water and feel no responsibility.

When the keeper sagged, Pomp cried out. Then he reached forward, touching fingertips to the corded neck. Mustering himself, he calmed his own heart's race.

"This is not how I would have things end," he said.

Pomp sat contemplating the slumped figure. It wasn't sadness exactly. It was a feeling he couldn't quite place. He'd felt it before, but not for a long time, and when he realized that, he knew what it was. It was defeat.

Abby spoke with soft urgency. "The others will come. We need to leave. There's a train in the morning. I have a friend who can hide us tonight."

She was right. Pomp stood.

"Pack your things," he said.

If not for their hurry, she would have thrown her arms around him. She went to the cot, bending to gather up her belongings. Only when she started to rise did she realize Pomp had followed her. This time, he applied the harpoon handle gently. He had decided, and she was not part of his plan.

He laid Abby in the cot, covering her with blankets. He went to the door and took his coat off the peg. Spreading the coat, he draped it over the slumped man's lap.

Pouring himself another whisky, he wrote out brief instructions. Folding the note, he placed it in Abby's coin purse. If she woke in time, she would not have to concern herself with coins any more. It was one of his prize caches.

He knew the surfmen would come, but he did not leave. He had one last decision to make. He sipped the whisky and considered the doll. The doll looked back with her lopsided grin. It were as if she knew that the final answer still eluded him. Faint scratchings came to his ears.

Pomp took the cages outside. It had stopped snowing. White hush and a fading mist remained. When he lifted the tops of the cages, the yellowlegs hesitated before erupting with a whir into the sky. The birds rose in a cluster, and then, as if on some collective signal, they burst apart, scattering to the four corners of the globe.

Pomp watched them go, savoring the answer they had provided.

Back in the cabin, he picked up his jacket, regarding Daniel Cole one last time. "A twist in the great current's course," he said.

They passed through the Provincelands, a great white horse ridden by an old man holding a doll.

Ezekiel Donne paused in his searching to watch them. When they disappeared from sight, he slipped easily down the dune. He stood for a moment at a loss. They were heading away from the sea. It made no sense.

Hiram saw the birds first. Rising above the dunes, they whirled in the distance, in a white ball against the stars, before dissolving to nothing.

The surfmen ran. Hiram's feet slipped and caught in the soft snow, the ache in his lungs and legs propelling him forward, but these feelings came to him as an afterthought, as if he were a step behind the world around him. Even when they entered the cabin and it seemed as if the entire world was shouting, Hiram felt mired beneath a great weight. The shouting and the sweetish smell made his head spin. Most of all, Hiram wanted to be away from the slumped figure that still somehow emanated power, gathering the world's hopelessness and crushing the very air from the room.

He fell back outside, stumbling across the wrecked porch and into the snow.

The door to the stable hung open. Hiram saw the jumbled snow where the horse had fidgeted, the furrow leading into the dunes. He followed the furrow to the steaming droppings. He looked back at the cabin, a scrap of feeble light. So easy to do nothing. So easy to wait.

After Mercy disappeared, he and his father had sat in the dinghy, the settling water *tap-tap-tapping* against the sides. Morning sun full on his father's face, Hiram had watched the words push past the curious convulsings in his father's throat. "I require your silence." Hiram had obeyed. He had kept silent, even after unrelenting guilt saw to his father's end, leaving him alone with their secret and the haunting tappings that still lapped against his memory, resurrecting failure, night and day.

He glanced back at the cabin and then he ran, following the furrow into the dunes.

31

The trail was as clear as a boat's wake. Overhead, the stars glittered. Hiram followed the broken snow. He cared nothing for the plans. He was chasing a murderer. Keeper Cole was dead. Isabella spoke in his ear, the voice not an angel but a child, innocent and broken and clear in what was coming. His anger gathered and changed him. Pomp could not escape punishment.

But even as he ran, Hiram knew the old man held every advantage. He was on horseback. A boy on foot would not chase him down. Hiram knew he was heading for the harbor. There were dozens of ships, and stowing away would be easy. By morning, he would be gone.

Stumbling beneath the stars, his failures laughed at him. When Willie informed them of the contents of Marmaduke Matthews' letter, Hiram's blunders had risen as one. He saw himself reaching to pry the doll from Isabella's frail arms, felt again the fierce resistance that wasn't fear. *"No."* He stood beside the wagon at the funeral, the doll in his hand, another little girl speaking to him plainly as a child would. *"She can't talk."* The words hadn't been for the girl in the coffin; they'd been for a doll with a cork in its mouth.

He had hidden Isabella's secret away. Had he not returned the doll to a dead girl, Captain Cole would still be alive.

And here, at the last, he was still a fool. Even if he caught Pomp, what then? His knife pressed against his hip, but what good was it?

The answer lay slumped in a cold cabin. He was a coward's seed on a hapless errand.

He did the only thing he could do. He kept moving.

Only when the snow beneath his feet turned dirty did Hiram realize he had reached Provincetown. He followed the horse's track until it dissolved in a muddy quagmire. He was on Commercial Street. The buildings rose like dark waves. Here and there, light fell from a window. Hiram turned onto Bradford Street as if the horse were still leading him. He did not stop running until he reached the foot of the main wharf.

Lanterns, set atop squat pilings, ran the length of the wharf, puddling the planks with light. The snowy shoreline radiated phosphorescent light. Two schooners were tied up midway down the wharf and a whaling vessel was moored at the wharf's end, men milling at the foot of a gangplank. Hiram's eyes swept the dark harbor. At least fifty boats, of all shapes and sizes, were tied to the smaller docks or swinging lightly at anchor.

It was over. Hiram felt himself sinking beneath the surface, dragged down by this last thing, slipping away. White as the snow itself, it was barely a movement at all. Hiram stared at the point of his imaginings, a spot on the shoreline just away from the wharf.

When Icarus moved again, Hiram's eyes framed the great horse instantly. The horse was walking away from the pier. There was no rider. No one appeared to be walking beside the horse either, though distance and the animal's size could mask a small form.

He slid the knife from his belt, the handle cold and heavy, and approached the horse cautiously. It walked slowly along the water's edge, reins swinging slightly above the sand and cobbles. It made no noise at all.

"Lord Almighty. All I ask is privacy and a piss, and I'm rewarded with more lunacy instead."

Hiram's heart bounced.

The portly man standing at the top of the berm wore a bulging jacket and a scowl. His fingers fastened the last of his trouser buttons.

"Only half-wits and drunks are out in this sort of cold," the man said. "Since you appear sober, I'll assume the obvious. I'll tell you, it irks me to see an animal suffer its owner's idiocy."

"It's not my horse."

"Taking an ambling winter's stroll by itself?" The wool jacket fell open. Hiram saw the truncheon tucked into the man's waistline. "By God, I'll discipline an insolent half-wit as readily as a drunk."

"Please. I'm looking for someone."

"So is every sailor in this godforsaken port, though most of them have the sense to do it indoors." The man's scowl deepened. "I'd put that away unless you want your skull rapped."

Hiram remembered the knife. He slid it back inside his belt.

The sentry's hand dropped to his side. "I'll presume the fellow you're looking for isn't a close friend." He spat in the sand. "In all my years, I've turned no stranger stand of duty than this night. First a gargoyle, then a splendid horse tended by a half-wit. The sooner I can be away from this freakish circus, the better."

Hiram felt as if he'd stepped into the icy water. "You saw an old man?"

"Aye, but wrinkles wouldn't be his most memorable feature. Face so ugly, even a mother would spit up. Passed him on the wharf. Felt sorry for him at first. Smiles at me, smooth as cream, and says, 'I ate a man who looked like you.' Bugger me and this town. Should've given him a pasting."

"Did he board a vessel?"

"Lord Almighty, I hope not. If I had stake in a ship, I wouldn't like to know my chances rested in the hands of a troll ferrying a doll. Last I saw, he was walking toward the end of the wharf. If we're lucky, he walked right on off."

"How long ago?"

"You're a nosey lad. Fifteen minutes at most. Though with all the fun I'm having, it's hard to accurately account for the passing time. What's he to you? You related? Two half-wits make a whole?"

Hiram looked to the wharf. A lantern went out at its foot. Easy as mist, the humped form rose and scuttled for the street.

"Half-wit hide-and-seek, is it?" said the sentry, but the boy was already gone.

The sentry trotted to catch up with the horse. It was a magnificent animal. Its whiteness gave light to the night. As he reached for the reins, someone spoke directly in his ear.

"No."

Whirling about, he received his last taste of lunacy.

The thrust was clumsy, but the blade, honed by hours of industrious attention, slid through the breastplate as if bone were snow. The sentry bobbed upon the blade, making queer faces. He remained puzzled as he was dragged carelessly into the black water.

32

Pomp had gone to the end of the wharf where the whalers milled about, delaying to the last the walk up a gangplank. Ignoring the obvious, the whalers gulped whisky and pawed their last shabby breast. A bottle shattered and a woman gave a falsetto laugh.

Pomp singled the man out as he came down the gangplank—about the right age, his clothing and deportment tidy, disdain clear on his face.

Pomp stepped forward before the man could begin haranguing his crew. "You, sir, are an officer aboard this vessel."

The man was surprised. The statement was phrased respectfully, but by not being a question, it assumed a note of superiority. Although the figure before him was veiled in shadow, he could still see that the man was exceedingly ugly. As officer of a whaling vessel, however, he had seen his share of ugly men.

"I am the first mate."

The white smile professed true joy. "One day to be captain."

"That is the hope."

"May hope spring eternal."

A hint of mockery? He wasn't sure. The wish seemed genuine. A putrid stench assaulted his nostrils. "What is that foul smell?"

The old man continued smiling. "Life is dirty."

"If you are looking for a berth, I'm going to disappoint you. We have a full complement of qualified younger men."

"You have children."

The first mate hesitated. "I do."

"Perhaps a young girl among them?"

"Yes. Our youngest is seven." It surprised him to volunteer it.

"A gift for the next generation." The old man held out a doll. The doll wore a new cherry-red dress. The blonde hair curled prettily. The doll's body was oddly distended and the smile was crooked, but a little girl's heart would see past that. It was fortuitous timing. They were putting out at daybreak. He had spent most of his wages on gifts for his Portuguese mistress.

Still, for a moment, his hand remained at his side.

"Who did the doll belong to?"

The gray eyes softened and the outstretched hand lowered slightly. "To a girl who needs it no longer."

A philanderer is not without a heart. The first mate took the doll. "I will see this young lady to a good home. Thank you."

The old gnome released the doll wordlessly. The first mate was not easily unsettled, but when the old man closed his eyes and began to sway, something crawled across his own skin.

"The sea," the old man said.

The officer resented his uneasiness. He was too important to be distracted by a malformed tramp.

"What of it?"

The old man swayed. The silence lengthened. "It is the last wild place."

The first mate turned on his heel. Pomp saluted Andrew Carnegie's hopes, disappearing up the gangplank.

When he had spied the boy and the fat sentry on the shoreline with Icarus, Pomp felt a prick of irritation. The boy was a wrench in his plan, and it would be worse still if the other surfmen were about. He quickened his pace. At this distance, the boy might not see him as he left the wharf. After several steps, he slowed and smiled, like a man suddenly grasping a joke. If life was spice, then here was a welcome dash of uncertainty. Neither was he so removed from vanity that he might not enjoy an audience.

He waited at the foot of the wharf. And when the boy looked his way, he extinguished the lantern.

33

Pomp was nearly certain the boy had seen him, but crossing Bradford Street, he had slowed to be sure. Glancing back, he saw the boy top the rise of beach. Touching a finger to his bowler, Pomp disappeared down an alley.

Now that the chase was underway, he was grateful for the added zest, a pinch of the unknown tossed into what was now an otherwise predictable undertaking. With the plans relinquished, a simple task remained, and it would be made more exciting by the boy's presence. But he did not wish to be thwarted. He showed himself here and there to keep the boy on the scent, but he moved quickly. He could handle the youth, but the others were capable men. Something foreign roosted in his nerves. To be caged was unthinkable.

When he reached the dunes without interference, he relaxed. The surfmen would not look for him here. Common minds expected him to stow away. Only the boy remained, following him through the untracked snow like a tame mutt. He smiled at the thought.

Briefly, he summoned all his resources to gain some distance on his pursuer. Lunging through the deep snow like a jackrabbit, he made his way for half a mile before coming to a stop in a spread of snowfield. Taking off the jacket, he turned it inside out.

In the shadows at the foot of the gangplank, the first mate hadn't discerned the source of the stench. Now moonlight showed the stained lining clearly. He saw with satisfaction that his shirtfront, too, was coated with Daniel Cole's blood. He spread the jacket on the snow and walked on.

Hiram knew Pomp was leading him. Moving through Provincetown, the humped form appeared at precise moments, passing beneath a candlelit window or pausing in the moonlight at the mouth of an alley. Hiram prayed the other surfmen would arrive, but it was clear Pomp was heading for the far end of town, away from any chance of help. Pomp's path made no sense. The harbor was his only means of escape.

When Hiram reached the edge of the great dune fields, he knew he was alone.

Regret wasn't courage, but it didn't matter. He plunged on. As he ran, his eyes went to the shadows. The old man could lie in wait as easily as run—a final game before he returned to the docks and made his escape. *No one believes a man can be kept alive forever.* But Pomp would have time enough. A dog howled. It was a sorrowful sound, a terrible craving.

Hiram nearly stepped on the remains of the jacket, shreds of cloth strewn about and ground into the ruined snow by furious lust.

Pomp waited in the next clearing, a child-like figure in the vast white expanse. The bowler lay at his feet. His shirt was stained with blood. He brandished the knife, but not for man. Overhead, the stars hung like countless candles.

Pomp regarded him fondly. "Not too close now."

The ragged forms padded atop the snow, circling and yipping. A bolder dog veered in, but Pomp turned him back with a lunge and a shout. The dog fell back, but not far. The noise they made as they scampered was like crying.

Truth crawled up Hiram's spine.

"Timid souls, made different," said Pomp. "My honor to execute your captain's revenge."

Pomp turned slow circles. The blade caught the moonlight. "Brave and foolish to follow me, though perhaps there is something more. Man's motivations are among life's greatest mysteries."

The thought seemed to rise from some other world, indifferent and far away. Hiram wondered if he was failing again. "Give me the plans."

The old man laughed, but his eyes did not leave the dogs. "For the second time this evening, man's narrow interests disappoint me."

Staring at Captain Cole's blood, Hiram felt an emptying, as if his own veins were bleeding away. He searched for the fury that had been there moments earlier, but he only felt lost.

"You killed the girl," he said. "You murdered Captain Cole."

"Neither event was part of the plan, but heroes sometimes come to unexpected ends."

"They were innocent."

"Man is not so simple."

"Where are the plans?"

"Set free."

A dog dashed in, ducking under the knife. Pomp landed a boot squarely in its ribs. The yelping dog tumbled back. The effort made Pomp pant.

"Do you feel as if you've won, Winter Man?" Pomp said.

Hiram stood silent.

"Then you understand." The gray eyes flicked to the left. The smile turned radiant. "Behold the warrior."

Hiram had not seen the dog. Gauging from where it sat, it had passed a few yards behind him. The dog was a half size bigger than the others. It sat comfortably on its haunches, watching its circling brethren, steam rising from the lolling tongue.

"To breathe is to yearn." Pomp tossed the knife in a lazy arc. It landed beside the dog, scattering snow.

The dog rose. Its front paws plunged through snow. Head down, it worked slowly to restore its footing. Weight distributed, it padded toward the gray circle.

"Go, boy. They love me now, but soon enough their eyes will turn to another." Spreading his arms, Pomp looked to the stars.

The dogs saw advantage, but they did not abandon instinct. Two of the smaller dogs fixed on the man's legs. While the man was distracted, the large dog drove soundlessly into the man's side.

The stars gazed down on the snarling melee. Had they cared, they would have noticed how the man greeted the snapping teeth with his own satisfied grunts, turning so the great dog had access to the organ that mattered. When the dog began ripping at his midsection, the man gave a viscous sigh.

34

Hiram ran until his legs buckled. He lay in the snow, mind tumbling, hot breaths thundering in his ears. He closed his eyes, but he still saw the dogs backing and shaking and leaping until the flesh relented, tearing away in a spattering of rain.

Oddly, the spattering still continued, faint and measured, a slow *tap-tap-tapping* that tiptoed deliberately toward another terrible memory. At first, Hiram resisted. Tonight's horrors were enough. But there was something in the familiar tapping, a prodding and nudging against the periphery of his consciousness. Hiram willed his mind back again to the pond, Mercy gone, their father silent; the murky water, condemning and uncaring, performing its final settlings; and the faintest, drawn out *tap-tap-tappings*, nudging the waterline of the dory.

His eyes shot open, watching, for a last instant, his breath melt the crystalline snow into a tiny droplet, and then he was on his feet.

The whaling boat. Pomp had walked to the end of the wharf. The fat sentry had seen him.

I wouldn't like to know my chances rested in the hands of a troll ferrying a doll.

Hiram ran.

35

He watched as the desperate boy returned to the foot of the wharf, nearly crashing into the other surfmen gathered and turning about like sheep. He stood close, but the men ignored him. No one familiar with him ever paid him any mind. In return, he hardly listened as the boy spat and spluttered. When he heard Pomp's name, he fleetingly wished his mind had not wandered to his happy jig and the pleasant jerking of the man dying at the end of his arm, but there was no changing it. He did not traffic in regret.

He watched the surfmen run down the wharf. He was surprised when, after a time, the whaling vessel, which had cast off all but two lines, secured all its lines again.

Turning, Ezekiel Donne walked out of town.

The horse was where he had left him, tied to a cypress pine. The pine was too small to hold the great horse—he saw that now—but the horse had not tried to leave. The horse had waited patiently, just as he would.

He touched its muzzle. "Faithful steward," he said.

Gently, he took up the reins. He looked at the stars. Swinging his head made them sway like a thousand lanterns.

Ezekiel led the horse through the dunes. In Provincetown, the church bells rang. Ezekiel paused for a moment in the blue-black darkness, enjoying the ringing like a ship's bell. Closing his eyes, he followed the last soft note until it was only a tinkling in his mind, the sound like pretty things spilling over each other. He had watched the old man for a long time. He knew every trick. No one would discover him. He moved as quietly as fog. He would do the work just so, collecting pretty things until the old man came for the horse. Maybe then, the old man would be so pleased that he would share his treasures, and he could stop his searching.

The thought of pretty things made his heart ache.

EPILOGUE

On Sunday, Hiram went alone as he always did to Provincetown Cemetery. With good roads in place and automobiles to ply them, the trip from Wellfleet took less than thirty minutes. It took him nearly as long to walk from the car to the graves.

Hannah made him promise never to walk too long; when he tired, his footing grew unsure. He kept his promise most of the time, although it was also true he had taken more than his share of orders in his life.

This autumn day was particularly fine, with a sun that radiated warmth and a cloudless blue sky, but Hiram knew enough to feel the first faint glance of cold, a herald of the season to come.

At first, he walked the crooked rows without stopping: Willie; Antone; the grave of Martin Nelson, a fresh bundle of salt spray roses atop the cracked earth; Enos Lombard, who had acquiesced to nothing in his life except a daughter's wishes (here he always said a thank-you); and Widow Mayhew, who, even in death, alarmed certain Cape residents with the naked Aboriginals intertwined on her tombstone.

He stopped first at his own family plot—Mother, Father, and Mercy long gone—though the memories that greeted him were as fresh as yesterday, and, these days, mostly pleasant, that comforting trick that allows man to continue on.

Had he been capable of it, a single long stride would have taken him to the three nondescript headstones barely reaching to the middle of his shins. He had briefly considered using part of the reward to replace the three headstones, but he knew at least one of the inhabitants preferred anonymity, and he had left them as they were. Standing in the warm sun, he gave a small smile. His mother and Daniel Cole lay close. He himself had had only one love in his life, but he knew this wasn't always the case.

At last, he walked to the foot of the oak, stopping before the memorial he had commissioned. It was nothing ostentatious, but large enough so that a passerby would not forget innocence must be cared for. The sculptor, recommended by Andrew Carnegie, had produced an astonishing likeness of a girl cradling a doll, though Hiram guessed many visitors saw the lopsided smile as a glaring blemish.

He bowed his head, but it wasn't the girl he remembered. A new world had dawned and war had come, steel serving its cause, men and nations rising and falling as they always do. But standing beneath the fluttering leaves of another passing season, the grand events drifted away. He recalled a wobbling bicycle piloted by a clench-jawed rider, a quail carved by an equally small and proud hand, picnics beside Great Pond, the constant shouts for him to come swimming seeing to it that he never ate, the slow spread of Hannah's smile on their wedding night when he broached his plan for the remainder of the reward money.

Rousing from his musings, Hiram looked to the clear sky. It would be pleasant to spend the evening with Hannah. He would build a fire and make hot cider. Maybe before bed they would take a short walk along the beach beneath the stars.

On June 3, 1883, the struggling Seamen's Society for Children and Families, founded thirty-seven years earlier to care for the children and widows of sailors lost at sea, received an anonymous grant that set it firmly on its feet. Through education, adoption, foster care, and other programs, the society continues to serve hundreds of children and their families to this day.

The dog, it's said, descends from wild stock, and though it adheres to the strictures of the Provincetown fisherman who feeds it, and shows a gentle fondness for the children it oversees, on certain nights it pads to the far corner of the fenced yard and howls. There is no deciphering the thoughts of wild animals, but there is no mistaking how the dog faces east, its melancholy sound rolling over the shopping malls, fast-food restaurants, and souvenir shops, out past land's edge and into the fog.

And in the Provincelands, treasures still lie.

CPSIA information can be obtained at www.ICGtesting.com
Printed in the USA
LVOW121723080413

328161LV00003B/365/P